Three Wrongs

Book One
Donovan: Thief For Hire

Chuck Bowie

MuseItUp Publishing
www.museituppublishing.com

MuseItUp Publishing

Layout and Book Production by Lea Schizas

Print ISBN: 978-1-77392-041-2

eBook ISBN: 978-1-77127-258-2

First eBook Edition *February 2013

Production by MuseItUp Publishing

Several people have helped me to understand how to write,
but Lois Williams taught me that my life is fuller when I write.
Thanks, Lois, for the unconditional support and for making me fulfilled.

Acknowledgements

Helping me along the way were some very special people: My editors: Paul Muller, Forrest Orser, Katie Hines, and Penny Ehrenkranz. My readers: Fred Stenson, Paul Muller, Victor Paul-Elias, Gus Funnell, and of course, Lois Williams. Special regard for the agent who found me: Paul Muller.

Thank you all so much for the alchemy.

Prologue

U*mbria, In the Year 32 BC*

Mercurio waited until after the moon had settled behind the swell of clouds that arose from the west. He exited his family's house and using a torch for light, stepped down to a door leading into the hill's rock face. Descending the steps to the sarcophagus, he swung open the hammered bronze and hewn-wood door and then pulled it shut behind him. A linen-wrapped object was tucked under the arm carrying the torch. Pausing beside the mummified remains of his great-grandparents, he peered into the stone coffin, bowed in respect, and then moved to the back of the small cave.

The previous evening's lightning foretold the fall of Etruria. Mercurio watched for the signs of ill fate: chain lighting, followed by several strikes to the south of the family house. From this, he knew the Etruscan empire would be overcome. Roman legions were marching up from the south and would be here soon. They had annexed the nearby provinces, and he felt his country's fate was sealed. He had no choice but to head for Po and thence on over the Alps. But before he left, he had this final task to perform.

The ceiling at the back of the cave bevelled downward until it met the dirt floor, and Mercurio was obliged to crawl the final few steps. He touched the stone wall and then lowered his hand until it met the ground. To determine where to begin digging, he gauged two forearm lengths outward from the wall, and then he dug into the cold dirt floor. His torch fluttered and went out. No matter. He continued digging until he hit something solid and flat. Other than the satisfaction of finding his target, Mercurio felt nothing. News of his father's death, the war, his task...all numbed him. He had a job to do, and he would see it through. He widened the surface area until he could grab the bronze case, lift it, and release the lid.

When he reached inside the family chest, his hands felt three familiar objects and heard the tiny clinks of the scores of coins lining the chest. His fingers touched two *speculae*, which were polished tin disks his grandmother and mother had used as their mirrors. By moving his hand just a bit, he found the *cistae*, the tiny bronze box passed down from mother to daughter for two centuries. He lowered the wrapped golden cup his father had forged. His father! The scribe was no more, called to the afterlife by his ancestors while fighting in Terni. He had shared a final message to Mercurio before leaving for battle. "If the fates so say, go and place the *ciborium*, the Mother Cup, in the sacred spot—the area in the cave closest to the east and therefore closest to the Gods—behind your grandparents' remains." The fates then spoke through the lightning of the previous evening, and Mercurio acted upon the message.

His father's bequest completed, the young man tidied up the distressed dirt on the floor of the cave, closed the door behind him, and headed for his laden cart. He sat on the cart, staring from the sarcophagus entrance at his family's home on the hill just above it. He noted the six marble columns lined up across the entrance, with his room behind the one to the right.

Less than a day before the Romans would arrive. As part of their conquest, they would confiscate the property, assign it to a centurion, and his home and homeland would be lost. Sighing, he grabbed a short whip and snapped it behind the ear of his donkey. The cart wheeled around and headed north.

SAN MARINO, ITALY
    January 1944
    A letter from Xavier Attanasio to Helena Ponza

Dearest Sister:

The world is turning on its head these days! Until just last month, I would have bet all I have earned that the Axis powers would win the war, but recent events have left me in grave doubt. My Nazi employers are still paying me handsomely to acquire pieces of art for them. But I'm not sure how long this partnership will last. You see, all around me now is indecision, uncertainty, and chaos!

You may recall I am collecting art pieces from the Italian villas in order to fund the Axis war movement. At least, that is what the Germans are telling the Italians. To do so, the Italians have given me a detail of Romanian prisoners, and armed with my knowledge of the art world, I am tasked to visit the villas to appropriate pieces of value to pay for the Italian war effort. Last evening, a group of Romanians broke out of the nearby internment camp. Unfortunately, this was the group of prisoners the Italian commandant gave me as laborers to confiscate the art as I visit the estates of Sienna, Florence, and Modena.

At any rate, as they took their leave, the Romanian prisoners, who knew the gold when they saw it, broke into the warehouse where these treasures were stored. Oh, they were very choosey. They stole only the best gold and bejewelled artifacts: necklaces, tiaras, and chalices. I particularly deplore the theft of an Etruscan-era bucchero chalice. Instead of being made from pottery like the others, this one was gold! It was to have been my pay for this month's work. Alas, gone. It is probably slung over the back of some Bucharest dog, halfway across Yugoslavia by now.

But now to my point. As I mentioned, I no longer trust that the Italian-German entente will survive the battering of the Allied armies. Tonight I travel to Portofino and eventually to Monaco. It is my intention to hide in the weeds, transform myself into a French resistance fighter, and voila! An allied patriot is born!

Be assured that most of the paintings and sculptures I acquired these past two years have been securely tucked away from prying eyes. I will return to get them once things settle down. And, of course, I will return to my Athens as soon as this giant mess resolves itself.

Until then, I will be thinking of you,

With fondness, XA

Chapter One

M inistry of Labor, Bucharest
Late Friday Afternoon, October 2008

This should be fun. Donovan opened the door of the former KGB headquarters in Bucharest. *Let's see what I can get away with. But first the guards.* The slender man in tailored business attire swung his attaché case in time to a silent melody. Walking through the modest front door that led to the Romanian Ministry of Labor, he entered and crossed the foyer to meet the two guards standing by the massive stairway leading to the heart of the building. Catching the eye of the younger of the soldiers, he lowered his briefcase to rest beside black Cordovan shoes, presenting both papers and passport to the soldier.

The two soldiers conferred for a moment, spoke the magic words: *Canada* and *Delegati* and nodded to Sean Donovan. He was in.

"*Plaicera!*" Please. The older soldier hesitated, his arm half-raised. "You will see...who?"

"Ah. Ministry of Labor. Security systems."

Once again, it seemed the correct words were spoken. The older man waved a weary arm to permit passage. "At the top of the stairs, you will turn right to find the Ministry door."

The Canadian in the ash grey suit took the sculpted steps one at a time, but he did not dawdle. At the top of the stairs, he glanced over the railing to the reception area, noting the soldiers were engaged in a conversation.

Instead of turning right to visit the systems shop, he headed down the hall and pulled a pair of the thinnest available leather gloves from his pocket, tugging them on. After passing three office doors, he opened the fourth with a key copied that day. Closing the door, he found himself in the office of Razvan Petruscu, a protocol officer for World Bank activities. Having phoned him earlier, Donovan knew Petruscu was out for the afternoon.

The only illumination was from thin cuts of sunlight shining through a half-shuttered window. Donovan wasted no time powering up the desktop computer, and by applying the LAN administrator's override code, he bypassed the user code invitation. He left the server system and sought out the C drive first. Once in, he performed a cursory search of the Word documents. It took just a moment to locate and jot down Petruscu's passwords on a scrap of paper, and then he keyed in the URL for the man's bank accounts.

So trusting. So careless.

He picked the only fat, out-of-country account, gained entry with the fourth password, and transferred the balance to his bank account in the Caymans. A minute later, the computer was powered down. As a double precaution, the keyboard and doorknob were wiped cleaner than Petruscu's offshore account, and Donovan was back down the hall. He headed for the stairs, gloves tucked back in his jacket pocket, swinging his briefcase to the same silent melody.

Chapter Two

B*ucharest, Romania*
    Sunday Night

"I'll tell you what to do, how and when to do it, and since I'm paying, I'll also tell you whether you're enjoying it while you do it." Edward Yorke leaned his thick bulk over Janos Dobra, a sullen man who avoided his eyes. Placing both of his ham-hands onto the man's shoulders, Yorke pressed him deeper into the rough chair to hammer home the point. Janos's brother, Tomas, watched, expressionless, nearby.

Yorke butted out a cigarette and continued staring down at the smaller Dobra. "My employer is not happy with that little gypsy brat you brought into this mess. You and Tomas have been stupid, and the theft of that passport from my boss was unforgivable. But you will soon shut the kid up, right?" He checked the date function on his watch. "You have two days. And don't slough this off on your imbecile brother standing behind me with his silly jaw hanging down."

Edward Yorke, a squat man with cheeks so round they all but hid his sharp, piggy eyes, had spent his professional life in the British government. He had first used his intellect to steal power and authority from his colleagues as he rose through the lower ranks of the public service. After, he had focused on international development and now held sufficient authority inside the Foreign Affairs department to be able to influence international contracts to his advantage. But something had gone wrong with this one, and he wasn't happy. Yorke glared once again at the two Romanians.

As brothers, Janos and Tomas looked nothing alike. Janos was smaller, with a narrow, bony face, and eyes that were set too close to each other, causing him to appear smarter than his brother, which was misleading. Tomas was an immense man with black eyes and a scar that created a map line across his shaved head. His sloped forehead and poorly-shaved face lent him the appearance of a Neanderthal, which was also misleading. What was accurate, however, was they were thugs for hire, and as such, Yorke had them in his back pocket.

The men faced one another in the foreman's semi-enclosed second-story room, square in the middle of a once productive marble-cutting operation. The factory was one of scores of abandoned buildings on the outskirts of Bucharest, all fallen into disrepair. No one paid attention to them, a perfect set up for a discrete meeting. Half of the foreman's room was walled in a continuous mural of dusty windows, the other half opened to the shop floor below, a flimsy wooden railing running around its perimeter. All of the industrial machines on the shop floor had rusted where they had sat unused for years, victims of a bankrupt Romanian nation. Of course, this didn't matter to the men on the platform above them. All they wanted was the privacy to conduct some business out of sight of government authorities, local police, or anyone else.

The room was empty save for a scarred table, a metal chair in which Janos was slumped, and a bare cable where a telephone had long since been disconnected. Tomas leaned against the wall not far from the table. Yorke presided from the middle of the room, a spot he always chose. He not only exercised control, he revelled in it, and the center of a stage—any stage—was where Yorke wanted to be.

He refocused on Janos and bullied him with his gaze until the man averted his brown eyes yet again. The Brit stepped back to the railing near the top of the stairs and smiled with satisfaction. His short arms were splayed as if in welcome. A quick glance at the exterior doors that opened to the production floor told him no one would interrupt them, so he returned to business.

"All right then, we're in agreement. You two stupid gypsies will tidy up this mess you made. First, you'll deal with that beggar brat." Using a handkerchief, he wiped drops of sweat from the back of his perpetually damp neck and changed the subject. "Now. We have a second job to do." He shifted his mass from one foot to the other. "Janos. You're supposed to be the smart one. When I say Donovan, Sean Donovan, what do you recall?"

Neither one answered. Yorke fumed.

"Come on! I've mentioned him before. Skinny Canadian. Piece of shit and in our way. Ring any bells?"

Janos shrunk a bit more in his seat and stared over at his brother for some hint of a response. His brother's face betrayed nothing.

Yorke's fat cheeks turned ruddy. "Well, here's how it will be. The man is a nuisance. I don't like nuisances, but hey, since I'm the bloke who pays you, life's all about me, innit? As for you miscreants, think of him as having his hand in your wallet, getting in between you and your money. Does that work for you? Not that I give a rat's ass."

He shifted once again from foot to foot. "Knock that Canadian bastard around a bit. Make him sorry he landed in Bucharest. Take his passport and lose it. Sell it, drop it in the Black Sea, I don't give a damn."

Janos half-raised his hand as if in school. "Canadian?"

Yorke threw up his hands in despair. "Did I not just tell you that? The money from the Romanian government grant was cut in half because Canada won the international development contract over England, and he is their rep. I worked hard to get that grant, and I'm not pleased. Not at all. Yes, that would be the same grant money paying you two losers. Might I remind you that you can't skim money off a contract you didn't win? The less successful this sod Donovan is this year, the more likely I get my entire contract back next year. And that means money for me, which means money for you. What part of this aren't you getting? For Chrissake, one of you focus, just for a minute." He looked skyward, as if beseeching an implacable God. "I could weep with their stupidity."

The Englishman crossed back to the centre of the tiny room, took off his size fifty-four-short tailored jacket and tossed it onto the table beside Tomas, who shifted position behind the table, a step closer to the two others. Yorke wiped his neck again. "Okay, here's the plan. You will follow Donovan tomorrow and shake him up a bit." He jabbed a finger at the larger brother without removing his stare from the smaller. "You, lazy arse. Hurt him. I don't want him dead because that would draw attention, wouldn't it? Listen. The Canadian needs to get the message to stay away, but don't bloody get caught." He glanced up at Tomas, whose dull expression carried...something behind it that made Yorke wary. He returned his attention to Janos and dropped his voice from peevishness to warning.

"If this comes back to bite me, mate, I will throw the pair of you under the trolley without a hello, goodbye, or kiss my ass." The man squirmed and dropped his gaze to the floor. Yorke leaned in toward him.

Tomas took a single step to meet Yorke and then launched himself upon the man. As Yorke straightened and turned his attention to Tomas, the big man caught the Brit with a perfect rugby straight-arm, ramming him backward. Off-balance and unable to regain his footing, Yorke was propelled step-by-step out of the walled area and through the wooden railing.

Yorke pivoted, a slow tumble into open air. His head hit the dusty plant floor first and halted the scream. The impact separated the skull from the spinal column at the top of the neck, snapping the Atlas vertebra with a sickening crack. The plates of bone around his bald spot caved inward, sliced into the brain, and erased the final, remaining sensation. The torso hit the floor, and all movement stopped with a final, minute twitch. A dark crimson pool crept across the filthy cracked tiles, snaking away as it enlarged to follow the grout lines.

TOMAS LEANED OVER THE space where the railing had been. "Now who is the stupid one, Yorke? And who is the dead one? I think maybe you are both."

Janos leaned over the remainder of the railing to peer down at the expanding arc of blood. He reverted to Romanian. "This isn't good, Tomas. What'll we do now?"

Tomas walked over to the table and emptied the dead man's jacket pockets, making little piles of the contents. "This isn't difficult. We go to his boss and say Yorke had an accident, we're in charge now, and we want more pay. It's simple."

"You know his boss's name?"

Tomas looked at his brother. "I really don't need to know his name, although I do because I have this now." He picked up a disposable cell phone from the pile of Yorke's possessions, scrolling down until he came to the name he sought. "Yorke phones this man, Gaia, regularly."

"Gaia! But...we met him! The time the Roma boy stole his passport. I don't understand how Gaia is connected to the Roma boy, other than the boy stealing his passport."

"Understand this. The Roma boy knows too much. He heard you talking about the government money allocated for street kids not getting to the street kids, and he's seen us with Yorke. He will be trouble before too long. We can't let him talk. To anyone, ever. Yorke is right. We have to get rid of the little boy. And, we need to get Gaia's passport back. That will get us in good with him. So, we only have to do our job, and we can keep the money.

"Now. It's time to leave. I will call the police after we're gone. Wipe down the table, doorknobs, and let's go." Tomas waved the phone. "Your English is better. Call Gaia tomorrow. I'll tell you what to say."

He stood, grabbed the passport and the money in front of him, and a minute later they were gone. Behind them, Edward Yorke's lifeless eyes stared without comprehension at the foreman's room and the splintered railing above him.

Chapter Three

Bucharest, Romania
Monday Morning

The dogs and children playing in the street awakened him. Yaps and growls floated through the open window, riding on bleached morning sunlight, sliding over the ochre window ledge. *So early in the morning for kids to be out. I wonder if they're orphans.* The air was so still he couldn't determine if they were playing just beneath his window, or across the boulevard in front of the Leitha, a disease of a hotel. But he was not at the Leitha; he was in the Majestic, four stars, and second best in Romania. No sense being pretentious. He had learned that if you made a living as a contract thief named Sean Donovan, it was best not to let your surroundings draw any more attention to you than necessary.

He had pulled back his bed linens the evening before, folding them to one side so he could lie naked in the warm October night. The sheets were ivory-colored and complemented the buttery color of the walls. *At least a four hundred thread count and Egyptian at that. Decent.* He rolled over and glanced at the cheap plastic clock radio that read eight o'clock. *Why the cheap radio and the gorgeous linens? Must be the technology lag. With the country just getting back on its feet economically, not all industrial sectors will rebound at the same time.* "Romania won't be rebuilt in a day," he murmured.

Once up, he turned on the shower, stepped in and soaped his body as he thought about his day. So, what does a contract thief do on his day off? Steal something just for the having? He smiled at the memory of Friday afternoon and the money he had made, on a lark, in five brief minutes. Maybe he'd get into the palace today and begin reconnoitering that most challenging opportunity he had been offered by Canadian Professor Umbra at Concordia, in Quebec. He would call the professor in a few minutes.

The problem, of course, was always the same. How did the professor find Donovan and figure out his reputation for such shady dealings? Was Umbra legit or was it a setup by the police? Donovan was, after all, being asked to steal some kind of heritage piece from Ceausescu's palace and find a way to get it back to Canada. *And I really don't want to end my days in a Romanian prison.* He was confident, and the challenge was intriguing. The professor's reference had panned out, and he seemed on the up and up.

Finished with his shower, he wrapped a towel around his waist and took one of his disposable cell phones, punching in the numbers to Canada.

"Umbra here."

"Professor Umbra. I am the, um, individual you approached to pick up a souvenir from Bucharest. Do you recall?"

"Absolutely, absolutely! I must say, sir, I am beyond excited you are in a position to take care of this for me. All right. What can I tell you, Mr...?"

Donovan ignored the hint to offer his name. "Tell me exactly what it looks like, precisely where it can be found, and how much it weighs. And email me the floor plans. I apologize because I don't have a lot of time, so please be brief."

"Of course, of course. It's a *ciborium*, a golden chalice. It weighs about two pounds, and it's fat, thick as chalices go. Here's the thing. It's a replica, probably made before World War Two. So instead of being a priceless relic, its value lies in it being literally the key to understanding the Etruscan language, which was the ancient language of the Italians. You'll see an etymological code etched onto the outside of the cup bowl and base. It was replicated from drawings that have since been destroyed. That's my interest in it, although the fact it is made from gold doesn't hurt, let's face it.

"Why this business of it being a replica is important to you, Mr., erm, sir, is because you may wish to unscrew it at the base, if that makes it easier to transport. Oh! And it's almost ten inches tall, with lion feet on its base. You will find it on the minus fifth floor underground at the Houses of Parliament, which used to be the palace of Ceausescu. I'll send you the layout of the palace, as you've asked. The elevator to take is located two hundred feet from the information technology offices on the main floor at the back of the palace. As you come off the elevator, walk straight to the warehouse doors, which are protected solely by a security camera." After he described how to navigate the warehouse, they agreed on a fifty thousand dollar fee, and Donovan rang off.

It was always motivating to start a new job, especially one with so many angles. And then there was the tidy transfer of Petruscu's funds three days ago. The opportunity to make money from his government contract and to profit from a contract job on the side made everything three times better.

If he wanted the cup, he had to get into the palace. He was assigned a Romanian government representative to accompany him, which was a requirement for all international delegates. *And he was 'delegati.'* These government reps who came to Romania on World Bank projects to improve the country's infrastructure were more than just diplomats. Their work was invaluable, so their status as *delegati* was appreciated. It made passage through all kinds of doors...easier. Donovan grinned at that. He had scheduled a brief breakfast meeting with his rep, Razvan Petruscu, from the Romanian Ministry of Labor to gain access to the palace. It was ironic, though. He had made the man a whole lot poorer with the computer transaction of Friday afternoon, although Petruscu didn't know it. Now here he was, currying favor with him in order to get at the chalice.

He padded to the window. The makings of another perfect day told him how to dress. He looked down the length of a small cul-de-sac and saw a slender woman hanging out her laundry in the shadow of a seventeenth century church. To the left, along the boulevard, he observed a Bucharesti cab up on the sidewalk. Its owner was washing it with water from a two-litre soda bottle. The cabbie was drinking beer as dogs and children ran around him and his tiny vehicle, the archetypical *Dacia*.

He returned to the bathroom to shave, taking care to avoid nicking himself around the clean white scar that dipped under his chin. Back in the bedroom, he glanced in the closet and chose a powder blue, short sleeved shirt and adjusted it to accommodate and conceal the transparent eight-inch knife that followed the contour of his spine. He loved its uniqueness, a one-of-a-kind dichroic ceramic weapon that could slip through airport security, yet promised to offer up a nasty slash when necessary.

Looking touristy in his shirt and khaki pants, Donovan picked up the huge room key from the writing desk and headed for the door. Everything about the Majestic was oversized for effect, from the vaulted ceilings of his room to the eight-foot-wide corridors; likewise, the half-pound cylinder attached to his key. He opened the substantial hotel room door and glanced down the ornate hallway. Once he arrived in the lobby, he checked the key in with the concierge, as was the hotel's custom, and headed into the dining room for bagels and lox, fresh fruit, and yogurt.

The food put him in a good mood, and he thought about how to enjoy this quiet day before the activity of the next few days. *Hitting the hotel gym is a necessity, and maybe I'll get to wander around a bit, perhaps take in a few sights. It would be so nice to have a break.* He rubbed an eye with the back of his hand. When he was finishing his second cup of tough, aromatic coffee, a compact man in a navy business suit approached him.

"Good morning, my friend. You slept well? I trust I am not so late for our chat." The man offered his hand.

Razvan Petruscu was a bureaucrat, a director in the Romanian ministry. It was his responsibility to smooth the path of visiting businessmen and government workers, *delegati*, in the interests of a better-running labor market. While only a mid-level public servant, Petruscu's position afforded him the opportunity to influence the outcomes of international contracts, a circumstance he had exploited for financial advantage on numerous occasions in the past.

His skin was olive, his eyes dark and moist. A small mole drew attention to his left cheek, and his mouth was compact, lips set in what seemed to be a perpetual smile. Petruscu's overall look reminded Donovan of an Italian businessman.

Donovan stood and performed the classic handshake with his left hand on Razvan's shoulder. For such a slender man, Donovan's grip was strong.

"Not late at all." *I wonder if the subject of your recent financial losses will come up.* Donovan's smile was thin. "I've only been here three days, and I've been treated very well."

"I'm most pleased to hear that. All government delegates help to bring prosperity to Romania, but in this regard, Canadians have been especially helpful." Petrescu offered a small bow.

Donovan shrugged, and the two men sat. "I hope some of what the Canadian government is offering is helpful. Building a labor exchange, upgrading the phone system... Installing a decent security system in support of your telecommunications and information systems should be helpful."

"Is going to be very helpful, I am confident." Petrescu changed the subject. "So, my friend. What is your schedule today? Do you visit the Ministry of Labor building today to start your work? Was former KGB headquarters, you know. Bullet holes still in walls." Petruscu leaned forward as if to tell a secret. "Their dining hall has the best sour cream mushroom *zupa*. I promise you."

Donovan nodded. "The KGB is long gone now. I like seeing bullet holes. It makes me happy they weren't meant for me. As for the soup, it will have to wait for another day. No, today I was hoping to visit the former palace where the houses of Parliament are now located. I know you have me scheduled to visit the palace on business later in the week, but it would be nice to see it today, if that's possible."

Petruscu frowned. "Ceausescu Palace? Today? I don't know. These things take time. I have...so many people to contact." The frown deepened, and he scratched the side of his head. "I would do much to make this happen. Canadians are..." he paused, "more than *delegati* to me. I repeat, these things take time. But I will make the...the effort." His voice was filled with doubt.

"That's all anyone can do. And you? What are you up to?"

"Up to? I make stupid phone call all the day... Australia all of the morning, Canada in the late afternoon, but nobody will be at work. Both the time zone make me crazy. I even work this night. But I will go to the symphony tomorrow night as reward. Is very cheap. Only four dollars fifty of your money. You should go with me."

"All right. Will you get me tickets?"

Petruscu looked uncomfortable. "Why we not just buy our tickets there? Is just as easy. Seats will not be filled of people."

Donovan took note of the navy jacket of Petruscu's suit, with its neatly mended cuff. It was the same jacket he had worn every time they had met. Although the tailoring was done in a professional manner, it carried a tell-tale shininess at the cuffs, elbow, and collar. But Donovan had discovered the man's off-shore bank account. Until that little fact had revealed itself, he had thought the purchase of things like an extra ticket were an issue of affordability. Either the man was cheap, or he didn't want to advertise the second income that padded his offshore account. Further, Donovan suspected Petruscu's ticket had been a gift, a benefit of office, like baseball tickets for Microsoft executives.

Donovan began again. "Perhaps I'm making things more complicated. But since you invited me, I insist on paying for our tickets and those of your guests." Petruscu opened his mouth to protest, but Donovan held up a hand. "No, I insist."

This was met with a shrewd look followed by some measure of relief. "That is very nice of you. Oh! You want to go to the sexy clubs instead? See the girls? Is whatever you want."

"No, I'd really like to see the symphony."

"Perfect!" Petruscu's cheerful Mediterranean mouth widened to a full smile as he extended his arm to shake hands across the table. "Then I must go. Mr. Donovan, the ministry team is going out for drinks after work tomorrow. Why don't you join us? I will meet you at seven o'clock tomorrow at the brasserie just up the street, yes? We will go to concert after that." He rose to leave. "*La Revadere.*" Goodbye, then.

DONOVAN FINISHED HIS coffee, grimacing at the thought of the horrible blue milk he had been obliged to pour into it. He really should learn to like it black. Wiping his hands on the exquisite hand-stitched linen napkin, he whisked some imaginary crumbs from his lap, threw a very ordinary tip onto the table, and straightened the cup in its saucer as he stood to leave.

As Donovan thought of his chat with Petruscu, he frowned. It hadn't gone well. To steal something from a public servant's office was one thing, but this next job would be more challenging. For instance, it would first be necessary to actually gain access to the palace. His only excuse to get through those doors was his security contract with Romania, and since that hadn't worked with Petruscu today, he would have to wait. He shrugged. *Tomorrow is another day.* For now, it was time to get outside and grab some fresh air.

He left the dining room and walked through the dappled morning sunlight shining through the tall arched windows of the hotel lobby. The day promised exquisite weather, but would the events match it?

"Mr. Donovan?" The desk manager crossed the floor to meet him. "Sir, you have a phone call. You can take it right over there, at that desk."

Donovan picked up the heavy handset. "Hello?" No response. "Hello. Who is this, please?" His answer was a click and then a dial tone. He crossed the window and checked as much of the street as he could. Nothing. No suspicious cars, no one at the phone booth that he could see. Nothing. *I'm being paranoid.* Shrugging, he left the hotel.

The rest of his morning was free. He would go to *Parcul Cismigiu*, the park. On a previous trip, he had taken the opportunity to visit it and remembered how the landscape appeared foreign to him. The tiny rowing pond for lovers, the flower beds toward the back end of the park, and the incongruous maze that had been placed at the very end of the park. He remembered the old-man plane trees, gigantic with bark that looked about as real as the concrete trees of Disney World. They had a shiny ash color similar to sycamore trees but in reality were unlike anything he had ever seen outside of Europe. Many of them were hundreds of years old.

This time, he thought he'd just wander through the park and see a bit of everything. He slipped out into the white gauze sunshine of an early Eastern European morning to catch a slice of Bucharest.

The Majestic was located in the heart of the city, not far from any of the major areas of the city. Through the exit at the back of the hotel was the street that could take him to the Ministry of Labor. From the boulevard outside of the hotel's main entrance, he could go left to the *Quartier Française*, the French Quarter, or right to the playhouse where he would see the symphony the following evening. He could even cross the boulevard and go down the hill to the park.

Donovan elected to cross the street, ignoring the moneychangers. In a short minute, he reached the intersection where five major boulevards met and took the one leading to the park.

The boulevard led down an incline, with buildings jammed together and several side streets leading away from the main thoroughfare. Near the end of the boulevard, he peered down a blind alley. One of the short-haired tan dogs played with her pups. Bucharesti dogs are owned by everyone because of a lack of space in the apartments. When she spotted him, she growled a short snarl, and took a step toward him, ears low. Donovan walked on, and the dog lost interest, but a small huddle of gypsy children poked their heads out of the next alley.

The tiny gang of six was led by what appeared to be an eight-year-old boy, whose filthy hands were almost as black as his hair and eyes. With one arm he balanced a cherubic three-year-old on his hip. Her chubby cheeks seemed to hold as much street dirt as her protector, but beneath the smudges, she was as striking as any of the angels in Titian's paintings. A cigarette dangled from the side of the little boy's mouth. He made a slight gesture to the right and left sides of the street, and Donovan saw the beginnings of a swarming, or a gang-begging at the least.

"*Nu* (no)," he called his voice soft. "It will bring you bad luck. Stay there." They stopped and watched him with no emotion. Remaining on the side of the street opposite the alleyway, he took out his wallet and made a show of placing three five-hundred lei bills on the cobblestones and covered them with a pebble. It was worth almost a dollar. Turning his back to them, he continued on his way to cries of "*Multumesc.*"

"*Placere* (you're welcome)." He kept walking, glancing back from time to time, just in case.

From a safe distance, he stopped to study the gang of street urchins. The leader had pulled out a wad of bills at least two inches thick and was wrapping half of the newest earnings around the outside. His shiny black eyes never left Donovan; they were narrowed, calculating.

In a moment, Donovan had entered the large park, relieved at the protection it offered. The massive pale trees lined the path as if marching in column formation. He passed each one, first left, then right, up an easy grade, and then down a shallow incline. By the time he had passed the tiny boat pond, the open areas began to close in, the number of lovers thinned out; the old caretaker trees became fewer. The massive trees in this part of the park seemed to cast longer shadows, their immense arms stealing sunlight. He neared the farthest end of the park and looked for a bench or table on which to enjoy the dappled sunlight.

He chose a bench near the mouth of a sizeable maze and sat down to think about his palace job. He got up, retrieved a willow branch from the bushes behind his bench, and sat again on the bench, leaning to face the ground, the better to draw in the dirt between his feet. With the branch, he traced the outline of a section of Ceausescu's palace that led from the great hall and down the corridor to the ballroom. The ballroom—easily a hundred feet square—had the unique feature of a retractable ceiling, presumably to present the stars above to the stars of the ball. It was there he knew he would find the unmonitored and unmarked staff elevator that would take him to the warehouse five floors beneath the surface.

From the left corner of his eye, he caught a slight movement. He glanced in that direction, toward a curve in the path, where a solitary man had just rounded the corner. Mindful of the "ghost" phone call at the hotel, Donovan dropped his eyes, but continued to monitor the man's progress. He stretched, taking a second to glance around, and then reached over his shoulder to loosen the knife in its sheath. Fifty feet now, the man following the dead middle of the path like a streetcar follows its track. Donovan could almost smell the trouble swirling up and around him. He slid the transparent knife into his hand, while shifting his feet, sliding one under the bench for leverage.

Donovan reviewed the vital spots to hit first and hard. Kneecap, genitals, kidney, heart, carotid, and eyeball, if he had to. At thirty feet, it was obvious the man was now avoiding eye contact.

He was a scrawny five feet seven and more Turk than Latin as Romanian looks went. Just over one-fifty, max. Nice tidy shape. No bulge inside the shoulder, but Donovan guessed there would be a knife, maybe a bar, up his sleeve. The man was now fifteen feet away and easing across the path toward the bench. Donovan watched the outline of a weapon drop down the inside of the sleeve and into the man's hand. Yes, knife or bar.

Donovan jumped up. "Excuse me, sir. Do you have a light?" He moved to cover the brief space between them. "Do you speak English? *Vous parlez Français?*" Before the thug could swing the weapon, Donovan whipped his ceramic knife down and across the man's arm, ripping a six inch cut. The man's eyes widened in shock and then narrowed in comprehension and anger, a bar falling to the ground between them. Donovan swung his right leg in a roundhouse that smashed the peroneal nerve above the thug's knee, causing temporary paralysis to the leg. The attacker dropped. Donovan ducked into the maze and was gone.

He estimated he had six to eight seconds to find a good corner for an ambush. He was in the process of tearing through the maze, giving thanks he had been through it once before, when he stopped short. Why not listen for his opponent, get out of his way, double back, and then get the hell out? So he did.

Moments later, Donovan was out of the maze, headed back down the hill, and congratulating himself on a great decision. That was when he found himself ass in the air, and the stark realization came, as he hit the dirt face-first, that he had underestimated his attacker. It seemed he had a partner. A kick in the ribs brought a wave of nausea and rolled him onto his side, knees up to his bloodied nose and consciousness beginning to flee. Something wet dribbled into his eye, stinging, and he tasted copper. A giant of a man, with part of his face obscured by his collar, leaned down and reached into Donovan's front pocket, withdrawing his passport. The giant thanked Donovan with a fist to the kidney and crushed Donovan's hand with his heel until something cracked. The man then kicked him again for good measure and left.

The last thing he remembered was watching the little gypsy boy emptying Donovan's wallet in slow motion, a curl of cigarette smoke around his sister's head, like a halo.

SEAN DONOVAN HAD REGAINED consciousness under similar circumstances in the past, and it was never pleasant. A familiar wave of nausea welled up from his stomach to his craw as he rolled over onto his side. Some grains of gravel and a bit of twig stuck to the side of his face. He drew a knee to his chest and moaned. He exhaled another groan, cutting it off to a grunt as he pulled himself up to one knee. Donovan looked around, preparing to muster the energy and balance to get onto his feet, which were in full mutiny.

Time to take stock. *Am I going into shock? No, not yet. What had been broken? Maybe a rib, but I can breathe without feeling faint, so there's probably just bruising.* Aware of a shooting pain originating in his hand, he looked at it, and saw the outside finger bent at an inappropriate angle. Grimacing against the pain, he pressed the finger down to rest against the others. Even as a groan escaped him, and beads of sweat formed on his brow, he wondered if he was still in danger. He looked around.

A few silent people had gathered, staring as he struggled to his feet. A young man unwrapped an arm from around his girl's neck and retrieved a stout stick from the underbrush, handing it to Donovan by the tip. The youth backed away and asked, "*Politia?*"

"*Nu,*" Donovan grunted in the negative. No police. Leaning on his new cane, he hobbled away from the small, silent group.

It took a half hour to return to his hotel room, normally a ten-minute walk. On the way, he determined he had one loosened tooth—an upper molar toward the back—a bruised rib, and a broken baby finger. Like that scene in the James Bond movie, he thought, not smiling. The patina was wearing off his perfect Romanian day.

Dragon, the very solicitous doorman at the Majestic, helped him to his room, fetching bandages for the rib, tape for the finger, and a bucket of ice for his bruises. He also brought a cloth from the kitchen to wash the blood from Donovan's nose and mouth. He asked no questions and for his discretion, received a tip worth a week's pay. After he left, Donovan pulled up a chair and sat beside a bathroom sink full of ice water, his hand sunk up to the wrist.

Did all of this begin with that phone call? Was he set up right from the hotel door? Two attackers! It hadn't occurred to him there would be a second thug. He had to be more careful. The questions were why he was attacked, and how he could prevent another?

He had an eidetic memory and conjured up every detail he could of the smaller man and his giant assailant, all to no avail. The collar had obscured their faces. Despite his efforts, he felt no tug whatsoever on his recall. It was possible the men wanted some quick cash for the passport, but that theory made no sense, since they had left his money behind. It was also possible the guy needed to get himself or someone else out of the country. He thought about how the little boy had emptied his wallet. Being robbed while he lay helpless was the insult to his injury, and it rankled.

He hobbled over to the wall safe to grab some more money, glancing into the steel wall box to confirm the forged passports he used on occasion were untouched.

Donovan sat for thirty minutes, staring at the pattern in the marble floor and thinking evil thoughts. It wasn't yet noon, and he'd already lost his passport and some cash. The cash wasn't worth fretting over; he had lots of money. What really bothered him was the look the little gypsy boy had tossed him. The look said *I win; you lose, because I am patient and smart, and you're not.*

He stood up and limped over to the nightstand. Tossing back enough Aspirin to alarm his liver, Donovan shrugged into a French blue shirt. He rolled up the sleeves and headed out the door.

First stop was the doorman.

Dragon was helpful. He not only knew of the boy but was able to explain the boy's begging route. With a thick Romanian accent and generous waves and gestures, he said, "Yes, he is this tall, with a liddle gorl what has yellow hairs. He is not nice. Steals thinks. Yes. Very bad boy. Where can you find him? He is in the *Quartier Française*, maybe two o'clock. Soon, soon. I see him there oftentimes. He is not living there, he just walks all the time to beg. It is not far. Ah. You know this place? You are welcome, Mr. Donovan. *Placere.*"

Donovan proceeded along Victory Road to the five-street intersection where he took a hard left into the tiny French Quarter. The three-block neighborhood was criss-crossed with narrow streets, and every alley darted in and then turned left or right into a labyrinth of paths. These ended at doorways or circled in behind a building, carrying the pedestrian toward small, alien courtyards that looked like nothing Donovan had ever seen.

Each alleyway was cobblestoned, and every building appeared to creep upward. Balconies hovered over alleyways and threatened to topple at any moment, although in reality they'd lasted for centuries. They shielded the sun and painted a sepia-toned twilight, even in mid-afternoon. On normal days, it took no more than three steps into this foreign landscape to change the mood from happy carelessness to one of wariness. He skirted the edge of the Quarter, avoiding the alleys for the moment, and followed the tourist paths.

Back on the main street, he sought a spot where he could watch for the little boy. He entered the first tiny church he came to. Crossing the stained and cracked marble floor, he sat in a pew on the street side, furthest from where the priest stood praying. The Orthodox churches in Romania hold services all day long, and members of the congregation come and go according to their schedules.

The room was round. He'd read this design was to prevent the devil from cornering the parishioners. It was empty, save for him and the priest. Donovan ignored the droning of the priest, scooching sideways in the pew as much as his aching side would permit, and watched the street from the narrow, ornate window at the back.

It took almost an hour before he spotted the pair. The boy and his sister were alone this time, begging from the edge of an alleyway across the street. He watched them work for ten minutes, with the girl sitting in the shadow and the boy darting out to accost each tourist as they'd pass. They then moved on to an alleyway closer to where Donovan sat, and each time the boy would step out and beg for money, before fading back into the alley. Donovan knew if he went up to them, they would evaporate into the labyrinth of paths. So he continued to watch and wait.

It took another half hour before the boy picked up his sister from the mouth of the closest alley and crossed the street, coming close to the tiny church where Donovan stood hidden in the entryway, face cloaked in a darkness that matched his mood. The boy drew close, and Donovan decided not to pull him into the church but rather to follow and choose his moment later.

After they passed, he slipped out of the doorway and mingled with the crowd, staying at least twenty yards behind the children. He followed them for two blocks, and the boy begged with much success. At the next intersection, the boy waited, giving his attention to one direction, and smoking. A black cloud of tangled hair obscured his eyes. The little girl seemed content to sit on his hip, arms about his neck, saying nothing. In a moment, a bus came along and stopped before them. The two got on and just before the bus pulled away, Donovan composed his face to mask the effects of his recent assault and slipped on as well.

Donovan stood by the door, noting the few passengers on the bus. He hid his face even as he watched the boy solicit from the passengers. Each one rejected him with a wave of a hand or a soft curse. Face expressionless, the boy continued to the back seat and placed the little girl on it. He took a quick look out of the window, his back to his sister, and then turned, startled to find himself facing Donovan, who was just approaching the bench beside the little girl. The few other passengers on the bus faced forward, seemingly disinterested in the activity of a filthy Gypsy boy, and averting their eyes from the beggar whom they had rebuffed. The three sat alone, the boy's eyes round with alarm and Donovan's left arm wrapped around the tiny blonde child.

"Remember me?" He spoke to her in a gentle voice as her tiny hand circled his forefinger. "Yes, I believe you do." Turning from her, he looked at the little girl's protector. "Do you speak English?" Donovan's voice was low and betrayed no emotion.

"Well, do you?" It took some self-control to keep his voice pleasant. He made a conscious effort to keep his recent pain separate from this little matter of a few dollars. Why frighten a little girl?

The boy shook his head. "*Nu*. I spik only liddle English. *Mais je parle un peu Français? Parlez-vous Français?*" He waited.

Donovan reverted to French. "Of course. Listen, what I have to say is very simple. I want my money back." He opened his shirt, just a little, to reveal the sheen from the transparent knife. He tapped it with his fingernail and then closed his shirt. He could almost see the boy's thoughts moving. "It's that simple." He looked into the boy's eyes. "That's fair, isn't it?"

The boy sat motionless, looking undecided. Donovan reached toward his shirt and the knife. The boy raised one hand and with the other, pulled out the thick wad of bills Donovan had seen earlier that day. He handed it all to Donovan, his eyes never leaving the dirty wad of bills. One of the passengers glanced back, and Donovan smiled and waved. The woman huffed and turned to face front. He took the bills, peeled off enough to cover his recent loss, and dropped it in his pocket. The boy's shoulders drooped in relief.

Watching him, Donovan sought out the largest remaining bill from the boy's wad, a hundred thousand lei bill worth about twenty dollars—a week's pay for a waitress—and ripped it in two. He pocketed half of the bill and returned the remainder of the gypsy's cash, brushing the ripped bill across the back of the little girl's fingers. She reached for it, and Donovan pulled it away, causing her to smile. His eyes never moved from the boy. "I will meet you, alone, in front of the Leitha Hotel at midnight. I'll trade you this for a little bit of information. Remember! Alone, at midnight."

He stood up, limped to the front of the bus and got off at the next stop, not bothering to glance back at the boy. He had heard gypsies never snitched, and although he wanted him to talk, there was no guarantee the little boy would even meet him later.

Donovan began the walk back to the Majestic, but with his body protesting, he decided to seek a taxi. The drive took just a few moments, all traffic lights and stop signs just suggestions to this particular cabbie.

In the lobby, he sat down beside the bar, a lone guest with his day eaten up, a glass of Romanian red to push back his headache. He listened to a pair of young men serenading each other on piano and violin, alternating between Debussy and Elton John, no vocals. They played as if they were being judged in a competition.

The music soothed him like a reiki massage, and he felt his energy return. But his spirits remained bleak. How did he find himself in Eastern Europe with the shit kicked out of him, robbed, and carrying three forged passports? When was that moment many years back, where it had occurred to him he could bypass the legal ways of working? How did he slip into a world that rewarded, richly, those people who were skilled enough to separate people from their possessions? And what if he had died? Who would mourn or even remember him? He sighed. *This was self-indulgent.* He pushed up from the sofa and was pleased to note that if he caught his breath as he arose, he could avoid the little moan caused by the pain in his ribs.

Back in his room, he took his time changing into shorts and a T-shirt. Feeling better, he began another list. The process of getting through the palace had to become intuitive by the time he was inside:

-Access using the CIDA Docs

-Lose Katya (an errand?)

-Dump tour guide

-Get approval to 'fix' monitors and security

-Media/security Room

-Floor Map

-Minus 5 Floor (No elevator button!)

-Special Entrance: Need an access code.

-Left, left, 60 feet, left

-12-12-25-9-9 Middle shelf

-10 inches by 8 inches

-Disassemble the cup

-Wrap: 10 minutes, tops.

Once the approach seemed feasible, he consigned the list to memory and burned it in a massive onyx ashtray. With luck, the strategy would work. He had received the floor plans in an email from his client, Umbra, so it was time to get to work.

He had to meet Katya, since it would be either her or Petruscu who would lead the tour of the palace. What could she tell him about getting around the palace? She'd refused his offer to take her out to eat, murmuring she was having supper with her sister, and how it was a long bus ride from her home to the city core. But, she would return to meet with him and others in the courtyard tavern for a beverage the following evening. *This was working out well.* He'd go to the concert with Petruscu and meet Katya afterward. But for now, it was time to try to heal. He lowered himself onto the bed, no careful folding of sheets this time. He lay on his right side, taped pinkie resting on his left hip.

WHEN HE AWOKE JUST before midnight, it was raining sharp knives. He drew the damp curtain away from the partially-opened window and looked across the street toward the Leitha Hotel. To see it, he had to peer through countless tiny black droplets that flung themselves to the streets and gutters and sparked against the cobblestones, making them slick and distinct. Every few seconds, the countless droplets coalesced into silver sheets of rain, pounding down to the street. Puddles fed the rivulets at the lower end of the intersection, carrying sticks and refuse, damming up corners. The cobblestones melted into small street corner lakes.

Two incongruous silhouettes leaned against the front wall of the Capital, just yards apart, seeming to ignore each other. They were indistinct, faces covered respectively by a hat and cap. The one closest to the hotel steps, standing just outside the light, was half the height of the other. Donovan knew it was the gypsy boy despite the slashing rain and the absence of the little girl. He squinted, wondering if the boy's hands and face would come clean in the downpour. He shifted his attention to the man who stood nearby. Built like a rugby player, he was over six feet, five inches. Why was he present? The streetlights revealed form, but the rain distorted detail. Nevertheless, the shadowy figure lurked just beyond Donovan's recollection.

Then it hit him.

Bastard! It was his friend from the park! "Bastard!" He said it aloud this time, backing away from his window even though his room was dark. He grabbed his windbreaker and threw open his suitcase to reveal what he called his toy box. Pushing aside the cell phones and timers, he picked up a monkey paw, which was a little rope-and-hardwood ball that could almost be concealed in the palm of his hand. Dangling from one end was a thin rope with a D-buckle on it. He thought about the monkey's paw as he took the marble stairs two at a time. It was no match for a gun, but a nasty treat if he could get in close.

Dragon was in the foyer chatting up one of the musicians. Donovan took advantage of the doorman's distraction to ease past the open foyer. He then took the long corridor to the back entrance. Once there, he ran along the back of the building, up the alley, past the strip club, the "sexy clubs," and the short, wet line-up of men.

At the edge of the darkened alleyway, he noticed the streetlights weren't working. The storm did not relent, and the lightning was spaced at regular intervals. With timing on his side, could he make his move across the street under cover of darkness? Too risky. He backed off and walked the long way around the building, traversing the street a long block away.

Soaked, he eased along the edge of each building, willing himself to be small, willing away the ache in his side. By following the contours of each building and not hurrying, Donovan hoped his approach would go unnoticed. Was it rain, or sweat on his hands? *I do not like confrontation, but I want my passport back. I want to know why I'm being singled out.* It was time to work around the perimeter of the last building. If the plan's execution went right, he would come out of the alley beside the shadow-and-a-half.

He didn't spy any bitches whelping their pups in the back of the alley this time, but one lone dog appeared. The thin animal met him halfway down the alley, stepping from behind a sodden cardboard box. He bared his teeth and braced himself to lunge. Donovan took one step back and with one eye on the animal, reached down, searching fingers finding a loose cobblestone. He grabbed it and let it fly, catching the dog on his hind quarter. With a yelp, the animal bolted into the darkness. With a grim smile, Donovan passed the spot where the dog had been hit. *The cobblestone might come in handy again.* He pocketed it and moved on, feeling his window of opportunity slipping away.

Aside from a rat scurrying to avoid being stepped on, Donovan met no other creatures of the night and arrived at the far end of the alley unnoticed and unannounced. He inched forward, paused to listen, and then moved forward again. The rain pounded down, making a terrible din. Despite the noise, he could hear the two speaking Romanian, but could pick up little of what they said. The giant was closer, and Donovan hoped he could use this to his advantage, or at least keep the boy out from between them.

The man wanted something, and the boy was unable or unwilling to get *or do* it for him. The man growled at the boy. Donovan knew trouble was about to rain down, and it was likely the little boy would find himself at the receiving end of it.

Donovan reached into his pocket and pulled on the cord attached to the monkey's paw, wishing he carried a gun.

But it was too late.

Like a snake's strike, the huge man grabbed the child, hauling him up by the hair. Donovan saw steel flash upward, the massive hand behind the blade lifting the boy off the ground, the knife's hilt stopped only by the boy's ribcage.

"No!" Donovan roared, the power of his distress not quite drowned out by the downpour. The man stopped dead. He bent low, as if to look under the pounding rain. Pushed up tight against the building, his head twisted to the left and right, and then he wiped the water from his eyes, trying to spot the intruder as the little gypsy lay in the street, dead or dying. Donovan lobbed the monkey's paw at the assailant, the weapon made visible by the lightning. It floated the fifteen feet to its victim, who tried to bat it away with his open palm. One hundred and seventy-five barbed metal shards as sharp as straightened fishhooks shot outward from every quadrant of the orb, attaching to, and in many places, pushing their way through the man's hand. Lightning flashed again, and Donovan saw the results of his effort as he ran forward.

With a howl, the man dropped his knife and tried to pry the monkey's paw from his bloodied hand. But it was impossible to find a spot on the ball not covered in barbs. The release cord attached to the ball of hooks would have been useless to the giant, given the threshold of pain required to surmount in order to pull it free. But by then, Donovan let loose the cobblestone towards the man's nose. It connected with all the force an angry man could muster. The giant fell face down and didn't move.

Donovan turned to the little boy who lay in the streaming gutter, his life leaking down the street in wet, shiny black threads. Donovan picked him up, cradling him in his lap, and studied his face for life. But the gypsy boy was gone.

Sighing, Donovan stood and placed the tiny corpse facing the building wall, to cover the face from the rain as best he could. With a shudder, he redirected his attention to man lying in the gutter.

Remembering his experience in the park, Donovan looked around, checking for any movement. Nothing. The three were all just inside of the shadow of the alley, and with no streetlights and an unforgiving rain, there was no way he could be spotted.

Unless someone was searching this particular place for one of them.

He thought about the man's partner, the smaller assailant he had slashed in the park. Was he nearby? Maybe. He might show up. But the job of murdering a little boy would be so straightforward, Donovan expected the man was safe and dry somewhere.

Returning to his work, he rolled the unconscious man to his back and hovered over him, grimacing at the mess of the man's face, but was unable to identify him. Holding the offending cobblestone high over his head just in case, and prepared to cave in the man's head at the slightest movement, he slipped his hand into the man's jacket pocket. A wallet. He probed further, but all he found was a key and some folded bills. No passports. Disappointed, he pocketed the contents, including the key, and stood.

He placed his foot upon the man's wrist and reached down, grabbing the rope of the monkey paw, and pulled hard. With a squishy sound, more than a hundred barbs released their grip on the gristle, flesh, and nerves of the offended hand. The shards from the monkey paw performed more damage on their way out than on their way in. The man didn't move. Donovan disarmed the weapon, rinsed it in the gutter, and slid it into his jacket pocket.

The thought crossed his mind that the man might be dead. *Don't care.* Donovan wiped the corner of his shoe on the man's jacket and headed down the alley.

Moments later, he was behind the dumpster in the alley beside his hotel. *With one or even two bodies showing up in the news, hotel staff would remember anyone walking in at three in the morning, especially if I show up covered in mud and blood.* Donovan had another thought. What if he had stumbled onto something bigger, some kind of crime or large criminal operation? That may not be the case, but knowing of Petruscu's bank account, some kind of shitstorm was swirling nearby. Someone had paid Petruscu that money to do illegal things. That someone could be looking for him for reasons he couldn't even suspect. And that phone call in the hotel, just before getting beaten. Someone knew where he lived.

Crouching down against the wall of this alley wouldn't work for long. He had to move. So deciding, he opened the man's wallet and found an address not far away. He began a long, wet trudge through the streets of Bucharest, Paris of the East.

Chapter Four

B*ucharest in the Rain*
Tuesday Evening

The apartment building looked like all the others in the neighborhood: rectangular and eleven storeys, sitting alongside a line of other rectangular apartment buildings, which Donovan presumed to be grey. The lightning offered few clues. Most of the lights were out in the building, and several hundred people were sleeping through the deluge. *I hope so.* Donovan didn't know Romanian culture well enough that he could assume anything. He opened the door and passed through the foyer into the heart of the building, with his footprints puddling behind him.

The lighting was non-existent along most of the first floor hallway, and he walked into darkness in the long space halfway between each bare, dim light bulb. At the end of the hall, he ignored the broken down elevators and chose the quieter, darker stairwells. Each floor's stairs had three left turns, and he counted corners until he was on the fifth floor. Taking care not to let the stairwell door slam, he eased into the hallway.

Apartment 505. He waited a full minute at the door before trying the key, his senses bristling. He didn't bother to listen for an alarm; who in this building could afford an alarm system? What he didn't know, however, was who, if anyone, was sleeping behind the door. A rustling a little way down the hall sped up the process. Then he was in, behind a closed door, listening.

After a moment, Donovan strode over to the bedroom door and pushed it aside. Two single beds, a closet, and a chest of drawers. No people. He stared at the remaining closed door. Another bedroom? He grasped the knob and turned it a quarter of a revolution at a time. The door opened into a microscopic, unkempt storage room, smelling of garlic and old turnips. He let out a slow breath; he was alone. Returning to the main living space, he placed a dishcloth over the lone table lamp before he dared turn it on. The living room was small, *barely big enough to swing a cat*, and it contained little furniture.

Wanting to know whom he was dealing with, Donovan began with a quick look-around for photographs. He spotted a couple of five-by-sevens in cheap frames, each showing two men. One was a summer scene at the beach, the other a winter scene that appeared to be of a somewhat formal event.

Donovan recognized the second man. It was the slight chap he'd tricked in the park. He seemed to be the brother or at least the best friend of the fellow now lying in the street, judging by the number of photos of the two of them. The photos were found on a tiny table holding a small stack of unframed snapshots. Some were of parents and grandparents (he supposed); others were of the two. The only other framed photo was a fetching Las Vegas publicity still of Celine Dion.

He entered the bedroom. The closet was tidy, with two suits, two jackets, and a pair of muddy wellingtons lying limp in the back. Donovan turned to the single beds and checked the first. Nothing. But, under the ragged mattress of the second bed, he found a stash of passports in a packet tucked in the middle of the board the mattress rested on. Scooping them up, he headed back to the main area to take a closer look.

Shrugging off his sodden jacket, he slumped into the sway-backed easy chair next to the muted lamp. He tossed the deck of passports onto the table beside him, looked around the room, and stopped for a second to listen for any new noises. All quiet, he picked up the first, revealing a middle-aged man with a grey moustache. Some American named Merle Overholser; Donovan shrugged, for the man's face generated no spark of recognition. Curious, he flipped through the passport. Lots of stamps. Well-travelled. The next passport belonged to the giant, Tomas Dobra. Apart from his recent experiences, the man was unfamiliar, and he knew he hadn't met Dobra before. *The little guy probably has his on him, so it won't show up here.* He tossed it aside. Next up was a Brit by the name of Edward Yorke. The photo revealed a fat man with a shiny forehead, who seemed to be sweating. No bells were going off. He noted the occupation: Parliamentary Staff, Government of England. *Hmm.* Donovan wasn't hopeful, since with the help of eidetic memory, he remembered almost everything. He set it with the passport of the American.

Third time lucky. Donovan stared at his real passport: Sean Joel Donovan, Canadian. Another well-travelled guy. He read the details, noting the photo made him look a little like Bono. Age forty, hair black, no grey. *Really? Am I forty?* He slipped himself back into his breast pocket, humming. Passport number four showed a man who had long since said goodbye to his forties. Galen Intos Attanasio. Greek. Stamps on almost every page. Donovan whistled. He knew this guy, Gaia, as he was known to the art world. *Bon vivant*, capitalist, art collector, cure-all for boredom. This passport was either useless or worth a pretty penny.

"I guess I'll have to see what the market can bear," he muttered tossing it back into the pile.

Somebody could drop by at any time—like the smaller, but still dangerous, friend of the giant. Time to snag a change of clothes and bolt before company arrived. Donovan rifled through the closet and chose something boring and huge but dry. Enough time for one last look around. He popped his sodden clothes into a plastic bag found under the sink and then proceeded to the bedroom. Nothing interesting in the stark chest of drawers huddling in the corner. Returning to the front room to retrieve the packet with the passports, he put it in the bag with his soiled clothes. Donovan reached behind the door at the last moment to grab a decrepit umbrella, smiling that it, too, had a bent rib. Holding his bag of clothing, he left the apartment building behind and headed toward the hotel.

It was almost three. On the way, he had dropped his muddy, bloodied clothes over a small bridge and tucked the packet into his shirt. Rather than walk around for the rest of the night, Donovan waited beside the Majestic, where he leaned against a wall and waited for Dragon to take his break.

As he waited, he thought about the giant, Dobra who, if he lived, would want revenge. If that happened, it would go down in one of two ways: Broken Face would either lie in wait to ambush him (again), a risky endeavour since Donovan would be waiting for him as well. Or, he would sic the police on him, which was by far the likelier scenario. If it was the latter, the idea would be to catch Donovan with the batch of stolen passports. In that event, things would not go well for him. The passports had to disappear, along with the oilskin packet and its contents.

He walked to the back of the hotel and found a crack in the wall behind the building's refuse bin. The packet fit by squeezing it deep enough to be invisible to passersby. It would be safe for a day or so.

Getting back into his room without being noticed was straightforward. Just before jumping into a scalding shower, he took Broken Face's pants and shirt and tossed them out his hotel window to the alley below. Some homeless bum or scrounger would have them on before six o'clock, he bet.

Chapter Five

C oncordia University
     Montreal, Canada

Roberto Umbra, Professor of Romance Languages, pulled a cell phone from the drawer of his desk and keyed in a thirteen digit number. He listened for the single word "Hello?" and then spoke.

"Hello. You and I are in the process of conducting a bit of business in Bucharest, a little matter of a chalice? Yes, that's it. At any rate, you had left me this number for emergency purposes, and I wanted to mention that after this, erm, business is completed, I may have another opportunity for you. Why don't we talk some more when we next meet? It might be very interesting, not to mention profitable, for you. Does that sound good? Yes? Excellent! So, until then. *Ciao.*" Umbra smiled and tapped his cell phone closed. "That hook is baited."

Chapter Six

The Majestic, Bucharest

The next day arrived sunny, with little wisps and puffs of humidity steaming from the sidewalks and streets, carrying away the moisture of the previous night. Donovan could enjoy none of it. He awoke stiff and sore, his body revisiting the punishment of the previous two days, thoughts of the dead boy at the forefront of his mind. His side in particular felt raw and unforgiving of the punishment it had received. He pushed the pain out of his mind because it was Wednesday, the day to visit the Houses of Parliament, former home to President Ceausescu, dictator and martyr to communism.

Nicolai Ceausescu's people finally ran out of patience with him in December, 1989. In an effort to quell the demonstrations led by the miners, he'd ordered the row of tanks standing between him and his people to open fire on them. Instead, their turrets rotated one hundred and eighty degrees to point to Ceausescu, and raised their gun barrels toward the balcony on which he stood. They caught him, killed him, and then unleashed a revolutionary firestorm. The people of Romania—miners, students, even the military—ran through the streets, shooting his few supporters, and defacing buildings and monuments, anything representing the way of life they were overthrowing. The country, now bankrupt and without a leader, ground to a stand-still. It would be a long ten years before the construction cranes would re-mobilize and the new agents of change—governments like Canada and Australia, as well as American corporations like Sun Computer Systems—would reinvigorate the country with infusions of equal parts capital and technology.

The buffet-style breakfast was comprised of a spectacular smorgasbord of foods from around the world. Yet, as with many travelers, Donovan had entered the "one week" tedium syndrome, where the food after seven days in a foreign country still looked wonderful but no longer settled well in the stomach. He passed on the eggs and ham, smoked salmon and bagels, and picked up a fruit cup and some yogurt. He had just tasted a strawberry when two men sat down, flanking him. It was obvious to Donovan they were police agents: similar dress, one leading with the other in lock-step behind, stern faces, and a glance around the room before sitting down without being asked.

Donovan chose not to smile at the apparent relish with which they approached their roles. He couldn't help but offer a tiny jab, though. "Really? Sunglasses at the breakfast table? Why don't you just wear a sign that says, 'I'm tough, just ask me.' And the matching suits; y'know they just shout 'I'm a cop.' Seriously. Anyway, how can I help you?"

"We have reason to believe you are in possession of stolen property. Security documents of a politically delicate nature. We wish to discuss this with you. In your room."

The second agent, meanwhile, had cadged a fork from another table and was spearing fruit like he had won it in a lottery.

Donovan thought. He had only just sat down, so there hadn't been enough time to plant anything in his room. It also boded well for him he wasn't yet going for the ride that led to a rougher form of questioning. Finally, the amount of information they had already shared with him told him they were not experienced agents and weren't Romanian ex-military who had been trained by former KGB agents. It also suggested they were fishing. He calmed down a speck.

"Sounds good, gentlemen. May I fetch you a glass of orange juice before we proceed upstairs?" He could swear the hungrier, more taciturn agent brightened behind the aviator glasses, but there were no takers. They stood and waited while he ordered a pot of coffee and three cups to be sent to his room, yet another act that furrowed the forehead of the lead agent. On the way past the main desk, Donovan asked to see the manager. Before the agents could protest, the desk clerk had bounced out of his seat and dashed through the door behind him. Donovan smiled.

"Sorry, guys. This won't take but a moment. Ah, Mr. Tufan. These gentlemen are escorting me to my room for an interview; however, I have business with the Ministry in half an hour. Could you send somebody up to get me in twenty minutes, please? You know how time passes when one is having fun."

The manager nodded, smiling. "Of course, Mr. Donovan. It would be our pleasure." He beamed at the agents, waving a generous hand toward his hotel guest, as if last night's storm itself could be explained away with but a smile from Mr. Donovan. "He is *delegati*. Please. Enjoy your visit with us, however brief, at the Hotel Majestic." And he withdrew.

They walked to the second floor in silence, three pairs of dark business shoes, two sets more worn than the third, all tapping on the polished, pink marble stairs. They hadn't got the door opened when a member of the staff appeared with a pot of coffee and some cups. When the heavy oak door closed behind them, the quieter agent moved straight to the bedroom. Donovan heard drawers opening as he sat down with his coffee.

"So. What exactly are we searching for?" He leaned forward as if the answer would be fascinating.

The agent didn't answer but sat, staring at Donovan's broken baby finger, which was taped to the one beside it. "A mishap while you are on vacation?"

Donovan looked at his two fingers. "Oh, that. At the airport, my hand caught in the luggage strap just as the trunk lid of the taxi came down. Clumsy, really. By the way, I'm here on business with the Ministry of Labor as I noted at the front desk. No vacation."

The agent sat pondering this response while his partner continued the search in the other room. "While we wait for my colleague to do his work, let me ask you, do you have a money belt on you, Mr. Donovan?"

"Why, yes I do."

"Show me the money. And the belt."

Donovan was willing to bet the contents of his belt this man had never seen Tom Cruise or any of his movies, so it was easy to contain a smile at the unintentional reference. He reached into his pants and pulled out a money belt, emptying its contents onto the table. He then turned the cloth belt inside-out to show the agent it was now empty. He handed over fifteen hundred dollars in U.S. cash—twenties—and his still-damp passport.

The agent sat, coffee untouched, riffling the twenties without even looking at them. He wasn't counting. *I bet the bastard is gauging his chances at walking away with a year's salary for ten minutes' work.* The more taciturn agent returned from the bedroom with a document in one hand and a jackknife in the other. He placed them beside Donovan's passport, took his coffee to the window, and fiddled with the drapes.

"Mr. Donovan, where are the documents?"

"You have my passport in front of you, and your partner has just presented you with a document signed by the Canadian International Development Agency and the World Bank Group. That document advises that I am a delegate, as the hotel manager downstairs said. My understanding is that the Ministry of Labor, *your* Ministry of Labor, believes I can be of some use to your country. I am of no use to your country if I have been physically abused, and believe me, I am also of no use to your country if I have been robbed or even pissed off. Am I clear?"

The agent's mouth turned upward to form some semblance of a smile, but no humor was shared. He dropped the wad of bills, reached over, and took Donovan's wrist. With his other hand, he grasped the broken finger and...did nothing. After taking a few seconds to regain his temper, the agent spoke. "It is my turn to be clear. We received a call from a trustworthy source, and...you did a bad thing last night. A man is dead because of you." His voice took on an injured tone. "Our country does not need murderers running around, killing innocent citizens." His voice returned to an impassive cadence.

"You are not in jail at this moment because we are still gathering evidence. But once we are finished, we will arrest you, and your status as delegate will be revoked, if indeed you are not thrown in some *oubliette* of a prison cell. Now, before we leave, would you like to help us with this investigation? Do you, for example, have anything you would now like to give back to us?"

There was a knock at the door; discrete, polite. Their twenty minutes were up, and hotel staff had arrived to save him.

"Um, before you leave, gentlemen, I seem to have forgotten to ask you for identification. May I please see your police papers?" The agents ignored him, rose, and brushed past the hotel clerk without another word. Donovan tipped the staff, closed the door, and heaved a sigh, touching his broken finger.

At nine o'clock sharp, he presented himself for the second time in three days at the entrance to the Ministry of Labor. The door itself was unprepossessing, with a modest sign advising visitors of their destination. Behind him, the former KGB headquarters had been converted into an annex of the ministry—the security division, Donovan noted. It was much older and like many of the buildings throughout the city, carried the hallmark of bullets fired during the revolution. They weren't holes because when the bullets hit centuries-old walls, they chipped off small pieces of stone, creating dimples. Any smashed windows would have been repaired ten years ago, but filling in the pockmarks was an unnecessary cost, however displeasing the marred stonework was to the eye.

Donovan entered and showed his passport and briefcase to the guard who, in turn, reviewed a paper list of potential visitors for the day. Again, Donovan heard the word *delegati*, followed by a smile. *Such a magical word! It's the key to anywhere in this country.* He noted the guards were different from the shift that had reviewed his papers on Friday. Relieved at not having to answer questions about a visit to the Ministry that didn't take place, he returned to the matter at hand: getting into this building today. This guard paid great attention to the document and passport but ignored the briefcase altogether. Donovan continued up a broad flight of stairs, marble of course and turning right this time, entered the Ministry of Labor for Romania, International Division.

The area was bright and busy. The director's office occupied a third of the Ministry, although it seemed to play host to numerous visitors. The remaining area was an open concept design, with desks facing one another and sharing ancient computers. The wall facing the mezzanine was comprised of windows, lending a fishbowl effect. Donovan caught the eye of the director, Razvan Petruscu through the glass.

"Good morning, Mr. Petruscu. Thank you for making time for me."

"*Placere*, it is a pleasure, Mr. Donovan. You slept well, I trust? It was a lot of rain last night, no?"

"Indeed." Donovan took his time to lower himself into the chair. Once seated, he leaned away from his tender ribs and assumed as pleasant a demeanor as he could. "Fortunately, I had no place to go and remained as dry as a bone. So, I understand you are going to sit me down beside one of your technicians, and together we will see what sort of security systems your servers maintain. I will check for weaknesses and write up a report, recommending which systems could be used to address them. Later this month or early next month, a representative from Canada will come to Bucharest and do the installations. Your entire directory system will be bulletproof from hackers in forty days. Is this basically what the Memorandum of Understanding states?"

Petruscu nodded. "So much work accomplished this morning, and I haven't even offered you a cup of coffee. You Canadians are hard workers!"

"Not so much. All of your staff were here working before I arrived this morning. But speaking of coffee, I brought you a gift. Canada is not much of a coffee country—too cold!—but I brought you a pound of dark roasted coffee beans for your apartment and a pound for your colleagues here at the office. And, of course, that makes a little more space in my suitcase for me to buy myself a fine Romanian tablecloth."

"This gift is not necessary," Petruscu chided, "but most appreciated. Here, let me pour you some now, unless you would prefer tea?"

"Coffee would be wonderful, yes to the milk and sugar, please. And with whom am I working this morning?"

"You will work beside Teresa today." He pointed to a woman who sat at one of the pairs of facing desks, keying something into her computer. She had strawberry blonde hair pulled into a bun, severe black glasses, and a businesslike attitude to match.

"And Petr over there will make any systems adjustments you may need." Petruscu pointed through the glass at a harried young man in a shiny navy suit, loose tie, and cigarette dangling from the side of his thin lips. Petruscu smiled. "So. You are new in Romanian security business."

"That's right. It's like house insurance. Ninety percent of the time my work is unnecessary. It's just that pesky ten per cent that makes you want my services."

"That sounds correct, sir." Petruscu grinned and then waved a sheaf of papers toward the staff in the open concept office. "As you saw in the proposal, and as we discussed on the phone before you came from Canada, we have a labor exchange service that we call the Job Bank. Your job is to install a security system to protect it."

The director again pointed to the woman closest to the window. "Teresa is very good at keeping our national job exchange running. Our staff are well-educated in systems infrastructure and platform maintenance. She'll explain what she does in more detail and how we use our software platform. Teresa can also explain how your security system will fit on the local system. The security system will also have to be available in the Labor offices in two other cities."

Donovan nodded in agreement.

When he and Petruscu were done, Donovan sat beside Teresa for a while, watching her work. He was surprised to note how cheerful she was in contrast to the seriousness of her look and how old her computer was. Teresa mentioned that most of the staff had been educated at the same university, so training wouldn't be an issue. Any challenges they faced would come down to hardware and access to pipelines, computers, and servers: the capital costs.

Razvan called the small team together and introduced Donovan, who in turn reminded them of the parameters of the project. The job bank software that would match people to employers and employers to people was already installed. Donovan, in turn, would be working behind the scenes to ensure the system was stable and could rebuff any hackers or malware from outsiders. From a technology standpoint, Donovan didn't worry about the equipment Canada had sent, so he anticipated a smooth roll-out. Judging from the questions they asked, the team was well-informed about the project, and they seemed competent to carry it out. He made a mental note to either chat with a contact at HP about a donation of computers, or even bring a new laptop with him and leave it here on his next trip to Romania.

After thanking the team, he sat down in a spare chair in the director's office to gather specs and map out an installation process. Petruscu had gone to his private office to make phone calls, leaving Donovan to transfer the software from his laptop to the Ministry server.

Just before lunch, Petruscu returned, accompanied by a tall, slender woman dressed in a cream pantsuit. She had a taut, angular face, framed by jet-black hair. Her lips were full and her chin strong. She smiled a warm welcome. Petruscu's tone was apologetic. "I'd hoped to take you to lunch, but, unfortunately, the minister has asked me to meet him at this time."

He indicated the woman. "You met Katya on your first visit to Bucharest. You've known her as a labor exchange specialist, but perhaps she could also be your hostess over lunch? As you know, she will be your escort to the palace this afternoon, so sharing this meal will give you time to get to know her work as our Public Affairs representative."

Donovan offered her his most winning smile. "Of course. That would be fine. Katya, do you mind using up your lunch time to hang around with me? I would, of course, be pleased to buy your meal, but you will still lose that time."

Katya, smiled, revealing even white teeth. "It will be my pleasure. I will practice my English."

"Your English seems to be perfect, and I agree we shouldn't let me massacre your language. We'll stick to English. I see it's almost twelve o'clock. Let's go eat now and beat the noon-hour rush."

Donovan looked over to Teresa. "We're finished for today. If it's okay, I'll come and see you first thing in the morning to pick up those directory files I sent to the printer. Okay? Great."

He turned to Petruscu, always mindful of protocol. "This morning has been very productive, and I'm confident we can fulfill the terms and conditions of the Memorandum of Agreement. I am pleased, but not surprised, at how wonderful and competent your staff are."

Niceties over, they followed the balustrade down the wide staircase, past the guard, and out into the city. The streets bustled with the noon crowd. Donovan noticed the money changer shops were all busy, with lines at every one. At the intersection, an individual even offered to convert American cash for Romanian lei. With a curt gesture Donovan found all too familiar, Katya dismissed the moneychanger. She explained as they crossed the street that visitors must have receipts for all of their remaining Romanian money, or security might not let them convert it back on their way out of the country.

"It could work out," she shrugged, "or you may end up giving them your extra lei, or you could even be detained. It is better for now that you pay a few cents more at the shops and get the receipt. Remember, the new currency since 2006 is the leu, and the plural of leu is lei. So that is your Romanian lesson for the day, okay?" Once again she was quick to smile.

She chose a Chinese restaurant he had passed but never visited. He noticed there seemed to be no Chinese running the restaurant. "Yes, maybe one Chinese," Katya explained, "usually not more. But the food is good." She paused. "I *hope* it is good." Again, she flashed her amazing teeth.

The food was indeed very flavorful, yet once again, it was the sour cream and wild mushroom soup that stole the show. "I just can't believe how good this is! Everywhere I go it's better than the place before. Do you have a restaurant where it's the best?"

"Of course. It is my mother who makes the best soup. Oh, I almost forgot. We will be doing the tour with some other delegates from Sweden, Australia, and Transylvania. Some of my friends, actually, who work at a Labor office up in the mountains. So, there will be seven of us, plus you and me. That is all right?"

More than all right. The higher the head count, the easier I can slip away. Aloud, he said, "Sure. Where will we all hook up?"

"Hook? Ah, where will we meet to walk to the palace? Actually, I will take you there, since we are going directly after lunch. It will be at the end of Unirii Boulevard. We will go to the first fountain and meet there. It is a beautiful walk, I think, so we will proceed along that route until we get to the palace. Actually, the boulevard was constructed to present the palace in its best light. I like this walk very much. It will be less than a kilometre. That is all right for you?"

A half hour and two blocks later, they met up with the Australians, Swedes, and the Transylvanians. Together they moved away from the first fountain, a loose collection of internationals walking toward the new Houses of Parliament, Ceausescu's Palace.

"...that Ceausescu built this boulevard to show off how grand the palace is. You can see it from here. The meridian is unusually broad, the streets quite wide, and the street lamps very, very special. Even now, it is only the best shops that are permitted to be in the buildings. See?" She pointed to a glass storefront. "That is the best jewellery store in Bucharest, perhaps in Romania. Pardon? No, I have never bought anything from there. Yes, I was in once. Just to look. No, no, just the one time. Too much money for me." Again, Katya was quick to smile.

She continued, playing the part of the knowledgeable guide. "The palace has almost the same floor surface as the U.S. Pentagon. But the palace is the world's largest civilian administrative building. In fact, it houses four thousand rooms inside of 3.7 million square feet. It takes half an hour to walk it."

One of the Australians interrupted. "I heard it took a million cubic feet of marble to build it. Is that true?"

"Oh, yes. And there is around thirty five hundred tons of crystal throughout the building, which can be found in the lighting, the mirrors, and numerous other pieces."

Donovan was aware of a few, less savoury, facts about Ceausescu's palace. He knew, for example, that between seven and thirty thousand homes were razed to seize the hill for the construction of the palace. Almost thirty churches, not to mention a hospital, had disappeared as well. The palace was also called "Madman's House." *Apt.*

"...followed a basic eclectic neoclassic style, both inside the palace and outside. But Ceausescu and his wife imposed various styles as their whim suited them. Anyway, we can now see the building. I find the fountains in front to be very pleasing. Refreshing, on a day like today, don't you think?"

As they walked along, Donovan noted just how attractive this part of the city was and how warm the people were. And the day was ideal, a perfect eighty degrees. The streets were clean. The Danube was not so far away as it finished its journey through most of Europe and coasted into the Black Sea. It was true the half-finished high rises and rusting cranes off in the distance were stilled for now, but he felt things would soon turn around for this beautiful country and its gentle people.

The group could see the guardhouse up ahead. Two guards in full military regalia, replete with Kalashnikovs, stood at ease, smoking. They appeared to be about thirteen-years-old, Donovan thought. He had, at times in the past, been obliged to take advantage of various kinds of security guards, but most of them, he recalled, did not have AK47s at their disposal. He wasn't sure if he preferred the casual diffidence of the older guards or the exploitable inexperience of youths. It was harder to put things over on older guards, but youth could sometimes go off half-cocked, never a good thing, and dangerous when automatic rifles were involved. He shrugged, and caught up with the group, insinuating himself into the middle.

Papers were shared—again, no peeking in Donovan's briefcase—and they proceeded up the winding driveway. It was six hundred feet to the palace, and the group took a moment to drink it in. The building was about a city block on each side, almost white and symmetrical. It was grand. Katya advised the group it was the equivalent of seven storeys high, with a further five floors below ground, and made from Romanian marble throughout. She commented, with no emotion whatsoever, that the construction of the palace, together with the smaller palace across the street (dictators' wives needing a roof over their heads as well), was the final blow that toppled the country into the financial abyss of bankruptcy.

They completed the walk up the drive to the entrance. A woman in a tan suit with a pin on her chest that read Communications Director welcomed them. Katya whispered that their host's name was Gabriela.

The group passed through the massive palace doors into a dark, busy ballroom-sized foyer. To the left, a wooden stage had been set up over the top of the existing staircase. It attracted all of the light, which shone from giant pots dangling from steel girders. The juxtaposition of dance music pulsing through the formal, empty palace halls was curious. Donovan smiled in approval as a series of tall, flawless women marched out from an entrance on stage left.

The models headed to the front to face Katya's group, Aussies front and center on the floor just in front of the stage. To a girl, they were dressed in jeans, flip-flops, and tees or camisoles. Each strutted down the runway, stopping halfway to offer a slow 360 degree twirl, and then continue to the edge of the stage. Once there, they eyed their audience and offered some attitude, either with chin and hip exaggerated, or with a stare-down to the Aussies. One model lifted the hem of her tee, just an inch, to reveal part of a tattoo before turning on her heel and strutting back to the dressing room.

The cameras placed on either side of the stage were poised to work but remained unmanned. He also noticed scores of chairs stacked around the perimeter of the foyer. It was a dry run, probably for some modeling event scheduled for this evening or tomorrow. He sauntered over to the Director of Communications, smiling at the two Aussies who behaved as if this afternoon's show was just for them.

"Yes, please?" The director offered her most solicitous smile. "How may I help you?"

"Hello, Gabriela. You seem busy today." He introduced himself.

She seemed grateful for this acknowledgement. "Yes, yes. We almost canceled your visit. We weren't sure we could meet your needs. We're having a fashion show this evening that will be televised next month all across Europe. And in two days, there will be hundreds of people from NATO here. They will meet here for one day as a massive, united group, and then a smaller group of bureaucrats—officers like me—from the NATO delegation will stay behind to do more work. So yes, we are very busy. You are due to meet with our IT staff at two-thirty, correct?" She double-checked her clipboard.

Donovan nodded.

She shifted her weight and dropped her eyes. "I'm so sorry, but the technology person assigned to be with you this afternoon has unfortunately a very busy schedule. He is obliged to provide the computer and audio-visual support for the fashion show as well as setting things up for Friday's NATO meeting. We can cancel your tasks for today, or we can place you in the systems area and leave you alone to do your work. It's certainly your choice. I'm so, so sorry for this inhospitable behaviour."

"I see." Donovan had trouble containing his pleasure. He pretended to ponder this latest development. "Okay, let's do this. You tell Katya that unfortunately I will have to miss the tour while I go survey your security systems. I'll hurry through the testing, and if I have time, I'll see if I can catch up to them at the end. And don't worry about me," he added, "I'll be fine." The woman smiled in gratitude and hurried over to Katya to explain this change of plans.

On their way to the systems area, Gabriela pointed out the unusual pattern laid in the marble, repeated every thirty feet. "As you enter each room, you will note a design about a square meter in size. It looks like a geometric, artistic pattern but in reality is a map of the palace floor, so you can never get lost. The floor will tell you where you are as you move along. By the time you have gone through three rooms, you will have noticed how the pattern changes just a little, to place you exactly where you are. Beautiful, yet practical. Also, since we are in this specific room at the moment, please let me point out that, despite its large size, this particular room has a retractable ceiling. Ceausescu enjoyed hosting balls under the moonlight."

In the alcove joining two immense rooms, Donovan stopped to stare at the window. He recalled thinking, as they had approached the palace, that the windows looked miniscule against the scale of the exterior. Now, standing beside them, he was dwarfed by pane after pane of glass. The window rose up thirty feet and owing to its height, seemed to continue even beyond that. He wondered what the final cost must have been to create such an edifice. And then he remembered: it cost the financial solvency of an entire country.

They arrived at their destination, and Gabriela thanked him for his flexibility. "I promise you I will be back to collect you in exactly one-half hour. Will that give you time to finish your task? And perhaps we can squeeze you into the last part of the tour. If you aren't finished in thirty minutes, I promise to offer you Georges to help you complete the work. All right?" She was already drawing the door closed behind her.

He had no choice but to acquiesce.

Once in the server room, he got busy. First, he went to the video surveillance system. It was archaic, comprised of a basic suite of cameras that captured 178 sites within the palace and around the grounds. The monitors revealed a different scene every ten seconds, cycling through the entire series every half hour. He'd seen systems like this in convenience stores across North America.

Donovan whipped through the cycle of camera shots, disabling certain sites throughout the palace. He also took note of guard placement. And then he swivelled over to the computer system. Gabriela had left him a LAN administrator's password, so he had access to the computer servers and slaves everywhere within the palace. First, he printed a directory map as well as the access codes for all secured areas. While he was visiting the directory that housed access to all entrances, he focused on the specific area of interest to him. Once the tracking application was disabled that recorded the doors to be accessed, Donovan exited the directory just in time to greet the real LAN administrator. Georges came in carrying a public address amplifier.

"Hello, how are you sir? Gabriela told me you were nice enough to take care of yourself today. I really appreciate this, Mr. Donovan. You know how the P.A. works?" Without waiting for an answer to his monotone questions, he swung the heavy piece of electronic equipment onto a work surface and grabbing a Phillips screwdriver, put his head down to work on pulling the guts out of the case.

"Ah, no, actually. Georges? Do you happen to know where the bathroom is?"

Without looking up, Georges said, "Straight down the hall. You will pass directly through the middle of two rooms. Once through the second room, you will see it on your left."

Thanking him, Donovan left carrying his briefcase, access codes stuffed in his pocket. As with all systems everywhere, the windowless server rooms were tucked away in a quieter part of the building, so he was seen by no one and met no one on his way to the elevator. That is, until the doors opened, and an older woman met him face on. She carried a tray of vegetables and brushed past him as if he were invisible. Inside the elevator, he reviewed the row of buttons that started at the top with the number seven, scrolled down through zero, and continued on to minus four. He chose the unmarked button located just beneath the minus-four button. He pushed it and watched the elevator doors close before him.

Five floors beneath the surface, the elevator doors peeled apart to face the archives room. The light from the elevator shone a few feet into the shadow to reveal two rows of switches, each one marked. Finding the security panel situated below the light panel, he keyed in the access code to the warehouse. To his left, a steel door slid open, and beyond it...darkness. He flipped on the lights, and a distant area of the warehouse sprang to life. Donovan squinted into obscurity, and then walked through the entry. Letting the doors close behind him, he stood for a moment until his eyes adjusted. He calculated the passage of time as he jogged down the main corridor to the illuminated spot. Five minutes had already passed. He guessed he had eleven more to get back to the systems area on time.

Both sides of the corridor revealed crate after wooden crate, the repetition broken by furniture draped in quilted moving blankets, table and chair legs revealed above the shelf ledge. Since Professor Umbra had armed him with the knowledge of what was where, it was easy to navigate within the gymnasium-sized room. Each alley was coded according to the Block Numeric Classification System, and he soon stood before a wooden crate marked with the Romanian symbols that in effect said, "Donovan, what you want is in this box."

His client had provided him with a precise drawing, together with the directions on how to find this room. Now he was here, his quest was for a vessel, not the kind to hold wine on the inside, but in this case, a chalice with words engraved on the outside.

He had picked up a crowbar near the entrance and used it now, cracking open the top of the crate. First out, a sealed urn. Placing it beside him, he then picked up a sculpture. Turkish, he guessed, maybe Russian. It was a nude woman about ten inches high, alabaster, and exquisite in detail. He placed it beside the urn and reached in again. Jackpot.

He unwrapped an ornate gold bucchero chalice. The exterior of the bowl presented a simple script that wound around the outside of the bowl, flowed down the fat stem, and wrapped three times around the base. It was as if the words themselves were threatening to throw themselves off the edge of the goblet. Turning it in his hand, he also admired the way the artisan had crafted it to appear as if golden wine had spilled over one side. The stem was thicker than normal, and the base was also constructed with more heft than a typical chalice, with stylized lion's feet flanking four sides of the bottom. "This would be pre-Roman, if it wasn't such a goddamn fake," he muttered to himself.

He twisted the bottom, revealing a crack at the base of the stem that opened to reveal a threaded joint. Off came the base. A second joint separated the bowl from the stem. He placed all three components into his briefcase, snapped it shut, replaced the other objects, slipped the top back on the crate, and slid it home. He wasted no time leaving the dim, cavernous archive. As he walked back down the short hallway between the archives and the elevator, he made a mental note to come visit again one day.

The systems area was as he had left it. It took him fourteen minutes to finish the ostensible work he was paid to do. He wrapped up his business and reactivated all of the systems he had disabled while he was up to no good. Then he straightened his tie, glanced back at his workstation to ensure even his chair was back in place, and left the room the way he found it.

Rejoining the group was uneventful. The tour was near the end, and he hadn't seen more than the two floors. But Katya made up for his disappointment by telling him she had missed him. He told her it was customary in Canada to make up for a missed opportunity by creating a new opportunity.

"That is a great custom." She grinned, while the two Aussies smiled at the flirting. "My girlfriend and I are meeting with the systems team this evening at the BB Bar. Razvan will be there as well. He already invited you? Perfect. It is an open air bar not far from the opera house. Open air is mean...open air means there is no roof over the top, but we will see stars tonight, not rain, I am certain. BB is not too far from your hotel, right?" She raised her voice to include them all. "And you are all invited."

The Director of Communications accompanied them all down to the guardhouse to see them off. When a guard glanced down at Donovan's briefcase, Gabriela made the characteristic wave of her hand, murmuring something in Romanian that included the trademark word *delegati,* and he was whisked through the gate with the others.

HEADING BACK TO THE hotel, Donovan decided he had time to change and afterward, go to Pizza Hut for an early bite before going to BB. He missed North American food and thought it would create time to think about the packet in the crack in the wall, as well as how to ship the *ciborium* out of the country. But first, a brief phone call.

He had received a text message originating from some cybercafé about a job that sounded intriguing. He opened the closet, chose a camel sports jacket and a white shirt with no tie, and then, from the bottom of his "two-day" bag, pulled out a set of four different brands of cell phones. Donovan chose the second one, crossing to the window for better reception, while keying in the number.

"Hello?"

"Hello. Ms. Storm, please. Um, Devin Koulos returning her call." In the pause that followed, he grabbed his suitcase clothes and tossed them on the edge of the bed to tidy up later. He straightened his shirt. "Hello, Ms. Storm...ah, Katie. I'm so pleased to have caught you off the set today. Not shooting until Saturday? Lucky you. I'm calling about that intriguing message I received from a mutual friend two days ago. It was Peter who suggested me? Well, thank Peter for me." There was a longer pause. "Yes, yes. I can meet you on Friday in London. The Strand Hotel? In the Strand? No,

I don't think that's best. It might be a little too visible. How about St. Paul's? None of the paparazzi would think to look for you there. No, I didn't mean anything by that. I'm just saying what I'm saying. Okay, how about Trafalgar Square, then? It's not too far, and Friday evening it will be full of teenagers. Yes, pigeons and teenagers...hang near one of the two lions on the Strand side. Friday at nine? Fine, I'll find you." He rang off. What would she have him steal, he wondered. What on earth would a rich, famous actress need that she couldn't buy, or out-and-out demand?

Donovan entered the Pizza Hut hungry for familiar food. He looked around the restaurant: plastic seats, plastic walls, and plastic ambience. No matter the country, Pizza Hut was Pizza Hut. To Donovan this was, in fact, what he was looking for: familiarity. The comfort of knowing your surroundings was something he needed just now. When the young server arrived, he smiled, asking her name. Noting she stood about five feet tall, he admired her black eyes and olive skin and asked her if she was of Turkish or Latin descent.

She offered a diffident smile. "We do not ask this question here." Regretting his impulsive question, Donovan decided to tip her a week's pay. His government protocol guy had told him the average annual salary in Romania was about $2,500 USD, so a fifty dollar tip would be most appreciated, and it meant little to him.

While he waited, he engaged in his favorite game: making lists. This time it was scheduling. He had to be in London by Friday morning and should leave Thursday afternoon to catch the right flight. He'd call the hotel to make arrangements for the flight and a cab for tomorrow. And then he thought about how to get both the packet and chalice out of the country. It would be necessary to figure out first how to prepare the cup in case it was discovered and then determine whether it would be better to carry it or ship it.

The packet hidden outside the hotel was another matter. What did it contain, besides those most interesting passports? And, he was being followed now at least some of the time, he was sure of it. So, who could he trust to pick up the packet? Someone had to get it to him today or by morning at the latest. And there was the challenge of getting two passports (plus his own spares) out of the country. All these logistical challenges! Why couldn't his job be to get the thing, no matter what it was, and hand it over? Most of his problems were about transporting the damn things after he acquired them. *I need an admin staff.*

His pizza arrived and he continued to organize as he ate. *And the other thing in the packet?* He'd have to wait and see what it was and then gauge the relative risk of smuggling it out. Or not. So much to think about, but there could be no solution until it was once again in his hands. "My grubby little hands," he murmured.

"I beg your pardon?" It was his server, breaking his reverie.

"Oh, nothing. Just the bill, please." He chose to hand the tip to her rather than leave it on the table to see her reaction. He wasn't disappointed.

HIS RECENT ADVENTURES made Donovan favor his left side, so he limped, just a little, over to the briefcase holding the cup. What could he do to get it out of the country? He popped the three pieces of the *ciborium* into his jacket pockets and left the hotel, this time heading away from the French Quarter. He stepped into a shop selling tablecloths and other handmade linens, purchasing a very colorful cover for a small table and a tasteful, sewn tablecloth of cream-on-cream linen, for his sister. Finally, he bought a pair of hand-carved wooden spoons. There didn't seem to be anybody tailing him so, emboldened, he left the shop with his touristy purchases and headed down the street to another area of the artisans community.

He had met David, the owner-operator of the pottery shop, back in Montreal when they were students at Concordia University. David had emailed him on a few occasions, asking for help in getting a job and a visa to return to Canada. He greeted Donovan as an old chum, and they chatted for a while about old times. After a bit, Donovan asked if it would be possible to make a couple of clay goblets to ship home.

David's eyes narrowed in speculation. "Why would you want to come all the way to Bucharest, just to make a cup?"

Donovan smiled and lied. "My interest is in the Romanian clay, one of my hobbies."

Shrugging, David left him with a potter's table, a lump of clay, and a task. Fifteen minutes later, Donovan called him back to the table and presented two rough-hewn goblets, asking him to please take them to a finer state of completion, and then fire them in his kiln. He bought a pair of bowls from David's shelf, asking him to ship the tablecloths, spoons, and pottery to his Montreal address after his works had been fired. He then headed for the BB Bar.

He hadn't thought he could enjoy himself while on two jobs, but in spite of himself, the evening was fun. After the sun went down, a full harvest moon bathed the courtyard in creamy white moonlight. Every table had a large bowl filled with tea lights to augment the natural illumination. Most of the people around the tables seemed to have settled in for an evening's drinking. Donovan was pleased to see *amuses-bouches,* little meat snacks, on each table. But by far his interest centered on the quart bottles of dark Ciuc beer. The lower-alcohol Bucharesti beer tasted just fine, and he looked forward to enjoying some, even if it meant breaking his beer-only-on-weekends rule.

Donovan spied a table of four. Katya's arm was linked through that of her best chum and co-worker, Magdalina. Petr, the techie, was there, accompanied by his wife, Paulina. The Aussies brought the number to six, arriving at the same time as Donovan, who was lucky seven to the table.

Katya stood and took him by the arm. "I am so sorry, Sean. Razvan could not make it this evening. He is still at the office and seemed quite upset. Magdalina said he said some bad words when he told her. I guess we have you to ourselves. Come, sit, I saved you a chair."

A round of beers was ordered by the Aussies, consumed, and more appeared. At some point, Petr made mention of something concerning the toilets, but Donovan just nodded, not really listening. At the other end of the table, Paulina was in the middle of a gentle, hilarious story of how she had survived American culture at Penn State University. She ended her tale by asking the table who could get her back to Penn State, or any other state, for that matter, to finish her doctorate. Petr cast a significant look at Donovan, who countered by changing the subject and ordering another round for the table.

At some point, he felt the need to go to the toilet, but yet another tale was being woven, and he didn't want to miss it. By the end of the story, this one told by Katya herself, Donovan was in some distress. It really was time to find a place to use the toilet. With Katya having pointed the way, he walked the inside perimeter of a small hedge that flanked the bar. As he spotted his destination, a small man stood up and placed himself in the middle of his path.

"Yes?" Donovan asked, unable to avoid looking around. *There must be some mistake. Is he speaking to someone else?* He could think of no reason why a stranger would interrupt a straightforward trip to the toilet. The man spoke in Romanian, and Donovan couldn't catch any of it. The man spoke again in accented English, "Five hundred lei," and held out his hand.

His response was a polite, but firm, "*Nu.* I'm not paying to piss. Forget that."

The man shrugged and took his seat as Donovan departed with as much dignity as a full bladder and a slight buzz could offer him. When he got to the table, there was yet another story, this one accompanied by much laughter. The table had reverted to Romanian and snippets of French since Donovan had departed, with the Aussies smiling and limiting their chit-chat to each other. He waited, trying to hold both his water and his dignity. Finally Katya looked over in curiosity, an eye cocked as if to ask why he wasn't sitting down.

"Do you know what just happened?" His indignation boiled though his words. "This little man is lurking around the corner, demanding five hundred lei for me to pee."

The table burst into a roar of laughter. Petr spoke up, a bit of peevishness tingeing his voice, "It is like I was told you. Two times. Is a charge."

One of the Aussies smirked. "So mate. How much is five hundred lei?"

Donovan did a quick conversion. His face reddened. It was about ten cents. He paused and then asked, "So, how do you say 'I'm very, very sorry' in Romanian?" Given this guidance, he trooped back around the corner and for the second time that evening, offered up a generous cash apology, this time to the polite little toilet attendant who waited.

Grateful for the imminent respite from his anxious bladder, he opened the toilet door and was plunged into darkness. In addition to there being no light, there also didn't seem to be any toilets, just a concrete floor. Knowing all of the washrooms he had been to so far had lights, he assumed this bar was different because it was an outdoor, patio-style bar. He unzipped his pants and proceeded to pee; however, it took only a moment for him to wonder why there was no sound of the urine hitting the bottom. He reached behind him and opened the door a crack to let in a little light. To his horror, his toes dangled over the edge of a precipice; he was peeing into space. What would have happened if he had slipped? And where would he have landed? He shuddered at the thought.

Clouds now competed with the moonlight, and the evening was winding down. The Aussies went to check out one of the nearby discos, and Petr and Paulina had gone home. Magdalina yawned, yet Katya seemed as fresh as she had been that afternoon at the palace. Donovan thought there might be a chance they could hook up, but even as she leaned into him, he knew there was still work to be done this evening. At the end of the next story, he rose. "My wonderful, beautiful hostesses, I am heartbroken to tell you I am falling asleep on my feet." He saw Katya's face fall and continued, "I'll be back in about a month, and I'd love nothing better than to take you to dinner and maybe a concert at the opera house. Will you let me make this up to you at that time?"

"Of course." Katya's smiled brilliantly.

"Then I will say goodnight. I'll see you in the morning. Please let me pay your cab fare home. I don't want to worry about you walking around so late in the evening, and the sky seems to have clouded over. You don't want to get caught in a downpour like we had the other night." Seeing them off, he wandered back to the hotel.

He entered the lobby and walked over to Dragon. Farther down the lounge, a woman dressed in a long glittery gown sat in a club chair, watching the piano player. She was out of hearing range, and her attention was riveted on the musician.

"Good evening, my friend. I have a favor to ask you. It will make both of us very happy if you will do this for me. Are you interested?"

"It is good, Mister Donovan. I make you happy and being a good guest. What would you like me to do?"

"Simply this. Tonight, please wait until you are on your break and then go outside—you will not have to go too far—and fetch something for me. Are you willing to do that? Yes? Good. You must wait until there is no one around. I do not want you to be seen, neither going on this errand nor coming to my room. Dragon, is it possible someone could be upstairs watching the door to my room?"

Dragon's face went deadpan. "I am a good guy to do this work. I will be there in one hour or maybe two. And no one is permitted to walk the halls upstairs. So no one can be there. And no one will see me. So for this thing I look for, will I know it when I see it?"

"Yes. Just go to the back of the hotel and look for the garbage bin. There is a crack in the wall beside the bin, with a small plastic packet stuffed with some papers. Bring it back to me. It will be worth a week's pay to you. Is that fair?"

Dragon's face remained stoic. "Is fair. Now you go to your bed. No one will see me."

IT WAS ALMOST TWO O'CLOCK when Dragon tapped on Donovan's door. He waited until the hotel room door was closed behind him before pulling the oilskin packet from within the confines of his concierge's jacket. Although he oozed curiosity, Dragon asked nothing. Paid well, he departed without another word, leaving Donovan with the packet.

Once the passports had dropped out onto the coffee table, he forced the packet wide open and examined the interior. Stuck to the back side of the lining was a single piece of paper. He peeled it away from the plastic and withdrew the velum sheet. The first thing he noticed was the letterhead: Ministry of Labor and Employment, Houses of Parliament, London. He skipped to the bottom and arched his eyebrows at the name: Edward Yorke, Manager, Systems Development, International Relations. So, what did this letter have to say?

It was addressed to Tomas Dobra, the bastard whose face he had caved in with the rock! There were no introductory pleasantries. Yorke advised that England had come in second behind Canada in securing the World Bank security contract for Romania. Any effort Mr. Dobra could invest in impugning Canada's reputation and enhancing England's chances at future contracts would be most helpful. *So, that's why they didn't kill me when they had the chance. There was no reason to. All they had to do was to mess up my*

entry and exit to the country by stealing my passport, and then make sure I was
seriously uncomfortable while I remained here.

Donovan sat back, his thoughts popping off like fireworks. What an idiot Yorke was to have dispatched a letter like this and on departmental letterhead to boot. Or was he just being cocky? And it wasn't a stolen letter at all, as Dobra was the actual addressee. And how in hell did Yorke's passport wind up in Romania? He had a lot to think about.

He looked over the remaining passport. He saw the link between himself and Edward Yorke. Perhaps even the high-flying Gaia, as the press hailed him, might be implicated.

Donovan paced around the coffee table, staying away from his window without thinking about it. Nothing came to mind, so he disassembled his laptop, placed the three less-than-legally acquired passports in between the back of the screen and the top cover. He added the poorly-thought-out letter and put everything back together, popping the computer back in its carrying bag. *So nice, having skills like this.* He opened his most boring security manual to page 140 and dog-eared the upper left hand corner of the page. He then took a Post-It sticky and wrote a few notes on user codes and passwords. After closing the manual, he put it into the middle of his five technical books. As far as sailing through security tomorrow, he was clean.

Thursday was taken up with security work at the ministry, but Donovan took the time to change his flight from Friday morning to the redeye at ten o'clock the evening before.

To prepare for security at the Bucharest airport and later customs at Heathrow, he wore his plainest, darkest sports jacket over a white cotton shirt, grey tie. At the airport, he checked in all of his luggage save for a briefcase carrying papers, a laptop, and a somewhat weighty book called *A Brief History of Nearly Everything.* Passing by a mirrored wall on his way to convert his Romanian lei back to US cash, he felt satisfied he looked like every male public servant who ever ascended the escalator at Phase III, National Headquarters in Canada's capital region. Boring as hell, it was the perfect attire to greet customs officials.

Initial security was fine, the security staff ran his passport under the black light, but as he met the final customs agent prior to entering the departure lounge, he knew something was wrong. The agent glanced over

Donovan's shoulder, and Donovan turned to follow the man's furtive glance. The two agents from yesterday's breakfast were leaning against the wall, stone faced. The sunglasses were still on, so Donovan could read nothing but the proverbial writing on the wall. It was the tiniest nod, however, that reinforced his sinking feeling. The customs agent apologized and invited Donovan to please follow him to a nearby room.

The room was less than eleven feet in any direction, with painted cinderblock on two walls. Donovan's luggage was opened on one end of the sole table in the room. His clothes were piled in a heap on the floor, and his manuals, cell phones, and assorted gear were lined up in rows along the table. The monkey's paw was nestled on the floor against his clothes. A security guard or military personnel, he wasn't certain, stood at ease in the corner, Kalashnikov pointed more or less at the newest guest. The customs agent invited him to stay here; someone would be with him shortly.

Donovan was left to measure the walls, note the presence of a single light in the middle of the ceiling, and watch the reflected light enter from the crack at the bottom of the door. He noted as well the absence of a window and chose to avoid eye contact with the guard.

A long minute later, a man he didn't know entered. He, too, was dressed in military garb, with a pistol holstered and an AK74 Kalashnikov assault rifle pointed at the floor. He got right down to business, no introductions. "Why do you have all of this equipment and computer manuals, Mr. Donovan? It looks like the kind of electronics a person could very easily use to spy on our country's computers. Is that what you do?"

Donovan tried to be pre-emptive. "May I open my briefcase, please? I have a letter from your Minister of Labor, inviting me to help your country with its security issues. These are the tools of my trade. I couldn't help your country without them."

The man waved the explanation aside as if it was irrelevant. "I know that. Let's try another approach. Give me your briefcase and that book as well, please."

Without a word, Donovan handed the two things over, giving thanks the monkey's paw on the floor looked like nothing more than a wooden souvenir. The man seized the laptop and handed it to the guard, murmuring something in Romanian. The guard left the tiny office with it. As his host rifled through the briefcase, Donovan took a moment to ask him his name.

"I do not have to give you my name." The man leaned across the desk as if he was going to jump over it. After a moment of staring, he sat back in the chair and waved one hand as if to present the room. "This is my room, my city. This is my country. For the moment, you are mine. I know your name. That is enough."

"So, are you looking for anything in particular? Perhaps I can help."

The man ignored him. He had gone through every page of the five manuals, double checking the passage Donovan had marked. He even took the time to riffle through every page of the history book. Another minute ticked away, and the guard returned with Donovan's laptop. Donovan wondered idly if his plane was still waiting. He noted the computer had been powered on, a good sign since the test had been about ensuring it wasn't wired for nefarious reasons, as opposed to dismantling it to look for hidden loot or a bomb. Once again the guard leaned into his boss and whispered something. The interrogator nodded.

"Your luggage appears to be satisfactory, and your briefcase and computer have been, ah, reviewed. Perhaps you can do just one more thing. Take off your clothes."

Donovan arched an eyebrow in question.

In response, the interrogator's jaw hardened, and his fingers whitened as they clenched the table edge. "You have a flight to catch, and I will be happy to have you leave our country. Perhaps you had better hurry. Our detention cells are very uncomfortable."

A moment later, Donovan's bare feet stood on his shorts, and he was naked. "Bend over." The guard walked around behind, letting the weight of the rifle barrel rest on the small of his prisoner's back. A drop of sweat ran down the back of Donovan's neck and onto the meticulous marble tiling below. The guard reached down—not unlike a quarterback, he thought perversely—and parted the cheeks of Donovan's buttocks with his one free hand. A second later, although it did seem longer, they left him alone to dress. The two men departed the room without a word of explanation or an apology. Donovan bundled up his equipment and clothing, closed his luggage, and opened the door, wincing at the unexpected brightness of freedom.

Chapter Seven

A *Cell Phone Call*
Tuesday Evening

"Hullo, this is Gaia, please?"

There was a brief pause. "Why do you have this number? Who is this?"

"Hullo, Mr. Gaia, my name is Janos. Janos Dobra. From Bucharest. My brother and I work for Mr. Edward Yorke, or at least we used to. Mr. Yorke had an accident, and he's dead. My brother Tomas has asked me to tell you we're doing the work that used to be done by Yorke. He doesn't speak much English, so he asked me to call you to tell you everything will be fine, and we'll be working for you directly." Janos waited until the delay became uncomfortable and then spoke again. "Is that all right, Mr. Gaia?"

"Do I have anything to worry about? Are you making arrangements to get my passport back? I expect the gypsy boy to be reminded of the trouble he's in."

Janos fell over himself explaining. "Oh, no, Mr. Gaia. He's already been punished for this."

Another pause. "And you have my passport?"

Janos squirmed. "No, not yet, but we're working on it. These things take time. And money." He heard a sigh in response.

"I want my passport. See that I get it. Some money will find you shortly. Listen carefully...Janos. I will be securing a replacement for Yorke, so don't think this, ah, promotion is in any way permanent. I'll have a new man on the ground to work with Razvan Petruscu shortly. Do not overextend yourself; do you know what I mean? You are not brains. You're brawn. Stick to that, and we will continue to work harmoniously together."

Janos replied in the affirmative, but by then the man at the other end of the line had rung off.

Chapter Eight

L*ondon*
   Thursday Evening

The late evening flight to England was uneventful. Other than an armrest-hogging seatmate, and no immediate offer of wine due to turbulence, he was alone with his thoughts. Donovan did recall in mid-flight, however, that his latest adventures seemed to be full of close calls, more than any of his previous projects. He touched his broken finger, remembering how helpless he had been as he watched the now dead gypsy boy staring down at him in the park. And he felt again the intrusiveness and fear as he leaned over to accommodate the guard at the airport in Bucharest. And now his finger, head, and rib throbbed.

Was this still fun? He didn't think so. He was used to coming out at the end of a hard week feeling the result was more of a lucrative adventure than punishing pain. It didn't seem so, anymore. "As long as I'm making lots of money." He gritted his teeth.

"Pardon?" The woman beside him had glanced over.

"I was just saying that bees make lots of honey." Donovan squinted at her and nodded in emphasis.

It worked. The woman returned to her novel. Her elbow withdrew from the armrest, and she buried her nose deep into the pages. Later, she wouldn't even glance at him as he accepted the wine the attendant brought.

Heathrow was chaos. The immigration and customs agents had tumbled into the throes of a collective bad day. Everyone in Europe either wanted to return to England at that very moment or was dying to leave. The lineups were staggering, and the cattle pens designed for people processing didn't seem to be working at all.

Donovan had the option of entering any one of forty queues, each one at least fifty people deep. The customs gauntlet seemed to stretch on forever. He took a moment to ignore the nattering of the family in front of him and listened to the background noise in the room. The hub-bub the crowd and workers created was an overwhelming white roar that bounced off the arena ceilings and echoed off the vast walls. Announcements to the three thousand international travellers went off like firecrackers, a cacophony of voices came from everywhere, electric vehicles whirred, and computer keyboards clicked at every desk and counter.

To his surprise, he didn't mind the mass of humanity. It was a bit like being in a forest; lots of wild animals, but overall it was calm. So yes, individuals were annoying, but nobody was being shot at, so, not a bad crowd here. He was surprised, however, to have found this spruce forest metaphor while at Heathrow. Could he possibly be missing Canada?

The shuttle to the train worked fine, and the Heathrow Express itself was on time. With a small amount of pleasure, Donovan took it to Paddington Station. London taxis cost a horrendous amount, and he enjoyed riding on trains. A minute later, he sat at the end of one of the cars in a window seat and this time had no companion to take up the other half of his seat. How pleasant.

The ride itself was no different from every other time. God bless English trains. He spied a little bit of green field underneath a dense night sky. He knew not everyone enjoyed the steely ch-chunk of wheels on track as the train passed by their flat on the half hour, day in, day out. But he loved the train and the destinations it promised. He stared out at grey factory walls and dark residence roofs. He thought of that song by Cream: black roof country, tired starlings. He still saw charm in the stark imagery. The train soon pulled into the station, and Donovan hailed a cab to the Strand Hotel in the Strand district of Old London.

He offered his credit card for the least expensive room in the house, since that was the only room available on short notice in this part of the city. Relative to his sojourn at the Majestic, a quick glance at his room told him he would now live the life of a monk. He shrugged at the paucity of creature comforts in the space around him; they consisted of a bed and a bathroom slightly larger than his luggage. He could almost touch the walls on either side of his room. The single window opened toward the tiniest courtyard of the hollow, inward face of the building. By angling his head, he could peer down onto a patch of grass leading around a corner to... He couldn't see what, so he couldn't say. It was now well past two in the morning, and to him, it felt like it. He unpacked his bags and tumbled into bed.

Friday morning dawned warm and sunny, but he didn't welcome it until after ten. All of Europe seemed to be enjoying beautiful weather, which belied a typical October London. It put Donovan into a splendid mood.

Breakfast at the Strand was traditional fare. He passed on the cold, unbuttered toast lined up on racks but picked out a couple of fried tomatoes and dove into the thick smoky slices of bacon. No kippers or sausages for him. He chose instead a couple of eggs sunny side up and back-to-back cups of unpleasant coffee for an unhealthy breakfast. His appointment wasn't until nine that evening, and since he had taken the earlier flight, he could play tourist or snoop the whole day, his choice.

Donovan left the front entrance of the Strand, turned right and headed away from the center of Old London, toward Trafalgar Square. Once he was close enough to observe the details of the four lions flanking Nelson's Column, he continued down the street. By veering to the left toward a large, official-looking building, he found the Grosvenor Street entrance, which housed the Canadian High Commissioner. Once inside, he identified himself as a Canadian citizen and presented his real passport. He would be Devin only insofar as his client, Katie Storm, was concerned while he was in London. A nearby computer was available to do a search on Edward Yorke, and armed with the man's position and work history, Donovan went looking for a consulate officer.

He didn't need to meet the actual Canadian ambassador or any of the immigration officers. Donovan felt the best person to help him was one of the communication officers, the younger and less experienced the better. He checked the staff directory and found Beth McLean.

Beth appeared to be in her thirties, medium height and very slim. As he approached her, she was finishing up a conversation with a young man carrying a backpack. After a few keystrokes on her computer, she turned her attention to her next client, Donovan. She extended a hand and introduced herself. Her handshake was firm, and her hazel eyes made contact and stayed on her subject. She pushed a stray lock of her straight, chestnut hair behind her ear, and they sat down.

Beth was personable and most helpful, once he showed his ID and government status papers. She was aware of all of the CIDA contracts across Europe, and she had some knowledge of the World Bank contracts as well. As such, she considered Donovan to be a co-worker. "Edward Yorke? I've heard of him, you know, heard stories, but I can't say I know him personally. Let's look him up and see what the system says."

Beth leaned over the keyboard, her chestnut hair falling forward, framing her oval face. She keyed in some information, stared at the monitor and typed some more. She gave the new screen a quick glance and then swiveled the monitor around to reveal the same script to Donovan. The document on the computer screen carried the heading: World Bank Activities: 2008-2009: Romania.

She spoke while he read. "As you know, the Access to Information Act states that any Information Resources of Business Value, basically any kind of files, whether electronic or paper can be accessed by the public. Well, from time to time, it does actually come back to bite us on the ah, behind, so we keep everything we input clean, with no extra notes. Unfortunately, at times it is so sanitized it's useless. But sometimes we take a chance and put things in a sort of code. This one seems to have that codey-jargon embedded into it.

"See? Here Yorke says he is involved in implementing government security systems. Yet in every CIDA meeting he ever attended, he always had techies attending with him, presenting the specific systems stuff. From what I'm seeing here, he's just a talking head. And judging by the length of these documents, we can put the accent on 'talking,'" she continued as she read the screen.

"He did the presentation as England's rep for the World Bank proposals. They didn't get it, as you obviously know. Not even a contract split. Hmm." She opened a second tab on her screen and looked around the monitor, casting an admiring glance his way. "I found you in here! You apparently know your stuff. The international development people like to split contracts and share the wealth between the countries. You know? But apparently we, most likely it was you, got both parts for this one."

Donovan demurred, waving a hand. "I was there, but it was my director who did the pitch."

Beth smiled. "C'mon, I know how these things go. We just spoke about talking heads. Your director ad-libbed one bullshit sentence to begin, read your proposal word for word, and finished with another bullshit closing sentence. Am I right, or am I right?" She flashed double dimples at him and tilted her upturned nose. He smiled, permitting her to draw her own conclusions.

She read more lines from the screen, scrolling down the text. "So, it says England appealed our contract. Said your team didn't have as much experience—seasoning was the term they used—as their group did. They were selling, but the sponsor wasn't buying." She read to the bottom of the document. "No grounds for appeal. Annnd...Romania put in a good word to the committee as well, since they had done business with you before. Good for you!" She glanced over at him, offering a warm, appraising look. "So Sean, where you from? Ottawa?"

"No, Montreal. Actually, in Notre Dame de Grace, if you know the city at all. I moved from the West Island to NDG to go to school. It seemed easier, and it was time to leave home anyway. So I headed downtown to where all the action is. But that was quite a while ago. You?"

"I grew up in Nova Scotia, in a place called St. Margaret's Bay, near Halifax. But when I go home, I stay in Halifax. Most of my family moved into town anyway. It's just easier."

"I understand easier. I should be living in Ottawa for work reasons, but Montreal's more interesting, y'know? Anyway, I'm really only working on an extended contract at this point. I took a leave of absence to do this international contract. It gives me a chance to see a country or two outside of Montreal." Donovan wasn't lying. At times, it was convenient to weave some explanations into what was the basis of his truth in order to let her conclude he wasn't so cosmopolitan.

"Anyway," he continued, "back to our Mr. Yorke. How high up is he? I see his position, but these can sometimes be misleading. Is he, do you suppose, able to touch the hem of the Pope, so to speak?"

"Are his contacts high up enough for him to be a person of influence? Is that what you mean?"

"Sort of. Okay, exactly."

"Mr. Donovan, your questions are making me curious as to why you need this kind of information. Knowing Mr. Yorke is a person of influence who happens to be a competitor of Canada, and by extension, you, I'm wondering where you're going with this line of questioning. I'm sorry, but in my line of work, a certain level of suspicion is healthy."

He expected this, sooner or later, and had a lie prepared. "Well, it's like this. England and Canada have contracts with Romania, and one of these agreements—the one I'm currently working on—has a wrinkle in it only Mr. Yorke can resolve. Since I've never met the man, I just wanted to know what he's like, before I approach him with a request for resolution. 'Know thy enemy,' y'know?"

She looked at him with a renewed interest. "Well, the role of a communications officer is to keep everyone, especially the government, safe and happy." Her eyes glinted, and a trace of a smile caused the double dimples to return. "One way we do this is by precluding people from doing exactly what I suspect you're considering doing. You seem like a really nice guy, but I quite like my job, and even if I knew you well, which I do not..." she colored a bit, "my counsel from this point is to not do anything. Period. You. Not anything." She gave him a preoccupied smile. "Okay, now that you know my answer is no to whatever else you're gonna say, what would you like to say?"

He couldn't help but smile. "Beth, you're great. As a guy in the security business, I've also been placed in the position of having to tell people they can't have what they're asking for. I do have a last question, but it's on the safe side. Where exactly does this guy work, and what's his boss's name?"

"I'm going to be shifty here, Sean." She scribbled a few lines on a scrap of paper. "Our security guys can easily review whatever systems screens I call up. And, they often do, so I'm going to do you a favor by asking you to find that information yourself. I'm sorry; I can't help you any further." Winking, she passed over a piece of paper with the extranet directory path for the British Houses of Parliament. He noted it was the half of the sheet missing her letterhead; this was a smart young officer. He folded it and gave her his most winning smile, which in turn raised another dimple. Donovan decided to push his luck, just a bit, and played a hunch. "Beth, may I ask you one more question? Have you ever heard of a gentleman, American citizen, I think, name of Galen Attanasio?" He waited as she pondered.

"Nope. I don't recall it, and I'm sure you'd agree it's unique enough I'd remember a name like that. Sounds Greek, actually." She looked for a follow-up question, but none came. He thanked her and left.

Once outside the building, Donovan headed towards the Thames. He wouldn't visit Mr. Yorke today as it was time to begin thinking about his next job. On his way toward Westminster Abbey, though, his mind kept drifting back to the young Embassy worker, Beth. She was so generous. Why? He couldn't wrap his head around the concept of a stranger being so nice and cooperative. And for no apparent reason other than to be, well, nice and cooperative.

He had not met very many altruistic people in his life—wasn't everybody out to get him and vice-versa? That was his experience. Even his father had screwed him over countless times before he left home. He shook his head and focused instead on the fact that he had all the money he could want and a sunny English day to lift him up. Once out on the street, he read the painted signs on the asphalt that warned him to look to the right before crossing. He thought again about Beth, the communications officer. *Wonder if I'll run into her again?* Shrugging, he looked right and then crossed.

He passed both the Abbey and a minute later, Big Ben and the Houses of Parliament. Standing beside the chariot of the good Iceni Celt, Queen Boadicea with her daughters, he decided to walk the bridge that spanned the Thames. Halfway across the bridge, he could turn back and see the Houses of Parliament from its best vantage point. Beyond Boadicea, he frowned as he saw the massive bicycle wheel being erected for tourism. He couldn't imagine the London Eye had been placed to compete with Boadicea, Big Ben, or Cleopatra's Needle, not to mention the Tower Bridge upriver. He did, however, think it might not be a complete waste of time to ascend the big wheel and have a look around. So perhaps it wasn't as gimmicky as it appeared on first glance.

With the exception of the London Eye and the endless streams of vehicles, everything he could see from the bridge was older than Canada, some of it centuries older. Shaking his head, he turned back toward Old London and proceeded to walk along the Embankment. The statue of the Iceni queen made him think he'd have dinner at the Boadicea public house at

Charing Cross Station. It would be busy, though, so he held off on a decision as to where to eat until he was hungrier.

The rest of the afternoon came and went. He visited St. Paul's Cathedral, thinking about its architect, Christopher Wren and the Great Fire of London that had destroyed the first version of this great church. Wasn't it ironic the Christian faith taught to avoid reliance upon material things, and yet... Donovan stared at this massive material thing, St. Paul's Cathedral. It had literally made the career and possibly the life of Sir Christopher Wren. *A paradox.*

Tiring from his hike and noting the time, he chose the nearest pub in which to eat. The Sherlock Holmes looked well-worn, unlike the bankers and investors around him. These were the businessmen who worked in the business district a few blocks away and who dressed as if their wedding was minutes away.

Donovan noticed the pub had been around forever. He thought about a story he'd heard from a friend who had been hiking in the Midlands. His friend had happened upon an inn at the end of the day and asked for a room.

"Do you want to stay in the new part or the old part?"

"What's the difference?" his friend had asked.

"The new part was built after the 1600s."

What a sense of history in the architecture! It was no wonder the Sherlock Holmes pub looked well-established. He had the choice of stout or a high-octane Canadian beer. A Guinness seemed appropriate, and the room appeared to call for a steak and kidney pie, cheese, and bread. "I've got to make better eating choices or leave this country," he joked to himself, ordering a salad on the side.

Soon it was nine—show time. He wandered over to view the Strand-side lions and stood in the shadow of Waterstone's book shop as night took hold.

No Katie Storm. *Well, what do you expect? She's a mega-star and a teen at that, commanding a gazillion dollars per movie. She's probably late because her entourage needed to rent a bus to accompany her here. Or, she's late because that's what mega-stars do. I wonder what she'll be like to work with. Probably difficult.*

Restless, he moved around, one eye on the lions while he studied the square. He noted Nelson's Column, wondered about the idiots who had scaled it in at least a half-dozen publicised events. One simple soul had even parachuted from the top. Donovan remembered the statue had always been promoted as being a certain height but when measured in recent years was found to be several meters shorter. Size matters, he shrugged, especially in self-promotion.

He found the statue of George Washington astride his horse, the pair resting on a plinth. In 1929, the State of Virginia shipped over a few pounds of noble U.S. dirt to place under Washington's horse. In this way, they argued, the general wouldn't have to set foot on British soil. He wondered what the good folks of London thought of this slight.

A slender figure in a belt-tied raincoat, wide-brimmed hat, and bug-eye sunglasses showed up. A large black man loitered nearby. Although he didn't look directly at Katie, the man had angled his body such that any activity near her would be apparent to him. *The bodyguard*. Donovan smiled, amused at the man's efforts to be close but not beside his petite boss. He stood a head taller than the group of tweens who surrounded him, mocking his fish-out-of-water presence in an area full of adolescents. He noted also the youths kept a safe distance, even as they prodded him with jeers.

"Ms. Storm?" inquired Donovan as he approached the slender young woman.

"Oh! Fuck, you scared me. Where have you been? I'm going to be mobbed any goddamn minute. Don't you keep me waiting again. Jesus, that fountain is making my hair frizz. It took my people an hour to straighten it!" She took a furtive peek around. "Can we get this done so I can get out of here?"

"You wanted to ask me to do something for you?" Donovan waited while she took a hand-written sheet of paper, folded twice, from the sleeve of her coat and handed it to him.

"These are the directions to an event I'm hosting tonight, starting at midnight. I want you to come to the party and meet my good friend and co-star, Nadia Kriss." She spat the name out. "She's gonna be wearing her lucky necklace. She never takes the fucking thing off when she's making a movie, except when she's in front of the camera. Well, I want that necklace. Get it for me."

"So, what's my timeline? Do I have three days or a week?" He knew enough to never ask why. It was immaterial to him why people wanted things. He had his opinions, but Donovan had learned over the years that delving too far into the whys of his thefts made the execution of those jobs more challenging. Who cares, really, why people want to do the things they do? Too much introspection might lead him to acquire a conscience, and then where would he be? *Poor and unemployed.* None of his clients ever said why they wanted what they wanted. All he knew was each transaction was illegal, and he had to watch himself at every move.

Katie took off her oversized sunglasses to reveal cheekbones you could cut yourself on, blue-violet eyes, and the otherwise delicate features of a tsarina. Her mouth, however, seemed to have come from Brooklyn.

"Fuck, you're a nosy little prick." She leaned in close enough that he could breathe her in, stretched on tiptoes, so her pouty lips hovered just inches from his neck. One hand rested gently on his chest, for balance. "When do I want it? I...want...it...now." She rubbed the tip of her nose with the back of her index finger, in the same manner that had been filmed and photographed a million times in the previous three years.

"It seems it's some sorta fucking good luck piece, and I want her taken down a peg. Bitch. I'm the star, and she's the washed-up old bag who needs to know her place on the set. So you will make this happen, got it?"

"Yes, I can do that. Anything else you want to mention before I leave?"

"Like what?" Katie pulled a pair of gloves from her purse and put them on.

"We actually hadn't got around to discussing a fee." Donovan waited.

She sneered her distaste. "You scum are all alike. All you want's a piece of my bank account. Talk to my associate over there. He'll hook you up. I don't carry money. You wouldn't believe the germs on it. But keep in mind half of what he gives you is to do the job, and the other half is to keep your fuckin' pie-hole shut before, during, and after."

Donovan turned away before he could shoot out an errant phrase that would wreck the deal. She called a stage whisper over his shoulder to draw back his attention. "An' don't try selling those personal handwritten directions to the paparazzi. Not my handwriting. Prick." He ignored her comment and turned toward Katie's bodyguard, who was still being mocked by the tweens.

Back at the hotel, he counted his cash. Two hundred thousand American dollars. A fine payday. He glanced at the time on his cell phone. Ten. Time enough to get the money into a safe, grab a cup of coffee, and head over to Notting Hill for midnight. A sunny day, a chi-chi party, *and* a fifth of a million dollars. What a nice place London was turning out to be.

But first was the tiny problem of what to wear. He had his casual bet-you-can't-pick-me-out-in-a-crowd outfits. He had a couple of business suits, and one gunmetal grey Italian-crafted dress suit. Having nothing in between, he chose to be overdressed rather than under and went Italian.

Knowing a little about entertainment industry parties, he chose to arrive at twelve thirty. As he ascended the stairs, he noticed Katie's giant associate standing beside a Bentley. They ignored one another. Devin's name meant nothing to the door staff, but as soon as he mentioned Katie Storm, the staff produced a second list with the name "Devin Koulos" on it. He was in.

The building itself looked modest from the street, but once inside, he understood the front was essentially a façade. The owner had lavished expenditures that made the building appear to be a series of apartments. Inside, however, it became clear the entire five-story building was one residence, with an interior that seemed to extend to amazing depths. As he crossed the threshold, the bass and drum beat caught him in the chest. He was at a party.

To further underscore this first impression, Donovan noted a gaggle of twenty-somethings, all female, clustered around the foot of the staircase. *Were they hired to decorate the newel post, like a chain of lotus blossoms?*

He passed a bar at the entrance, and the next one was within sight. Wait staff cruised through the more than fifty partygoers, lubricating each conversation as they floated from group to group. He recognized a few individuals from the film industry, and at least one rock star whose eco-sensitive lifestyle seemed to garner more headlines than the models he serial dated.

Donovan was quite certain the man diving into a tray of martinis under the chandelier was one of the more colorful ministers from the British Parliament. The man floated off, hands full of crystal. Without so much as raising an eyebrow, Devin was presented with a glass of sparkling wine. A *prosecco*. He took a sip and was then obliged to fend off the advances of a young lady half his age who should not have had as much bubbly as she had.

Katie Storm spotted him and broke away from a cluster of what Donovan guessed to be film industry types. His glance took in the group and then shot over the ordinary looking people to a statuesque woman standing toward the back. Her eyes caught his, and her lips were fixed in a half grin, as if she knew a secret worth telling. By that time, Katie had glided up to him.

She met him in the middle of the room, just under the massive chandelier. "Devin! So glad you could join us." She proffered a cheek for the obligatory pair of air kisses. "Please, come be introduced to my friends." Under her breath, however, she whispered "Look at you. A little overdressed, aren't we? All James fucking Bond. What's up with that?"

Donovan decided to set things straight. Taking her arm in a firm grasp, he leaned in to her, smiling for the room. "Listen, brat. I don't walk in front of the cameras when you're filming. Just let me do my job and shut up. I presume you want me to succeed, right?" He patted her shoulder, and she smiled on cue for the group waiting to be presented to this stranger.

"Beautiful people! Please let me introduce to you my good friend, Devin Koulos. He is from Canada and is doctoring a script I'm working on. He's a security guru and is going to make my character look all brilliant and clever. He works for the government, but in Canada, so he has no authority over any crimes we commit here, right?" Everyone laughed as if it was the best joke, although Katie's laugh was a bit too hearty. She reciprocated by flitting from one individual to another in her group, in turn clutching an arm with both of her hands.

"This is George, a producer." Her slender arm grabbed another elbow. "Dear sweet Tom, another producer, and this is poor Mark, he's the lowly director..." Everybody laughed again. "And this is Mary Beth, my long-suffering assistant, and last but not least, I don't have to introduce you to Nadia Kriss, my co-star in *The Two Donnas*, which is going to be galactic! Nadia, please let Devin get you a drink. You've been so quiet this evening. I'd hate to think we've been boring you." This time the laughter was tinged with a trace of nervousness.

Producers one and two parted to reveal a tall, slender ash-blonde woman who looked to be in her thirties but who carried a maturity about her that made her seem a bit older. Her eyes were the calmest green and crinkled at the corners when she smiled. When she did speak, however, everyone listened, as if she knew life-affirming answers.

"How do you do, Devin? What a pleasant surprise, to see a man dressed so handsomely. Have you moved to London, or are you just visiting?" Her voice was rich and a chuckle lurked behind her question.

"Well, I'm here on business as you just heard, but I must say, I hope business keeps me here awhile. It's been wonderful so far. Not a rainy day since I arrived."

"And when was that?" Mark the director asked.

"Last night." This provoked genuine laughter.

Mark countered, "You Canadians, always concerned about the weather."

"Yes, indeed. Canadians say there are only three things wrong with Canada: January, February, and March."

Nadia seemed to appreciate the quip.

Katie feigned puzzlement. "What does that mean?"

Devin saw an exit. "It means a segue from cool Canadian weather to cool London drinks. Ms. Kriss, may I get you a glass of something, or would you like to accompany me the great journey of twenty feet to the nearest bar?"

Her mouth turned up, just a bit more, and the smile carried to her eyes. "Yes, a walk would do me good. Life can't be all business, right? But can it be a leisurely stroll? All that exercise can't be good for you."

They passed through the archway to what Donovan thought was a quieter room, but the sound followed them. Both chose to switch to Chianti.

"The better to make a tasteful scene all over a white shirt if one of us gets fresh," she joked as they toasted one another. To her "Cheers," he responded with the Gaelic, "*Slainte mhath* (good health)."

"You impress me, Mr. Koulos. Is that not an Irish toast?"

"Irish...Gaelic, it's one or the other, and it's probably the only phrase I know in whichever of those languages it's supposed to be. I remember it phonetically. It's pronounced like, 'It's a lawn chair, va,' so who could forget a salute so cheerful and ridiculous?"

Nadia laughed, leaning in toward him, the better to be heard above the din. She rested one hand on his forearm and with the other, pointed through a stone archway, toward a set of French doors. "We'll have to step out on the balcony if we are to hear each other at all. I really don't know how the neighbors let them get away with this amount of noise—I mean, music—at this time of night. I confess I do like it, although in small doses."

"It is Friday evening. Perhaps this is typical Friday evening noise in Notting Hill."

"Perhaps. I wouldn't know," she responded. "Anyway, I saw a table bowed in the middle with food. D'you want to raid it and head out to the balcony with me? We can still hear the music, but we can also hear ourselves think. I think." She chuckled.

"I thought you Hollywood stars never ate anything! What if it's all spare ribs and fried chicken, and prime rib and pasta? What if there are no soy-rice sawdust cakes? Then what?"

"Then lead on!" She grasped his arm. "It's a gamble I'm willing to take."

They headed for one of the buffet tables where he chose a pair of Thai spring rolls and a ramekin of peanut satay sauce. Nadia, upon much reflection, decided upon a generous helping of lobster pot pie and on the side a golden churro with one end drizzled in chocolate. The evening was warm, with cool air that ribboned across an arm or cheek from time to time, refreshing where it touched.

"Good choice on the lobster dish. I may have made a mistake in not going with the lobster as well."

"You're in luck, Devin. I'm willing to share. Just mind, this seems to be Atlantic lobster, judging by the claws. So, Mr. Koulos, if you go for a claw, I have a fork with four pointy reminders that I picked lobster for a reason." She brandished her steely weapon and offered up a fierce look, followed by a grin. Nadia ran her right hand through a lock of blonde hair, pushing it out of her eyes.

"How do you know so much about lobster? I thought Americans only ate the ones with no claws."

"Ah, but Mr. Koulos, you're dealing with a girl who knows a rock lobster from a Maine lobster. I spent a summer or two in Massachusetts. I know where to find a great clam shack with an awesome lobster roll. Here's a little secret. Butter is my sworn enemy, and you know how butter and lobster go together like Chianti and Friday nights. I've made many a trip to the gym because of butter. It's my downfall, my deep shame. That and train robbing." She cast a glance up from her dish to see if he was smiling.

"Yeah, I've always had a hard time resisting a good train robbery myself. Okay, let me have a taste." She held out the dish, teasing him by covering the only visible claw with her fork. As he pulled in the salty-sweet morsel, he watched her mouth move in concert with his, as if she tasted it from the same fork. It made something stir within him.

"It's wicked good, isn't it?" Nadia's smile withdrew, just a fraction. "Mind if I ask a question? When Katie ran over to greet you, her words were cheerful enough, but I thought I saw a bit of tension between you. Did I imagine that?"

Acknowledging the lack of warmth between himself and Katie, he thought, would cause no harm. "Good call. I'll have to remember to keep my face deadpan when I'm around you. You're good!" He smiled, thinking he hadn't smiled so much in a long time.

He decided to share the nature of the relationship he had with the teenage actor. "Um, as far as my work for her is concerned, and certainly for the next few days, she's my boss." He paused, the better to give the impression he was sharing something unpleasant. He wanted Nadia to know he did not condone all of the teen's behavior.

"The Storm girl is very young. Let me give you an analogy. In the town of Piss Ant, Missouri, there's this kid, twelve years old and tall for his age, who plays amazing baseball. He has this sinker nobody under twenty can touch. Everybody in the town knows he'll make the big leagues one day. And ever since he turned eight, they've been treating him like Kid King Tut. Okay, after five years of being told you're the best thing Piss Ant, Missouri, ever created, how can that not screw up this seventeen-year-old's head? So. Tell me why Katie shouldn't think she's the best thing Dustbowl Kansas ever popped out?"

She paused. "Wow. Insight and compassion. So, she's not just a little bitch-brat spawn of Satan. Hmm."

He chuckled. "Actually, she's all that, or a part of her is for sure. I called her a brat two seconds after we met this evening, which wasn't very nice of me. So, one compartment of my brain is awful. Just awful! But there might be a smaller section in there that might contain a little niceness. The Buddhists say, 'Buddhism is kindness.' It's their..." he paused, "metta, I think. But kindness is certainly a work in progress for me." He stared straight into her face. "Believe me, I'm not all nice."

He changed the subject. "So. Nadia. You're an actor, and I apologize for not knowing your work. I don't get to the movies much. How's that going?" He noted that for the second time in fifteen minutes, she rested her hand on his arm. He got the impression this was not a come-on. She was probably a "touchy" person. He liked it.

"First of all, I adore that a huge part of what the Buddhists focus on is loving kindness. It's the center of their meditation mantra. Kinda cool, I must say, that you know this stuff. We will have much to chat about this, I predict, if we become friends. Anyway. Back to the word 'actor,' I sort of still think of myself in the old-fashioned way. I call myself an actress, as opposed to the word 'actor.' Something about keeping my femininity, I suppose. I was talking with an actress friend of mine, Anne Smith, and she says the main difference between an actor and an actress is: an actress is guaranteed to arrive on the set with perky breasts and a killer little black dress tucked away somewhere."

Donovan smiled again. "Wait a minute, I'm just picturing those breasts, and yes, there it is, the dress as well. You'll have to show me that little black dress, perhaps tomorrow, over dinner."

She tapped his arm and chided, "I'd say you were forward, but I guess if I'm going to drag my breasts, so to speak, into a conversation, I can't fault you for staying on topic, hmm?"

He smiled at the thought and then decided it was time for a change in venue. "Listen, this music is all right, I guess, but it's still pretty loud. Why don't I finish up your lobster, and we go find a quiet bar that plays some blues or something. Wouldn't that be nice?"

"Well, I have been to London several times, but this time I've been locked on the set on location here for weeks now. It would be lovely to bust out and have some fun for a change. As a matter of fact, I've heard of a place in Camden that would be perfect. Or, we could go to the Maple Leaf Pub in Covent Garden, if you want a Canadian beer. Which do you prefer? You decide while I finish up my own lobster, thank you very much."

"I've never been to Camden, whereas I confess I may have had a Canadian beer before. Camden it is. Do you think you can keep me safe there? I hear it can be a little rambunctious." He winked.

"Absolutely. I even promise not to be the one who is rambunctious there. You get us a cabbie, and I'll thank the hostess. Sorry, but I'm *not* inviting her along with us." It was Nadia's turn to wink.

The area of Camden where the taxi let them off was decrepit but based on the dress of the passersby, in vogue. They strode across the street to the Barfly and stood outside the bar in the queue, listening to the din coming from within. Nadia tapped the shoulder of the young lady in front of her. "Excuse me, I know this is a great bar, but is it a blues bar?" The young lady looked Nadia over and shook her head, wrinkling her nose. "Nah. Ya want the Blues Kitchen. This is all new music here." They left and found the right place in no time.

Inside, the atmosphere was warm, the music was cool, and the crowd appreciative. The opening act had finished, and the main event was yet to be. Nadia leaned across the table to chat. "You said in the cab you're from Montreal. I call New York my home now. Okay, tell me one reason why I should visit Montreal."

"Easy-peasey. Besides the cheesecake and smoked meat sandwiches, which I know New York is also pretty good at? You could actually go to see how beautiful Montreal women are. How beautiful? Almost as hot as you."

She rolled her eyes. "You're so full of it. But it might be nice to test both cheesecakes. That would be fun. It's interesting how there's this product called Montreal-style cheesecake and the same for smoked meat. New York brags up the very same things. So we have a few things in common.

"I do know a little bit about Canada, too. For instance, I know if I have a cousin in Toronto, and you're from say, Vancouver, you might not exactly have met."

Donovan smiled. "That's good. That actually happens, y'know. New Hampshire? I like the part where three states meet. New Hampshire meets Maine meets Massachusetts, all within something like twelve miles."

Nadia's smile widened. "I'm from the mountains, but you just pointed to the part of the Northeast I like best. Durham, Ogunquit, Portsmouth. Nice towns in the summer. Dover. Beautiful beaches that are just minutes away."

"You'll have to show me sometime. I haven't had much time to actually see places. Been to quite a few places—just didn't get to see them, you know what I mean?"

"Sweetie, I'm an actress. Other than scam artists and the military, no one visits more and sees less than the people in my industry. This..." she gestured to the room, "this is what I need more of in life. Less London and more Camden. You see, an actress has no balance in life—at least not that I've noticed.

"The in-demand actors are working all the time. They never see their fabulous homes. Then after a while, they still work, but it's sort of all work for nine months, followed by sitting by the pool doing nothing at all. Of course, while they sit by the pool, they obsess that nobody loves them. This is literally how Hollywood works. Jesus Christ, no wonder we're all in therapy!" She stopped, startled. "Holy smokes, where did that come from? Devin, did you pull that out of me? I've never said anything like that to anyone before. You a magic man?"

"Not really, I'm actually not much of a listener or a talker. But I felt you could have been telling me my own story. And listen, if you are, do not tell me you're my long-lost sister because I have to say I don't feel that way about you. I'm attracted to you, Nadia." He leaned in and kissed her.

The spell broke when an American accent interrupted. "Miz Kriss, can I have your autograph? I'm a big fan." The buxom woman was about thirty, a man standing just behind her, embarrassed.

"Well, as you can see, I was having a moment here, but sure, anything for an American cousin."

The woman's satisfaction showed as she waved the treasure. "An' can I have yours, too, sir?" Devin shook his head no, but Nadia prodded him. "Go on, Dirk. Don't be stingy with your fans. Give her your autograph. And be sure to put your latest movie title underneath your autograph. But no photos, okay? We're hiding from the paparazzi. You'll help, right?"

"My goodness, yes, Miz Kriss."

Afterward, Nadia asked him which movie he took credit for. "Couldn't think of one since I haven't been to a movie in ages, so I made one up. I wrote 'Dirk Dunn, in the fake movie *Three Wrongs.'"

She held up an open palm. "High five! That was fun!"

Keb Mo sauntered onto the stage after a bit and offered up a pensive, tight acoustic set that allowed for chit-chat. His skills on both slide and regular guitars commanded their undivided attention throughout his time on stage.

Donovan studied the features of the woman beside him. He was surprised at how comfortable he was, sitting beside this person who was able to offer up small witticisms, yet comfortable enjoying companionable silences. He even loved that she tapped her foot to each song and knew the words to some of them.

They stayed until just after two, and Nadia invited him back to her hotel. The pair entered the lobby and got to her room without any paparazzi spotting them. He stayed the night, the sex was great, and he was out and up the street by six.

While she slept, he had taken a few photos of her necklace, a simple string of tiny silver freshwater pearls holding a thin, roughly-forged grey bar about three inches in length. The bar was covered in runic symbols he couldn't make out. She had tossed it on the bathroom countertop, a fact he filed for future reference. He wrote a note, *"Dinner...9:00...Indian Butter Chicken (I know how you love butter) or a juicy American steak, your call...West End...DK @ the Strand"* and tucked the edge of it underneath an emptied wine glass on the table near the door. As he glanced across the table, he noticed a single framed photo. It was a version of Nadia, but it wasn't Nadia. The young woman's elbow rested on the window of an old Buick, her ash-blonde hair blowing across her cheek. It was Nadia's mother. In the photo, the woman was studying a serious little platinum-blonde girl who stood on the driver's seat. Her tiny hands were positioned on the wheel at two o'clock at ten o'clock. He straightened the photo and left.

Saturday morning weather was London weather, and he was soaked to the skin in the brief dash from the cab to the hotel awning. Donovan went straight to bed, and his expensive, wet Italian suit was strewn in a careless heap across the floor. A "Do Not Disturb" sign hung outside his door.

The morning rain had subsided to a drizzly fog, full of atmosphere in both senses of the word. Once up and about, he sent his damp clothes to be laundered and set out to get additional reinforcements. To squire actresses about town would mean an investment in clothes and where better than the city that hosted Savile Row? Once that task was finished, he headed out along the Embankment. He walked along the Thames past the Egyptian Obelisk—known as Cleopatra's Needle—in the general direction of St. Paul's.

He would have to go back to Montreal to drop off the Romanian cup and pick up his pay. After depositing the cash in even amounts between his off-shore and American accounts, that task would be done. It made him tired, thinking about heading off to New York to do the art gallery theft. An American (he assumed) client wanted to get his hands on the floor plans and electrical wiring blueprints of a tidy, high-end gallery in mid-town Manhattan.

Now. How to get the necklace? The tiniest, mostly unfamiliar pang crossed his mind as he thought of its owner, and he shook his head, thinking of a speech made by Churchill in which he said, "Men occasionally stumble over the truth, but most of them pick themselves up and hurry off as if nothing ever happened." He shook his head again and blinked, wondering whether grabbing it on the set, or at the hotel, might be the better option. He decided to keep both possibilities open, although he respected on-set security.

It was early in the afternoon, with plenty of time to work out a Plan B, just in case simply lifting the necklace wouldn't work. He went back to the hotel, tossed his sodden umbrella in a corner, and picked up the digital camera with the images of Nadia's necklace in it. He called a friend who knew people with specific skills in certain criminal activities. He chose one of them and managed to track him to a down-at-the-heels neighborhood by the docks, out in the East End of London. He noted the address and headed out.

A short walk along a narrow street took him to three side-by-side jewellery repair shops. They even offered the same "Cash for Gold" cardboard signs in the window. He rang the bell beside the building number he was given.

Once pleasantries were exchanged and Donovan's friend's name was mentioned, they got straight to work. The old man bent over the prints and studied the images presented on the digital camera. He remained motionless for some time. "Yessir, I believe I could do that fing what you ask. Here's a pen and paper, squire. You will need to bring back to me responses to vese questions."

Donovan offered a steady gaze in return and then nodded at the diminutive man. "You ask the questions, I'll remember them. I'm not a big fan of putting things on paper. Call me eccentric."

"Right you are, sir. Vis is what I requi-ah." He squinted at the image of the necklace, muttering to himself. "Right-o. Must have a bettah image of the clasp." He scratched his whiskers and looked up at his client.

"I must know how many pearls are on the string..." he continued to study Donovan's face, "on each side of the bar. I need somefink what represents the exact shade o' grey o' the pearls and of the bar. Having the precise diameter of the pearls would be helpful. Finally, I must have a bettah image of the bar itself. All four sides, if you wish it to be precise enough to dupe the owner." He smirked. "Oi presume this to be the point, in'it. And o' course, I need to know the weight of the bar, don't I? An' if you would be so kind as to weigh it in grams, that would be brilliant. A wax impress of dese parts would be helpful but not expected. Can't have every fink, what? We still innerested, squire?"

"Yes. Of course."

"Art'll be free hundred quid. Four hunnerd, actually. An it will be a fink of beauty."

"Euros okay? No? Okay, I'll give you 500 pounds if you can provide me with a serious fake within four days of my dropping off this information. Deal?"

"We have a deal, mate."

"Then you'll hear from me in a couple of days, latest. Our mutual friend tells me you are like me in that you understand the value of keeping information to yourself?"

"Absolutely. Ahm a man what can hold his tongue."

"Then I'll see you soon." He pulled out a small wad of bills. "All I've got is three hundred at the moment for deposit. Let's begin thinking about what a good job you're going to do. Listen, on second thought, I'm going to require two necklaces, exactly the same. We'll call it an even 800 pounds, okay?"

"Fanks, mate. It is awready a pleasure doing business wif you. Stop by my local an' I w'let you draw me a pint."

From there, Donovan headed out to purchase a better, high-pixel, short-focus camera and the tiniest metric scale he could find. Once that task was accomplished, he was back at the hotel by six and headed down to the bar for a drink a half hour later.

He had dissolved his ceramic knife prior to leaving the Bucharest airport, and his monkey's paw had remained on the floor in the airport in Bucharest. He didn't worry about it, as he had another back in Montreal. But he was always cautious, always waiting for the unexpected to come at him from left field. So, in his pocket he carried a *bagh naght*, an Indian cat's paw bar that, when held at his side could not be detected. Each end of the metal bar morphed into sculpted cat's paws, each holding a small loop. While the paws could do some damage, the loops themselves were coated in the same nematoblast poison that gave the Portuguese man-o-war jellyfish such a nasty punishment. He'd found it in a research lab in Australia, where an Indonesian scientist had found a way to pull the nematoblasts off the jellyfish stingers and coat the loops with the poison. The pain was brutal, anywhere it touched.

He had downed half his drink when he found himself flanked by a familiar pair of Romanian agents. As before, Donovan ordered them a drink, this time gin with tonic on the side.

"Welcome to London, gentlemen. I can be as good a companion as the next guy, but all this popping up unannounced makes it extremely challenging to—" He was interrupted by the leader and felt something prod his side.

"Shut up. Come with us now. We will not kill you this time if you do as I say. Get up." The bartender was serving drinks to a French couple, and there was no one with whom he could make eye contact. Leaving two ten pound notes on the bar, he led the pair out of the bar and down one flight to the public toilet of the hotel.

As they entered, the silent agent grabbed his arm and punched him in the gut with an intensity that took all of his wind. It left him down on the tiles, aching for just a gasp of air. A boot to his still-bruised side assured him nothing in the way of air was going to be forthcoming any time soon. Job accomplished, the silent agent left the toilet area to stand guard outside the bathroom while the leader continued with his task.

"Do I have your attention, dog shit?"

Donovan could only moan. He spat a mouthful of blood. The agent persisted, "I want Mr. Yorke's passport. You will give it to me in the next few minutes, or I will not be responsible for what happens to you. Mr. Donovan, I have never killed a man before, but my government will protect me this time, because there are greater things at stake than your dog shit life. At any rate, I will be home long before this country is aware I was even here." He emphasized his point with a placed kick to the groin that left Donovan in despair of ever taking a breath again. The cold from the tile floor on his cheek was the only thing keeping him conscious.

"Wait. Just wait!" he gasped. The agent sat on the sink counter and stared while his subject fought to get his breath. In a minute, Donovan raised himself to a sitting position. He lifted a hand as the agent threatened to slip off the counter. "No more. Yes, I have it. It's not worth all this to me. I found it...somewhere, and it means nothing to me."

"And it is your lies that do not mean anything to me. You found it in the Dobra apartment. I am curious, though. You injured Tomas because he killed your friend the Roma. But why you kill Mr. Yorke?"

"Roma? What's a Roma? And wait... Yorke is dead?" He stared at the agent's feet, trying to process this new information through the fog of pain.

"Roma is gypsy. He was of the Roma people. And you say you did not kill Mr. Yorke? This may need to be discussed later, but for now, I need to get the passport back to Mr. Yorke's body before it is discovered. As you can imagine, there is some urgency to this. The government of Romania does not want an incident. It will be bad enough Mr. Yorke has met with an accident while hiking in Transylvania. That's it! Get me the passport. Now."

The agent hopped off the counter and then grasped Donovan's sleeve to drag him to his feet. But Donovan came up wielding the cat's paw. The steel bar caught the agent hard, just under the chin, and the poisoned loop slapped his cheek in a tight circle from the jaw right up to his eye socket.

The agent grunted from the impact of the bar, and then he screamed as the skin on his face lit up in pain. By then, Donovan had the agent's gun and had pointed it at his temple when the silent partner burst in. He demanded the second agent's weapon and then stood back. He sat the agents back on the sink counter, keeping one of their guns trained on them, and began asking questions.

"I am a nosy man by inclination, so while I shouldn't care about this Edward Yorke bastard, here I am asking. Why do you care why he died, or if he has his passport? He won't need it where he's going if he's as dead as you say he is. Perhaps if you start at the beginning, I'll try to give the passport back. Okay...I can't promise you'll get it back, but it *could* happen." He waited while they considered their position. A brief conversation in Romanian followed. "Better hurry. Someone may need to take a piss."

The silent agent said nothing, but the leader spoke up, holding his crimson cheek and wincing from the locus of pain. "Mr. Yorke had a United Nations contract to work with the Youth Ministry, trying to get the children off of the streets. Unfortunately, he is, or was, not a nice man. He took the contract money, did not do a thing, and left the ministry in the unfortunate position of having nothing to report back to the United Nations just before election time. Worse yet, he had a small business on the side. He had your Roma boy stealing passports for resale. Further, he blamed ministry officials for the lack of success of the children's program and for the missing money. The night before he was to leave the country, he was killed. One of our informers found Yorke's body, not far from the dead Roma boy.

"So we tracked down Tomas at the hospital. Janos informed us when his brother came awake...um, came conscious...Mr. Yorke was lying dead in the street. Janos says he did not know how he came to be there, but he is certain you were gone before the body was discovered. We do not really know the truth yet, because both Janos and Tomas are liars. We will find out the details in time. We do think Yorke's head was crushed by the same rock or cobblestone you used on Tomas.

"We believe Mr. Yorke paid off Janos—he was a weak man—but if we present the body back to England without a passport, more, um, shall we say specific questions will certainly be asked. Mr. Yorke told his government he was going hiking just before leaving Romania, so we will be able to create a mountain accident for him if we can get the passport back immediately. But we have failed." The agent wouldn't look Donovan in the eye.

How can I get these people off my back? Donovan thought a second as he rubbed his side. Then he spoke, pointing the gun at the more vocal of the agents, just to keep them attentive. "Gentlemen, I am a nice guy. I want you to succeed. So, how can we arrive at a win-win situation, eh? I have an idea."

TWENTY MINUTES LATER, he was sitting on a park bench, just across from London's Kensington Palace Gardens. It wasn't long before the agent with the raised crimson loop imprint on his cheek exited the Romanian embassy on Kensington St. and walked through the fall darkness toward the park bench. He handed Donovan an envelope almost half an inch thick. He, in turn, handed over the passport, and both men headed in opposite directions without another word. It did occur to Donovan he might have to watch his step when next in Romania, or even in London for that matter. He shrugged the thought off and whistled a tuneless tune as he re-entered his hotel. It was time to lie down and try to heal up a bit. *This getting beat up every day is getting old.* He cupped his swollen balls as he entered his room.

Chapter Nine

L*ondon*
  Saturday Evening

    With the exception of wincing every time he turned to the left, Donovan (or Devin) was a more-than-congenial companion to Nadia. Further, he was an entertaining raconteur to her dinner companions that evening, although he chose to limit his stories to those with a Canadian setting. At one point, he asked himself if he thought he was in some movie, or was he actually having a good time? He had to confess both acting like a boyfriend to Nadia and actually becoming one seemed to be mashing up into one surreal scene. Which one was real? But what was the harm, as long as he could keep his lies straight? He closed his thoughts and chose for the moment to just be.

    They didn't speak as she opened the hotel apartment door for him, and in a moment, their clothes were on the floor, and they lay together, silent, on her bed. Their lovemaking was almost theatrical. She came straight to him, kissing him, needing him. Her tongue probed his mouth, and he felt her hand on his chest, caressing upward, and then moved lower. Practiced. After a moment, although it seemed in the moment, she moved so they touched from mouths to feet. They were engrossed in this terrain, each step in the dance a bold adventure. It was now carrying her away, and he was moved by the feel, the touch, the sensation, the small sounds he teased from her. He began to rock, slowly. Could an act performed so many times become new? But it was because they had just invented it. He let himself go and felt as if he had lost nothing, not self-control...nothing. This was what he had always sought.

    Later, as body heat dissipated, and the slight coolness of the room overtook them, they drew closer. Nadia traced a finger, light as a breath, across the redness on his side. He rolled over onto his back, hiding the welt.

    "Devin? You aren't taking very good care of yourself. What's with the bandaged finger, the week-old bruise on your left side, and now this new, huge welt on top of it? Are you really script doctoring or is stunt-doubling your game? Actually, I've seen stunt doubles with many fewer injuries than you." She waited in the faint glow from the hall light.

He was caught; time for another lie. "Just before I came to England, I was trying a new sport, called parkour. It's a very physical activity, from the French word *parcours*, or running a course. It's where the athletes use city property as their exercise tools. I was researching it because it's got this security angle. People who do it can get into buildings because the security systems aren't designed to anticipate entry from these areas, such as over a fifteen foot wall. Nobody expects someone can run up a wall. So there are...vulnerabilities to breaking and entering."

She began to smile, and he joined her. "I know you're thinking, 'really. This skinny guy running up walls?' Well, I didn't say I was good at it! As a matter of fact, I suck at it, thus the bruising and contusions and whatnot. Anyway, I was at it again today. I was trying to avoid banging the hand with the broken finger, so as I fell off this ledge, I let myself land on my left side. I know, I know, not nearly as good a story as my earlier ones. I had everyone laughing with that anecdote about being driven along a beach by my tipsy brother when I was fifteen, right?" He smiled and kissed her navel.

"Parkour, huh? So, you can now run up the side of a high-rise and use telephone poles to launch into space?" She caressed his bicep. "Devin," she whispered, "you a tough guy?"

"Yup. Hey, want a sip of wine before we nod off?"

She didn't answer but continued talking, almost as if to herself. "You know, my dad was a tough guy. Unfortunately, he was tough at home, too. He kind of popped me a few times when I was young. I used to 'spout off and wise crack,' he said, so he would say it was my fault, and I got what I deserved."

Donovan stiffened, listening.

"But after a while, I noticed he didn't seem to need a smart ass remark to set him off. One day, I walked out of the schoolyard, and instead of going right, I turned left and never returned home." She looked up, locking eyes with his, her forehead creased. "The bastard actually called me up a few years ago. He said carrying a grudge wasn't right, between a father and his daughter. I reminded him that smacking me around wasn't cool, either. He asked me for a loan." She looked away. "Can you imagine?"

Donovan's face softened in sympathy. "First of all, I could never be the kind of tough guy your father was. That's not what I'd call tough anyway. Secondly, let me guess. You sent him the money and changed your phone number afterward, right?"

She nodded. "Yes, I'm what my grandmother would call a dumb chickie. It was my grandmother who kept me mostly safe until I left home. She's Canadian...perhaps you know her? I'm sorry, a bad joke. I really do know how big Canada is, honest. And, I'm running off at the mouth. I'm so sorry."

He leaned in and kissed her forehead, smoothing a worry line away. "About that wine?"

"Perhaps a glass of water, if you'd be a dear? I have to work tomorrow, and the director wants to see my rapidly aging face by the dawn's early light. Bastard." She chuckled.

"Just one rapidly aging face in this room, and it's not yours." He grabbed her robe, draped it over his shoulders to make her smile, and wandered down the hall, past the closet to where his camera and scale rested in his coat pocket.

Nadia's voice remained chatty. "Honey, the bathroom is to the left!"

"Of course. Sorry."

"You Canadians...always sorry about something."

He took a second to measure the necklace on the side of the sink stand.

She called into the darkness. "Honey, did I mention I'm getting up in just a few hours? Now would be an excellent time to prove to me that at least some of your body parts are still in good working order. And I promise to use your ribs sparingly, or abuse them, as the case may be."

He took no time returning to bed, transferring the camera and scale from his shirt pocket to the floor, just under the bed on his side. She lifted the coverlet, inviting him in.

NEXT DAY DAWNED GREY and misty, and he found himself alone in the hotel apartment of a Hollywood actress. He took a quick tour around the apartment. Nadia had laid out the bits and pieces of her life throughout these few rooms, making the rooms hers. In this way, an actress could make a hotel suite her home for two months. She had placed the photo of herself and her mother near the door. He saw a set of worry beads tossed on a bookshelf, noting combinations of how-to texts for yoga and Buddhism, interspersed with travel literature—they had that in common—and historical romances. The coffee table sported a square copper pan half-filled with beach sand, featuring a sea star and a small variety of shells. He smiled when he saw most of the sand was pushed to one end of the pan to denote, he suspected, low tide, or perhaps a sand dune. A script with an unfamiliar title sat next to the copper pan diorama. *The chapters of her life. I guess the necklace will be an unhappy chapter, if she finds out.*

Nadia's work was to take her and the entire cast out of London to Bath for the day. How did a Canadian non-actor find himself in the middle of an American film being shot in England? Shrugging, he drew the hotel room door behind him and sauntered down the hall, nodding at but not speaking to the chambermaids as they began their long workday on Sunday, the day of rest.

He had breakfast in the West End, in what the tourists called "Theatreland." He chose a high-backed stool at a counter in front of a street-facing window, the better to people-watch. It was one of the few times he permitted himself the luxury of leaving his back to the restaurant patrons. The omelette arrived, and he discovered he was starved. He noted that, as long as you didn't mind paying a bit more because of location, you could have a great, unassuming meal. And if you ate early, you could avoid the crowds Theatreland would have later in the day. He was finishing up his first cup of coffee when his cell phone rang. It was Katie.

"Hello, Darling. We're just getting on the set now, and I'm watching the old cow try to remember her lines." Donovan chose not to speak and waited a long twelve seconds. "Well? Aren't you going to defend your lover?"

"What can I do for you, Miss Storm?"

"Well, let me see." Her voice chilled and then oozed vitriol. "How about your fucking job? You could do that for me, I suppose."

"It is under control. I will have met the terms of our agreement in a few days."

Her voice went down a tone without thawing. "I see. So you're doing what I paid you for?"

Donovan's spine tingled. His fingers tightened on the phone, and he chose his words with care. "I'm going back to college now. If you want to discuss this further, please come see me at my hotel after classes. Otherwise, you may conclude my consulting work with you will finish shortly. Sound good? See you." He flipped it shut without waiting for a response, setting it on vibrate.

What was that about? Was she impatient to get the necklace, or was she trying to get him to incriminate himself over the phone? He reviewed his words and didn't find anything he should worry about. But he didn't trust her. Not at all. He thought it might be time to wrap up this project and get the hell out of here.

There were other reasons to leave as well. He needed to get the chalice to his client at Concordia, in Montreal. Professor Umbra was convinced the script that wrapped itself around the bucchero chalice was some kind of translation aid, the only key of its kind that could unlock the Etruscan language. The original cup had been looted and disappeared sometime during the Second World War, but the Romanians had somehow taken drawings and created an exact replica. So, here was this chalice with some sort of *Etruscan for Dummies* code on it. *This was a more valuable commodity than he had imagined.*

He watched the pedestrians pad across his line of sight before the cafe window and considered his current project. He noticed one passerby averted his gaze when Donovan caught his eye through the window, but Donovan shrugged it off. *Too early in the day to be paranoid.*

It occurred to Donovan the main reason to consider leaving town was Nadia. He was beginning to think of her when she wasn't around, which wasn't normal to him, and it wasn't good. She liked the same kind of wine as he did. She tapped her foot to the same kind of music he liked, for Christ's sake. *Ordinary things, but they add up.* Only bad things could come from being vulnerable to, well, anything. He'd have to watch himself. His phone vibrated. He ignored it, nibbled on his croissant, and took a gulp of strong, harsh coffee from cup number two.

It wasn't difficult to pass a day in London. The rooms and tombs beneath Westminster Abbey and the alcoves within Saint Paul's Cathedral, carried the remains of some of the most memorable Britons of the past two millennia. The Tower of London was guarded by ravens, not to mention the colorful Beefeaters with their even more colorful stories, and the Tate Modern was absolutely world class. A simple walk-about through Piccadilly Circus was always fun for a people watcher. And then there was Abbey Road, just a street crossing in one sense, but the backdrop of one of the best Beatles albums, recorded at the height of their career.

It was, in fact, true what he had said to Katie; he was going back to class or at least to a library. First, Donovan traveled all the way over to the East End docks to drop off the necklace specs to his jeweller. Then he headed all the way back to Piccadilly Circus for lunch and a little more people watching. It was always a curiosity to him to note the street buskers who dressed as statues along the broad sidewalk beneath the video screens. He had seen them in Italy and France as well. It used to be an Elvis who was gilt from nose to toes, but he'd been supplanted by Johnny Depp's Captain Jack Sparrow. The silvery Statue of Liberty, however, could still be found. How did they find the patience to stand stock-still for hours on end? Further, what was the appeal to the crowd? *I just don't get it.* Another tourist tossed a Euro into the golden pirate's tin cup and watched him doff his tricorn hat and bow, ever so slowly, from the tiny, three-legged stool on which he stood. Donovan shook his head in disbelief.

After lunch, he took the bus to Euston Road. His first thought had been to visit one of the nineteen colleges of the University of London and charm his way into the library. But he concluded a simple day membership at the British Library would grant him the information he sought without the need to be charming. He knew the Senate House Library would also permit him a day pass. But, while the Senate Library was the larger resource, in most cases you had to know what book you were looking for. This wouldn't work at all for Donovan since he himself didn't know.

It took no time at all to find the library and receive a day pass. He hauled down a few books on the history of languages from the shelves. It was his thought to go online and use some passages from the books to trace a few key words and phrases out in the Etruscan language background. Looking around, he spotted a girl in a headband and tie-dyed sweater rising from a work station and counted himself fortunate to be able to grab a computer. Once online, he saw several examples of bucchero cups, but none that were made of gold and none with words forged into the sides of them.

It turned out the fellow who was able to translate Etruscan would be a fortunate fellow indeed. In addition to receiving a chair at any Ivy League university in the Western world, there was no telling what treasures might be unearthed by translating the few pieces of Etruscan writing that remained, up to now. In hindsight, he was annoyed with himself for undercharging the prof, Umbra. *That'll teach me for not doing my homework. Stupid of me.*

The afternoon was swept away like the first autumn leaves swirling around his feet as he walked back to the tube. At about four-thirty, he came out opposite Harvey Nichols in Knightsbridge and meandered along past the shops. At one point, he ducked into a side street to admire the holly bushes peeking out between the wrought iron gates and fences. And then he returned to the main street and his destination: Harrods. Within sight of the massive department store, a BMW coupe pulled over and spewed forth a trio of young teens. They were fresh from some sporting event, soccer perhaps, judging from their uniforms. As the car pulled back into traffic, the girls reached into their backpacks, hauling out makeup kits, boyfriend jackets, and stylish berets.

In the quarter block it took to catch up to them, they had aged four years. In fact, they led him to Harrods. He overheard them mention they each had an allowance of fifty pounds, and all seemed determined to go home without it. Donovan remembered a childhood where every day seemed to end with two options: "Will we have food on the table at suppertime?" and "Which one of us will get beaten tonight?" He suspected none of these three young ladies was worried about the availability of food or the proximity of a father's belt or fist. As they entered the store, the young ladies danced right, leaving him to find his path through the mega-shop. He took a moment to watch the dinnertime crowd lining up at the deli section in front of the neon-pink tandoori.

Donovan bought flowers, paid in cash, and had them sent to Nadia at her hotel. By using cash and avoiding all use of plastic cards, people wouldn't know, for example, he had visited Harrods unless they were watching him.

Generally, he paid cash wherever he went so as to increase the challenge for authorities or victims who sought to trace him through his purchases. Same with his cell phones. He had his Devin phone, his Donovan phone (which he seldom used), and a couple of European phones. Each of these was a burner phone with separate SIM cards, which he switched or threw away and replaced as necessary according to which country he was in. He then ambled over to the jewellery section, a recent work-related preoccupation.

In a cluster of kiosks in the open area of the store, he noticed several jewellery pieces costing a pretty penny. But in a nearby room, he could see even nicer rings and other items without price tags. The attendant smiled at him through the doorway. *Bet if you have to ask, you can't afford those*, he concluded. Moving on to stationery, he chose a leather-bound diary. After paying, he headed upstairs to the music section, bought a book containing the sheet music of Robert Johnson, and tearing out the lyrics and music to "Crossroads Blues," folded it and tucked it inside the cover of the diary. He smiled. What would Nadia infer from that? He focused on her voice, the timbre of which fell just into the lower mid-range for women. Contralto? *Sexy*.

As he headed for the exit by the nearest subway entrance, he thought he saw the man who had averted his gaze through the restaurant window. The man didn't glance his way, yet Donovan's senses tingled. This was not a coincidence. He considered following him, but the stranger had already disappeared into the dinnertime congestion. Donovan left Harrods of Knightsbridge, following the holly and wrought iron back to the tube.

UPON OPENING THE DOOR to his room, he was surprised to see Katie lying on her belly on his bed. She had crossed her legs at the ankle in the air, her head facing the door. Her tanned arms rose from the bedspread and supported a bemused smile. She wore crimson panties and matching pumps, delicate gold chains dangling at earlobes, throat, and ankle. Nothing else. Donovan closed the door, walked past her to the bathroom, glanced in. Empty. He returned to the foot of the bed, unbuttoned his naval pea jacket, and tossed it onto a nearby chair. Her eyes widened, and she turned, just a little, to reveal a pert, rounded breast.

"Small room."

Ignoring her, Donovan glanced to his left. He found no one in the closet either, and owing to the size of the suite, he knew they were alone. "Toss me your phone," he commanded. Her smile faltered as she obeyed. He powered it down, noting her displeasure. He took a moment to lock eyes with her.

Her frown lasted two seconds. "Come admire my panties," she purred, "and we can talk business."

"I have three daughters your age," he lied, "and I'd rather screw one of them than a little brat like you. Does your momma know you pull tricks like this?"

Neither of them smiled at his cruelty. He moved over to the window to close the drapes, not bothering to glance beyond them to the building across the street. Now that the situation was more to his liking, he took a moment to study her.

Her eyes darted from his bandaged finger, to the scar on his chin. He felt reassured to note her uneasiness. *Maybe she's beginning to understand you can't hire people like me—criminals—and think everything's a cakewalk.* He moved to the phone by his bed, lifted it, and with a final gesture, disconnected the wire without even looking. Alarmed, she sat up, grabbing three times for her dress before managing to capture it. Her cocky smile had faded.

"Now. Go sit in that chair over there and start over. Brat." Donovan grabbed a chair and slid it beside the bed, propping his feet on the edge of the coverlet. He slouched into it, inches from the hem of the dress that now covered her. He glanced at her crimson bra, laying on the nightstand. "What's this about?"

"Just you remember who I am." She thrust the words at him and then hid behind them. Her voice quavered, just a little.

"I know who you are, Katie Two-Shoes-And-Panties. You're a spoiled brat who gets her way ninety-nine per cent of the time. Ninety-nine." The corner of his mouth turned up, just a bit. "Seriously. Rich Girl with Bad Judgement. What's with the red undies and black designs? I've got a Hollywood joke you might appreciate. Did you hear about the stupid

Hollywood starlet? Oh, yes—dumb. She was so dumb she slept with the screenwriter to get ahead." He saw from her face she didn't get any of it except that it was probably a put-down.

His voice softened. "Listen, brat. You're a rich, talented, famous kid. But that still makes you a kid. There's no need to screw your way into or out of anything. Certainly nothing to gain from bedding down the help. If you want me to do something for you, just pay me in cash. Let's be old-fashioned about that. As I said, what on earth could I possibly do for you besides get you a lucky necklace? Give me a wad of bills, and I'll let you call me names. Take me to bed, and well, depending on who I am, there's danger in it for you. You don't need danger."

He saw her confidence returning now that her perception of trouble had diminished. She straightened up to face him.

"You don't tell me what to do. You're my hired help, remember? I-I just wanted to protect my investment. What's to say you haven't gone soft on the bitch, maybe told her what we're up to? And I do mean 'we,' you know?" Her voice rose, reminding Donovan he was implicated as well, but he also saw, once again by her tone, just how young she was. "I know you've hooked up with her, so maybe you're falling for her."

"Hmm. You were just about to bed me. Does that mean you're falling for me?" He grinned as she appeared to think that through. "I thought not. Listen, sex is just another tool. People use it all the time to get what they need. Now me, I prefer money, but if I can use sex to get money, well...I will." He drew a knee up and knitted his hands across it, careful not to bend his broken finger, and turned his gaze to the ceiling.

"So. Brat. Your investment is safe. And you're still a virgin, right?" He winked as Katie scowled at these words. "All in all, I think you're having a good day. Let's not ruin it by calling your giant-killer in from the hall. I'm sure he's holding the key that got you in?" She looked sheepish. He leaned over to pat her thigh. "Beat it, kid. It's all going to work out for the best. Now scram. I have a date." He picked up the sheer material from the nightstand and tossed it across the bed to where she stood. "And for god's sake take your bra; why complicate my relationship with the maids?"

His laughter followed her as his hotel room door swung closed behind her arched, rigid back.

He heard her mutter from the other side, "And I'm not a brat. Fucker."

HE STOOD IN FRONT OF Nadia's hotel suite door at nine and hadn't finished the second rap when the door swung open. She was dressed as if to go dancing. She wore her ash blonde hair swept up, and white gold bars shaped like bamboo reeds dangled down each ear lobe. The earrings caressed a flawless swan throat. The dress was a show-stopper: shimmering emerald to match her eyes, low-cut on top, tea-length on the bottom, with a flirty slit down one side from mid-thigh. The open toes of her black shoes peeked out through emerald piping, and their height permitted her to look him square in the eyes. She completed the ensemble by sporting a diamond necklace whose facets showcased a single square-cut emerald. He smiled, taken aback. "I'm sorry. I was looking for Miss Nadia Kriss, Famous Starlet. You must be Queen Noor of Jordan?"

She twirled, received an approving smile, and then leaned into to him, the better to receive a kiss low on her neck. While she accepted his caress, she held the back of his head to her as drew her closer. "Devin," she whispered, "I've decided you're trouble."

He stiffened, waiting. Where was this going? What did she know? Was this about her comment that he was a tough guy? He permitted the door to close with a swoosh, followed by a discrete click.

"I've grown accustomed to your face, and well, what started out as a harmless way to enjoy London seems to have become a little, just a teeny, bit more. I'm beginning to think we go together like Saturday and Sunday." Her voice stayed light, airy light, but he couldn't see her face as she continued to hug him. He knew words were just half the story; what did her face say? But Donovan knew even if he could see her face, reading it might prove a challenge as she was, in fact, a good actress. He pulled away at any rate, the better to meet her gaze.

She continued to smile, but her eyes searched. He felt as if she was attempting to read him. Then she stopped, appearing to lose her nerve. Her voice became casual, almost businesslike. "That said, we're both wrapping up our projects soon, and I thought we could have a great dinner, an awesome evening, and a remarkable roll in the hay...whaddayasay? How easy was that to get me in bed?" She laughed, nervousness in her voice. She walked away from the door and turned to stand near the bar table. He couldn't catch her eye.

Donovan recovered, letting his feet follow her to the bar and a waiting carafe. He asked permission with his eyes and then poured some wine, rolling it around to watch her through the side of his glass. He took a sip, stalling. "Pinot Noir?"

She nodded but with a guarded smile, her eyes a tiny bit shinier. "From the Yarra Valley. It's called 'Long Flat Destinations,' and yes, I bought it for the name. We, ah, we both like the Aussie stuff." She paused, not sure how to continue. "I guess." Her voice trailed off.

It was only ten seconds, but it seemed like ten minutes to him, when he finally spoke. "Baby, you know me awfully well for us being, well, us, for less than a week. This afternoon I was sitting in a window seat at some restaurant, thinking to myself that you were pretty much the same kind of trouble. To me." He walked back to the doorway, to where she still stood, and kissed her, his mouth gentle on hers. Did she believe him? Was he beginning to believe it as well? The half-lies were beginning to meld into something approximating the truth. Maybe he was feeling...something for her.

"Nadia, I can't tell you we're the 'it' couple of the year. I'm certainly no Brad Pitt. I do know I care for you, that you've got way under my skin. And I don't know what to make of that, because it's never ever happened before. Look. Let's do just as you say. Let's go eat, have some fun. Chat. Let's see where we are...who we are. Let's find out who has the most freckles on their ass 'cause let's be honest, it's mine. Let's...let's just be Devin and Nadia tonight, and who knows, maybe we'll become this couple called Devin and Nadia. Hell, we've already been a couple longer than some marriages."

"Certainly longer than some Hollywood marriages." Her voice rose, grew stronger. "But I wasn't talking about marriage. I was...just thinking it might be...a loss, of some kind, if we were to just, ah, part as if this week never happened, 'ya know?"

Donovan nodded and gave her a reassuring look, although his stomach was in knots. "Yes. I know. Well, then. It would appear we have something to chew on in addition to a nice steak. Can a fella, in fact, get a nice steak in England? Let's go find out."

She nodded.

It would be somewhat less tense talking this thing out in a public place, he was certain. He grabbed her wrap, and they headed out, stopping by the concierge to see where the best chop house in London was.

LATER, IN BED, SHE rolled off him and lay on her back, making little noises of pleasure until her breathing was almost normal. The room was still, so still even the traffic below seemed to be tiptoeing past her hotel. "Thank you, Devin, thank you so much for this amazing evening, from the flowers, to the dinner, to, well, this!" She patted his abdomen.

He smiled in the dark. "We did laugh a lot, didn't we?"

"Yes, we did."

Silence, and then she spoke again. "Darling, what do you really think of Katie, your boss? It's been several days now."

He kept his voice and words noncommittal. "She's a brat. A brat who pays very well." He paused to pass the back of his hand across her cheek, gentle-as-breath. "My read on her is she didn't have much as a child, and that lack of things has now turned into a control issue. She likes playing all the pawns around her, and to her, everyone is a pawn. She likes to hear 'yes' to her questions. If she ever hooks up with someone, her partner better have a backbone, or he won't last as long as a martini in Vegas."

He rolled over onto his side, wincing as his weight settled on his bruised rib. He watched her silhouette through the night glow emanating from the slight separation between the drapes. "That said, I wouldn't trust her. Not because she's evil but because in a way she's still a child, not quite grown up. She still carries that same wilfulness that makes her decisions so reckless. Add a bucket of money and a score of yes men, and she's absolutely unpredictable. She's insecure, so she's also dangerous. Why do you ask?"

Nadia's voice was even, stripped of inflection. "She doesn't like you very much. She told her assistant you copped some cash from her." Nadia's hand stole across the coverlet to grasp his. "I don't believe it for a New York minute. The thing is, that scene was staged as a set up for me. I know she waited until I was within hearing range to say her lines. Couldn't have been staged better if she had used a director. So I know the message was for me. Now, it could mean one of two things, from where I'm sitting. Either she loves me and wants me to be happy—which I sincerely doubt—or she hates me and wants us not to be an 'us,' as you said before. To be honest, Devin, I'm leaning toward the 'she hates me' scenario. She's certainly made it clear in a hundred other ways. And I don't give two shits about what she thinks or says, but I absolutely agree with what you said. For whatever reason, she's trouble. I wanted to warn you."

Donovan frowned, looking at her lips, so soft and swollen from lovemaking just minutes ago, now pursed in concentration, all business. "Baby, you know I'm no spring chicken..." his frown lessened as he heard her sniff in amusement, "but this is the first instance, in my entire life, where someone has actually had my back. And I'm almost forty."

Nadia sat up. "Really? You're not yet forty? Christ, I'm just over forty. Apparently I'm a cradle-robber in addition to being worthy of a famous child actress's hate. Shit!"

He couldn't tell if she was joking or not. "Nadia! Focus, dear. We're in the middle of my insecurities, not yours. Don't you think it's weird a guy can go the better half of a long lifetime without having someone who'll stand beside him, or at least within sight, who'll, you know, worry about him? What kind of life have I led that I'd be in this position?" He was musing to himself now.

"I mean, come on, I really have little to show for my life but a fistful of..." He'd gone too far. Better to stop now, before he revealed everything. And did she have that power over him already? It was possible...

"But what? You have all these gifts, Devin: techie knowledge, Hollywood consulting," he heard a throaty chuckle following that one, "travel experience. You are obviously well-read, funny, clever, good-looking in a beat-up kind of way, have some money and great abs, and I have to tell you Devin, the sex is pretty damn not bad as well. And if that's not enough, we like the same wine. Plus, you're nice. So shut up. You're good, in a world where hardly anyone is good enough."

"How do you know I have money?" He feigned suspicion.

She roared her laughter. "So everything else I said was true? And that's all you got from my little speech? You know what Carly Simon would say: 'You're So Vain'!" They shouted it together, hooting.

Both lay still for a moment, and then Nadia slid a warm thigh across him and eased back on top, sitting just above his waist. She put her mouth beside his ear, where she kissed him, and then whispered, "When are you leaving? Tomorrow?" He nodded, and his arms rose to cup her head and pull her down to his mouth.

"Yes. Red-eye tomorrow evening, or I'll have to catch the morning flight the next day. I finish my work with the little brat tomorrow afternoon, and then I'm off to Canada. I'm there for a day or so, before I have to go to the States for three or four days, followed by Ireland for a few weeks. After that, I'm back to Canada. You?" It was mostly lies. He'd thought he would stay in Canada for a few weeks at least before heading down to New York to do the art gallery job, depending on timing.

He made a quick decision and then acted. "Before you answer...um, about that name. Devin. I, um, I'm not Devin. There is no... My name is actually Sean. Sean Donovan. Devin's just a name I gave to Katie while I made up my mind how legal the work was she had for me."

"Oh!" She appeared startled. "Well. That raises two questions. Why do you trot around a second name, and I have to say, what you said does beg the question: would you have taken the job if it had turned out to be illegal?" He felt her probing stare.

"Good questions." *You don't know the half of it.* "Remember when I said I wasn't nice, but I was trying to be? Well, in the past, I must say I've done some sketchy things, and to be honest, the very fact I've done a few things that could require a visit to a confessional *(or jail)* is probably the biggest consideration I have when thinking about us becoming an 'us.'" He stopped, waiting.

"Hmm. And did this past mayhem involve hurting nice people or selling drugs? These are basically deal-breakers for me, Dev...Sean."

"No. I can honestly say I don't like taking advantage of nice people, so I avoid it when I can." He winced at his lies.

Nadia paused, weighing her next words. "Sean?"

"Yeah?"

"Sean, I just wanted you to know... Well, I've done bad things, too. So this isn't really about going to confession, it's about being honest, okay?"

"Okay."

"Listen. My scenes are all done. I'm here for a couple more days to shoot some post-production promo shots for the trailer. And then I'm off to New York for a week of sleeping, eating, and maybe slip in a couple of interviews to help pay the bills. Hey, maybe we'll be in New York around the same time...give us time to find out more about who this Sean guy is. What are the chances?"

"You never know." He inflected doubt into his voice. "We could try, but..."

"Yeah. I know. Ireland, followed by Timbuktu." Her voice deflated with the last three words.

"Well, we could keep..."

"Don't say it. I don't want to keep in touch, Sean. I want to touch."

At times like this in the past, Donovan would harden his heart, think of his chosen path, and with a few facile lies, extricate himself. Not this time. He stared at her, as if staring right into her, as if he was searching within her heart for a parking place for himself, as if he was searching for a home. He almost quit the job and offered to stay.

Almost.

While she showered, he switched the necklace with one of the two copies.

He thought about leaving before she finished showering but decided against it. When she came back to bed, it was his turn to take a quick rinse-off, and then he lay down beside her, memorizing the arc of her throat, breathing her breaths with her until dawn.

HE LEFT WITH JUST A brief kiss and a promise to phone if there was a possibility of meeting. Yes, he had her number; did she now have his (Donovan) number? No, he wouldn't wait too long to call.

Getting the necklace to Katie took no effort. She phoned around ten, impatience sewn into every word. She had the second copy in her hands before noon. She couldn't know by looking at it that she, too, had been scammed, and her triumphant glimmer told him she was satisfied she had got the better of Nadia in more than one way. He had seen that look in someone's eye before: in the eyes of a little Roma boy whose triumph was so short-lived. Donovan shrugged as he walked away. Wasn't this the business he was in: selling people a moment of triumph, one cash transaction at a time?

He wandered Old London for the rest of the day, pondering Canary Wharf, Nadia, and his life. Last night's lovemaking had been gentle, tantalizing, and slow as they came together in a full, rolling boil. He had cried out. This had never happened to him before, and he was left stunned, confused, and unsure of what it all meant. By the time he got on his flight, fingering the true necklace like a set of worry beads, he still didn't know what to think of her, of his career, of any of it.

Chapter Ten

M ontreal
        Wednesday Evening

He finally pushed open the apartment door off Sources Boulevard in Montreal sometime after ten, propping it open with his valise while groping for the light, dead tired. It was now almost eleven, and he had taken a minute to splash some water on his face and hands in an effort to keep awake. It was late October in Canada, so after turning the heat on, he unpacked. Only then did a slip of paper on the kitchen table catch his eye. His sister Madeleine had placed it to the side of his other mail so it would stand out, but he had missed it because it was so small. It read, simply, "Meet me at our Deli at midnight on the twenty fifth, if you're back. That gives us five hours to get caught up. Friends will be joining us afterward to create chaos all around. Bring anecdotes, small bills, and that get-out-of-jail-free card." He smiled, remembering his sister's ways.

He pulled out of the parking garage, turned onto Saint Simeon, and then out onto Sources Boulevard. It was fifteen minutes to Schwartz's, so he connected his phone to the stereo and rode the wave of traffic to Centre-Ville, the downtown area. He crested on some of Llasa de Sela's world music, and then he played Sam Roberts's "Bridge to Nowhere" twice in a row. Maddie was waiting in the lineup on the sidewalk outside of the deli when he pulled in. It was a minute or two after midnight.

"Brother, wherefore were you? I had to duck back to the end of the line twice so we could eat together. Man! So glad you're here, though. What country were you in this time? Somalia? Was that you I saw on TV fighting the pirates, or were you teaching them how to pirate?"

Madeleine Donovan was thirty-one-years-old and looked twenty. She was five foot ten and a perfect size four, although her eating habits were those of a teenager. She seldom combed her strawberry blonde hair, yet it fell in curls any model would envy. Her green eyes sparkled like a fresh idea on Madison Avenue, and her lips were always poised as if to kiss.

"I was, ah, in Europe. You are ridiculously young and beautiful. Remind me to look in your attic for a portrait of Dorian Donovan." His lips brushed one proffered cheek and then the other. "I thought we were giving the whole 'both cheeks' thing a rest. Too bourgeois, you said?"

"That was last month. This month, people haven't put enough love in their hearts. So, more kisses, even from cynical brothers. Damn, I'm glad to see you. Don't know why, just glad."

She clasped his hand, and though he held hers, he did not prefer this show of affection and began to plot his hand's extrication. Greetings over, they moved a slow step further along the sidewalk and could now see the entrance.

"So, how was Europe, Italy, did you say? I was in Toronto while you were away. My boyfriend's from there, and we had to take in a concert. Research for his master's."

"Masters? How many masters does he report to?" Donovan teased. "You can't mean a master's degree. Why, that would make your boyfriend, um, seventeen?" He received a punch on the arm for his troubles.

"You know what I mean. And yes, he's a little young, but he's an old soul. He's so smart, and unlike my other boyfriends, he pays his own way to almost everything. And plus he's hot! Did I mention he's hot?"

"Of course, Maddie, I can't see you with someone who doesn't have massive quantities of interesting and hot."

"And," she continued without a breath, "he's writing his thesis now, so I get to bring him with me on business. He stays in the hotel writing away while I'm in meetings, and then at night we get to eat out and..."

He patted her back. "I don't need all the details, sweetie. What's important is I'm hearing he's a good guy, and you quite like him."

She smiled a knowing smile. "Not that...although that's going quite well, too, thank you very much. I was just going to say that lately we've been going to take away concerts. You know about take away concerts? They've been around for a while. Famous and almost-famous musicians set up secret concerts for fans. They hold 'em in the subway, on certain street corners, and only the few people who've heard the news about them, or who stumble upon them get to attend. You might have seen Tom Jones do one in a hotel room. They made a YouTube video out of that one. They're way cool, in addition to being a sociological, if not anthropological, phenomenon. As a matter of fact, that's where we're heading after a bit. You'll meet him there."

"Meet...?"

"David. My boyfriend. You'll get on with him like gangbusters. You'll see." She nodded to emphasize her point.

Donovan tugged his scarf to ride a little higher on the throat and pulled the collar of his pea coat up around his ears. "We're almost in. Know what you want to eat?"

"Of course, the same every time, else why come here? And I know where I want to sit, right beside that little coal stove that spits out cinders. I wanna sit so close to it I have to keep checking my pant legs to see if I'm on fire."

She looked up, tugging one lapel of his collar down and stared into his eyes. "So be prepared to make a scene, Sean, 'cause we may have to squeeze some of the Beautiful People to the back of the bench. I swear to God, if Celine is sitting her tiny size zero bum in my seat, I'm taking her out, and you're taking out her bodyguards." She patted his bicep. "Seriously, you should work out, Seannie."

He couldn't help but smile, wondering in passing what Nadia would think of his hyperkinetic sister.

"We're in! At last!" She turned around to face the lineup that stretched half a block behind them and cupped her hands to create a makeshift loudspeaker. "*Courage, mes amis! Pas long temps maintenant!* (Take courage, my friends! Not long now!)" And they were in.

The deli itself was rustic to say the least. The room sported long red walls with matching tablecloths. One narrow aisle ran down the middle, flanked by ten picnic benches on either side. The aisle offered enough room for the runners—they flew down the aisle with abandon. Clients meeting the runners were obliged to squeeze to the side to let them pass. Adding to the potential for chaos were the armloads of steaming plates each runner carried. Every spot in the more-than-full deli was packed with people who were ordering, eating, or paying. Madeleine spied the only two patrons who were leaving at that moment and elbowed her way to their table, which was almost across from the tiny pot-bellied stove.

"Close enough!" she shouted back to Donovan, who had chosen not to barge ahead of a server. He slid into his place beside her on the bench. A glass of water and a tangy, vinegary coleslaw was dropped in front of him before he had time to unbutton his jacket. He marveled at the runner, who was covered with plates of savoury food from fingertips to shoulder and who moved with so little effort among the throng. It was as if each plate was affixed to his sleeve with clothespins.

"So." He turned back to his sister. "How's work?"

"No, no!" she whined. "Not work. Do you hear that sound, sort of like the gears of hell grinding out a sordid dirge on a hurdy-gurdy? That's my job, sucking my soul out through my Irish-Canadian you-know-what. It's a job; it pays very well; my co-workers love me, and I hate it. I really need a job that challenges me more, y'know? Maybe start up an ad agency, manage a band. Oh! I could fly to resorts all over the world, recommending to rich people who drink champagne and piss money, which place is hot just before it gets hot. I bet there's a market for that."

"Yes, I expect there is. But promise me you won't quit your day job until you land your first half-dozen clients, be they bands, TV commercials, or rich money-pissers, okay?"

"Yeah, I can do that. You know, I only hate my job on Monday mornings and Friday afternoons...okay, maybe all day on Mondays, so it's really not so bad. I can stick it out till the right one comes along. And you?"

Her eyes stopped people-watching to focus on her brother. "How's your job? Still good? And have you met anybody special? What's with us all, anyway? Not one of us has a husband or wife. We are one messed up family, y'know? Look at Julian; he doesn't even acknowledge we exist!" She took out a cigarette, made a face at either Julian or the cigarette, and then returned it to its pack.

Donovan looked down at the red and white vinyl pattern in front of him. He spoke in a quiet voice. "Your brother Julian is broken, Maddie. Our loving father fixed it so our brother's no good anymore, not to himself, and certainly not to us. But we're not him. We're not broken. We got out with no snapped bones and no twisted brains. Nobody slipped, and nobody died. We're all right, I guess, maybe even stronger because of it, who knows?"

Madeleine put her head on his shoulder, smiling, her voice soft. "Well, I *guess* I'm okay." She drawled it out so the sarcasm showed. "I must be. I've got a boyfriend seven years younger than me, I talk a mile a minute, and even I don't listen to me—who knows what psychological shit that shows—and I seem to be fifteen years old in everything I do or say. And plus, I have a favorite brother who I adore, yet I haven't a clue what he does, where he goes, who he meets, and why he meets them. Oh, yeah, I'm okay. Sure." Madeleine's lips pursed, face closed in, forming a barricade. Even her bright eyes shielded her from the world, just for that moment.

"Maddie, you are perfect. Listen. That amazing runner with the armload of plates is coming back to take our order. After we eat, let's hit Montreal until it hits back. We can see who we run into tonight. I'd like nothing better than to have a chat with Leonard Cohen or Sam Roberts or...who's that chick who played in Courtney Love's band, her dad, Nick, used to hold court on Crescent Street on Thursdays, um, Melissa van Something? I bet if we wandered around long enough we'd run into one of 'em. We could give them our autographs. Whaddayasay?"

He drew an arm around her as her face softened, and she murmured "Auf der Maur. Her name is Auf der Maur."

She perked up a bit, and the simple act of ordering a smoked meat platter and the decision to include a nice dense slice of cheesecake, seemed to bring her back to her usual ebullient self. Minutes later, they were talking with their mouths full, arguing the relative merits of Indie Folk music versus Indie Roots music, teeth sunk deep into smoked meat sandwiches that rivalled any in the world for flavor, size, and personality.

"Wow, that was special!"

"Yup. Pretty damn good, Seannie. And you know, if you hung around long enough, you could eat there regularly, say, daily, if you wanted to." She wrapped a neck scarf to cover up to her chin and tucked an arm in the crook of her brother's elbow.

They walked downtown to Crescent Street, having decided the jumping nightlife on St. Lawrence Boulevard would make things a little too claustrophobic, given they just wanted a drink and to meet up with friends. The plan on the fly was that, after a brief chat at Churchill's, they would all head somewhere below Chinatown, toward Old Montreal. The night air was fresh and pushed them into the pub, appreciating the warmth as it embraced them in the foyer. Madeleine's friends hadn't yet arrived, so they grabbed a table with a street view and a confident microbrew that promised loads of dark, yeasty flavour. Madeleine checked her phone for messages, texting her friends to ascertain their whereabouts.

"I'm not going to be too old for this, am I? Because I can go home if you want."

"Sean, Sean, it's not about how old you are, it's about how far ahead of the curve you are, and believe me you are far enough ahead to not worry. Tomorrow your co-workers will be bowing at your oh-so-sleepy feet, if I can mix up body parts to make a perfect but stupid metaphor. *Worry pas*. You are going to like where we're heading, if our secret organizers pull it off. And speaking of co-workers, where do you work, exactly?"

They received their beers and leaned back in their overstuffed chairs to watch the passersby and await the rest of the party.

Sean pondered the question. "Well, I used to work for the feds, the government of Canada. In the security field. And while I was there, I accepted a couple of assignments to work overseas, still for Canada. But after a while, I was offered contracts that didn't necessarily involve Canada, so I took a leave of absence, and now I'm freelancing. I'm a consultant, a hired gun. I know stuff, and when I don't happen to know the stuff people pay me to know, I just happen to know who knows that stuff." He shrugged. "It's a living."

"Sounds kind of spy-like. You a spy, Seannie?" Her voice was conversation-casual, but her countenance held a contrived lightness that meant business.

"No, Maddie. It's just security. I am sometimes, um, involved in things I can't talk about while I'm in the middle of them, but that's more of a 'don't let the competition know your trade secrets' kind of stuff." He tried to lighten her mood. "Why are you the least bit interested in me, Sweetie? I'm the boring middle child. I'm supposed to be invisible!"

Her forehead wrinkled. "Well, there are four of us, right? You, Julian, Mary, and me. You're the strong, silent one. Julian's the oldest, and he can't bring himself to talk to any of us now. Mary lives—basically she's given up on people—on a research vessel somewhere off Antarctica, and then there's me, the female Peter Pan who never grows up.

"Okay, so Julian's broken and can't be fixed. Mary is in hiding. And I just can't seem to get my shit together. How come you came out of this mess we like to call our family, in one piece? How come you're okay? And why aren't I?"

FOR A PREGNANT MOMENT he sat still, looking at her chin so as to avoid looking into her green, probing eyes. He shifted in his chair, feeling cornered. He had buried the thought of his family from the day he had left home. As soon as his mind said the word, his memory careened back to his sixteenth year, to a warm autumn afternoon. He had walked into the country kitchen and stared at his father, who was leaning over his mother. She was sitting on the floor holding her shoulder the way he later saw skateboarders hold their shoulders, the ones who failed to land a grind: clavicle broken, shoulder probably popped out as well. His father was still screaming at her for making him slam her, something about waking him up, or supper not being ready—some lie that didn't matter.

It was such a surreal moment. His thoughts, all red and bruised, flew somehow to the Troubles in Ireland, to Sinn Fein and their specific form of retribution. And then he didn't think at all.

Sean had grabbed the bat that was always behind the door and strode over to stand behind his father. The first strike would have been a home run in any ball field in Canada. It caught the big man right beside the left kneecap. The patella disintegrated, and his knee blew out. It brought him down like a roller coaster that had jumped the tracks. The second thunderous blow caught his father, his flesh and blood, with a screaming uppercut just under the man's left arm. It splintered four ribs and drove one bone through the lower lobe of his lung, stopping just shy of the left ventricle of his heart.

He didn't remember the third pounding assault. But Julian, who was cowering in the corner, later recounted it to him (in the very last conversation they had). He said Sean had screamed, 'Sinn Fein!' as he put the weight of both of his feet on top of his father's ankle, the better to pulverize the man's already crushed kneecap. His brother finished by telling Sean there weren't enough bone fragments to put it back together.

And then Sean had reached into his father's wallet, found the hundred his father always bragged was hidden in the back, and slid it into his pocket. *And why did that C-note never, ever buy groceries?* He had leaned over to haul the groaning man off his mother's legs without glancing at her. He couldn't meet her gaze. He...couldn't. Just then, his father grabbed his son's forearm, almost as if to haul himself up. His slack jaw trailed a string of pink spittle, and his jaundiced eyes caught Sean's.

Sean knelt down on one knee, grabbed the bat halfway along its shaft, and pressing it hard against his father's throat, told him, "This is the last time you'll ever touch my mother, dear old Dad." He tapped the bat against his father's throat to emphasize each word of his next statement. "Or Julian, Mary, or little Maddie. Next time...I see you...I will kill you. I just don't care. Don't be laying a finger on anyone else, ever again, or you'd better sleep with one eye open and a gun in your hand. It's over, you prick. You never were a man, let alone a father. Now you are nothing."

He walked out of the kitchen and the two miles down the road to the bus station and thence away to Montreal, where a new life began.

WHEN HE CAME BACK, he realized his sister was still watching, waiting. He smiled an apology. "Honey, I'm probably the most broken one of us all. I met this special, special woman in London recently, and in a weak moment, I told her, 'I'm not a nice man.' And I'm not. But here's the thing." He reached out, taking her small tear-stained hand into his and rubbed in the salty wetness from where she had wiped her face.

"We went through hell for many years. Well, that drove us all a little crazy, some more than others, but still, I was no exception. I should have gone to jail for what I did to Dad. If Mom hadn't pressed charges against him, he would have bullied her, the cops, and everyone else to throw me away. But Mom stood up that one time, thank God, and I got away with a big one."

Madeleine's eyes welled up again. "You saved us, Sean. You saved us all, then and there. He didn't lay a finger on us after that day, not one of us. Lots of bullshit words, but no more smacking us around."

"Maybe, but part of me kinda went bad at the same time. I remember telling Dad I didn't care anymore after that, and I didn't, not for a long time, not about anyone except maybe you. Listen, Sweetie. Let's forget this. I'm feeling kinda sorry for myself now, and that's not my thing. Never was. Let's leave it like this: you're full of love, you're a good person...with a brain, let me add, and you'll find your way. People adore you, and you're beautiful. You have to admit, Maddie, that's a hell of a head start on some of the shit-rat people we come across in the run of a day, eh? And you have me, to boot. I would do anything for you. Except no more of that double kissing thing. Too bourgeois."

Without a word, she leaned over to hug him, tears still streaming, but now trailing down onto a brilliant smile.

"Okay, Sean. Okay. I can't promise you I'll try, but I'll try to try." They both laughed out loud at that old salesman's phrase they had shared as a joke all of their lives.

"All right then. When are your friends coming? It's one o'clock, time to listen to some music or something. What have you got in store anyway, Maddie? Better not be politics or religion. Or food. I must say I'm pretty full."

She pointed to the window. "Here they are! Jenn's the one in front. Alain is right behind her, and then there's Marc in blue, Anne-Sophie who's preggers, and that's my David herding them in. Oh, and the straggler is Meaghan—she's a rugby player at McGill—watch out for her. Guys! Guys! Over here!"

And then bedlam broke out, beginning with hugs and kisses all around. Madeleine tried to introduce Donovan to the gang and David to Donovan, but as at any close-knit family reunion, everybody wanted to talk at once, and no one was interested in listening. He also noticed Madeleine smiling at him as each woman proffered her cheeks to him for a welcome double-buss.

In the time it took to have one quick beer (and a hot chocolate for Anne-Sophie, who really was newly-pregnant), Donovan had discovered David was indeed quite bright—not to mention hot—and the two got along very well. Donovan, as he had all his life, put up a bit of a guard, but the gang's good humour was infectious. At one point, Anne-Sophie put down her empty hot chocolate mug and asked, "Okay, the wait is over. First, where are we going and second, why? Somebody has to spill the beans. Who's the indiscreet one? Come on, there's one in every good gang."

Madeleine looked over to Alain, who shushed the crowd. He pulled out his smartphone and held it out for Donovan to see. It was a text message, and Alain held his thumb across the top so as to obscure the author. He read it aloud, translating to English, "Blogosphere two-dash-four. Take-away concert, Locker Seven, Marine St., door at the corner. Guys?" He was quizzical. "Seems like we're going to the bottom of Chinatown, just above Old Montreal. Okay then, let's go!"

They chose to pour into a couple of cabs, since time was against them. A few minutes later, they stood within sight of the warehouse. As they watched, a young lady strode up to the very door they were looking at, tried it, but was refused entry. She read something on the door, walked to an abandoned hotel that stood just beyond it, and without hesitating, entered what looked like a boarded-up entrance. Madeleine, unfazed, grabbed David's hand and set out behind her, and her troops followed suit. She passed the notice without even offering a second glance and then hurried over to the boarded-up hotel. In she went.

Anne-Sophie and David both remarked how nice it was to find the heat and lights on in the massive foyer. In the corner just under the tiled mezzanine balcony, a few musicians were setting up. Madeleine grabbed his arm. "That's Patrick Watson. They're gonna do a show here in a couple of minutes. Let's grab a seat."

Donovan told his sister to save him a spot on the floor, there being no chairs. He wove through the twenty-five or so in the audience, ascended the stairs, and looked over the balcony. He recalled something interesting about the old chandelier, so he made eye contact with Madeleine, waving her to come with him. Instead, it was Anne-Sophie who trotted up, out of breath.

"Sean, the roadie with Patrick Watson says we must not wreck anything, or it will ruin all the take-away concerts down the road. I know you wouldn't do that, but he is watching me to see if I tell you. Okay?

"What could we wreck in a wrecked hotel, I wonder? Anyway, no; I'll be good." He waved down to the roadie, who looked self-conscious. "Hey, let's look around."

As they wandered down the hall pointing to things that had been dismantled, the light from behind them grew dim, and with it, the fickle heat chose to stay with the light. It slid away from them with every step they took down the corridor. Anne-Sophie pushed open a meeting room door, the knob of which had been dismantled and placed inside the entryway on the otherwise empty floor.

"Geez, not even the loose doorknobs in this hotel get a seat." Sean thought about the chair-less concert below as he looked around the shadowy, vacant room and then smiled when he noted she had got his joke.

She threw back, "Hey, I'm pregnant, so I'm missing *two* seats." She made a sweeping gesture to encompass the whole hotel area. "Sean, do you know the story of this hotel?"

They ambled back toward the growing crowd and heard the first chords from an electric piano and the amplified sound of wind and rain. Anne-Sophie watched him pick up the door knob from the darkened room.

He answered her with a smile. "You do know I'm twice as old as you and from Montreal, right? So, yes, I know the story very well. Now, it may not be the true story, but I do know a story. It was built during Prohibition and catered to the booze crowd that floated up from New York and Boston. They were a step up from the bathtub gin crowd. They say the Bronfman family got their start right here, serving drinks to the American hoi-polloi, but I don't believe it. I think it was just a grand old hotel that helped create modern Montreal. I also think I'm going to keep this doorknob as a souvenir. Look at it. Probably not real porcelain, but beautiful still, with the tarnished brass against the white. Oh, come see what I remembered from the balcony."

Anne-Sophie went to within three feet of the edge and then hesitated. "I don't like heights, Sean. Can I see what you want me to see from here?"

"Well, of course you can. Just stand right where you are. Okay, now look slightly down toward the big glass crystal thing in the middle of the chandelier. What color is it? White? Okay, now scrunch down just a little bit without taking your eyes off the crystal. Pretend you're five feet tall."

"Sean! It's blue! It turned blue? How did you know?"

"When I was twenty—about a hundred years ago—I brought a date here. She was pretty cute, I must say, and short, around five feet tall. Anyway, it was close to midnight, and we stood, um, just where you're standing now, watching the dancers below. I said something about how pretty the white reflection was in that crystal, and we got into a little tiff about whether it was white or blue. Turns out we were both right, depending on whether you were around five feet short, or almost six feet tall."

Anne-Sophie watched the crowd grow. "That was a long time ago, Sean. Do you know whatever happened to her? The date?"

The muscles that contoured his chin hardened and then morphed into a bruised smile. He spoke, but it was almost to himself. "She got knifed out on Isle de Montreal. I lost track of her after that. She moved away, I think." His eyes grew distant.

Anne-Sophie grabbed the crook of his arm. "Let's go back downstairs, eh? The music is starting." Without a word, they descended the balustrade as the band started up. Donovan lowered himself to the floor, beside his sister.

The music began with just piano and then added voice. At some point, a fascinating array of instruments including toy pianos and machines hammered, barked, and practically sawed through the high, clear melodies that were the trademark of Patrick Watson's industrial symphonies. Donovan didn't know much of his music, save for "The Great Escape," but he smiled with the others when the band added the sound of generators whirring, or gears grinding, or wind-whipped rain to the intricate melodies. After a bit, Patrick gave the band a break and invited a young lady to sing some of the songs of Elliot Smith, accompanied by him and a piano. The audience was okay with that because the crowd was intimate enough and open to the band's experimentation.

"Okay, last song," Patrick Watson called out. "Then we have to get some sleep. We're just back from the West Coast, and I must admit I'm a bit spacey from jetlag. But let's do this again in a few weeks. I'll tell you a cool place to try for next time, Silo Five down at the Port. Used to be a grain elevator. The building has a built in, ten-second echo. how crazy would that be with our music? As usual, getting permission to play there will be the problem, but hey, we've made our way into better joints than that, *n'est-ce pas*?" To a round of cheers, they launched into a closing song, and within minutes of its closing refrain, the reconstruction site was all but empty.

It was approaching three-thirty, and they had stopped at an intersection on their way back up the hill. Madeleine let go of David and walked over to her brother as they turned to face Ste. Catherine Street. "Hey. You look asleep on your feet. I guess all you jet setters need shut-eye, eh? You should head home, unless you want to come with me. I've got a sofa."

"No. Thanks. I'll be fine. Nothing that a half-day of sleep can't fix. I'm on my way." He reached out to shake David's hand. "Nice meeting you, David. You guys going for more smoked meat and cheesecake?"

David smiled. "One more bar and then bed for me. I've got work in the morning."

He smiled at the other men and women. Anne-Sophie called back to him, "Thanks for the bathtub gin story and the chandelier story." Then he headed toward Crescent Street, where his car was parked. On the way back to his apartment, he noted the endless trail of cars traversing the streets of Montreal at that time of night. Exhausted, he then thought of nothing but the exquisite voice of Rose Cousins coming from his sound system until he pulled into his parking space.

When he opened the door to his apartment, it was after four o'clock. He felt almost as if he was walking behind himself. Jetlag. He sat on the edge of his bed, shoes off, cell phone in one hand. Nadia's number was punched in, but he hadn't hit SEND. He sat. Waiting. Deciding. His brain began to wheel around inside his head, just behind his eyes. It was a feeling akin to a serious drunk on Southern Comfort and cola. Refusing to succumb to the roiling sensation, he went to the kitchen and returned to the living room with a couple of Aspirin and a bottle of water. Despite the beverage, the tablets scratched on the way down. He grimaced and swallowed hard. Feeling himself beginning to tip, he let himself go. Cell hitting the floor with an innocuous tap, his head met the sofa's cushion, and he was out.

He slept like a stone until noon and lay motionless for an additional hour. His mind was clear, worries and issues tucked away to review on some other occasion. He watched the sun's rays bleed across the gunstock-stained hardwood floor of his Spartan living room and then began to feel the inexorable tug of the day. By three-thirty, he was back from the gym, clean, dressed, and if not at his best, at least functioning. He phoned Professor Roberto Umbro, chair of Romance Languages at Concordia University. Yes, Professor Umbro was in.

Chapter Eleven

M ontreal
Concordia University Campus

"Please. You can call me Rob." The professor's voice carried a trace of Italian. He opened the door in an exaggerated welcome and even tossed in a small flourish as Donovan grabbed the first of two visitor chairs.

"Your accent suggests I can't. But I'll be pleased to cease calling you Professor. We'll split the difference at Roberto." Donovan didn't offer any name at all.

Roberto nodded, his face unsure. He rose from his desk and came around, reducing the formality of the meeting. He ignored the second visitor's chair and sat on the corner of his desk, making idle conversation. But his eyes never left the backpack resting between Donovan's legs.

He smiled down at Donovan. His face was beatific, framed with coal black curls he tucked behind his ears at regular intervals because they were so unruly. "So, Mr...." He still had no idea what Donovan's name was, and again Donovan offered no help.

"You want to know how I did. If I succeeded." Donovan chose not to drag this out. "Yes. I have the chalice you want." He raised a hand to stop Roberto's questions as well as to prevent his eager hands from reaching down. "However, you made it clear you didn't care if it was the original, a copy, or a copy of a copy, as long as it was faithfully reproduced. I can assure you it is not the original, but for reasons I will keep to myself, I will not reveal whether this is the copy from the palace, or a copy of that. But I can also assure you, it cannot be distinguished from the one that came from the palace. You okay with that?"

Roberto's curls shook in the affirmative. "Yes, yes. But may I see it? Please! How did you get it? Did you actually go into the palace to retrieve it yourself?" A look of alarm overcame him. "You're keeping a copy of my cup? You wouldn't...share it, would you?" He looked aghast.

Donovan smiled. "Now, how would I have earned my pay with duplicitous behaviour like that? No, yours will be the only one in circulation, I assure you."

Roberto calmed, but the set of his chin revealed a trace of doubt.

Donovan left the bag undisturbed. "All right then. Let's discuss money, or rather, payment, since we've already agreed upon a fee."

Roberto stood, went back to his desk, and rummaged through a bottom drawer. Donovan continued, "You should know I incurred an additional couple hundred bucks of costs during my hunt, for which I won't charge, a contract being...a contract. I just thought you'd like to know you did indeed get a deal. People like to hear these things." He reached down and pulled up the bag that had been tucked tight against the front of his chair. "I had to acquire the services of a potter and the cost of shipping. Unreal, man!" Donovan was in a very good mood. He allowed himself the luxury of this gentle humor.

Roberto seemed not to mind. He came back around the desk, a broad smile on his face. "Ha! I give you fifty thousand dollars, and in return, you offer me a two hundred dollar discount. You are a generous man, my friend." He leaned forward. "Well, sir, you will find me a generous man as well, which I will explain in a minute. But first, let me see it. Let me hold it. Let me hold the bucchero chalice." He began to reminisce while Donovan untied the cords of an old army issue canvas backpack.

"Ha! That's funny." Roberto pointed to the green canvas backpack. "I imagined you would arrive with a steel-sided briefcase, with the cup on one side and thousand dollar bills on the other. And maybe a tiny pistol." He gave a nervous laugh.

"You've seen too many movies. Why would I advertise I'm carrying something valuable? Look at me. Do I look like I could beat off crooks and various other bad guys?"

"Hmm. Now, that makes sense." Roberto shrugged. "You know, this first came to me while working at Oxford. I was getting my doctorate at the time and had sent out a hundred practicum proposals to the best universities. I was willing to go anywhere to finish my thesis, which centered on the Etruscan language. Okay, you probably don't want the details." He twisted in his seat and pointed to a burgundy leather-bound tome of his thesis. "That summer, I got work in Romania, in Bucharest at the university. In exchange for marking assignments and invigilating exams, I had the run of the library. I even met a girl there. From Transylvania." He looked self-conscious. "We were serious, but..." His voice trailed off.

"You know, from way back, the Romanians are mostly either Turkish or Italian, just like the Mexicans are mostly Spanish or Indian. It's not literally true, of course. Their national makeup is a little Russian, from recent years, and a little Hungarian of which they are not particularly proud. Let's be honest, the Turks want to be Turks, and the Italians want to be Italians. They don't want to be confused, one with the other." He stopped and smiled.

"But I have digressed! Shit! Sorry. But anyway, let me finish. It is a good story. There I was at the university, visiting the library—basically living in the library actually—when I came upon a crude drawing of the Etruscan bucchero cup.

"Oh! It was startling and beautiful, although the drawing was rudimentary. It was so frustrating because I could tell based on the facts I gathered from the libraries of three universities in three countries, this was the cup that held the etymological key to the Etruscan language. And drawings don't reveal all sides, right? So it was just a tantalizing...thing!" Roberto stood up and paced.

Donovan wasn't certain Roberto even remembered he had company. The professor ran a nervous hand through a mass of curls.

"Carefully, discreetly, I asked certain colleagues about the chalice. Had they heard of it? What was said of it? Was this crude drawing the last vestige of it, the only remaining archival evidence? And oh," he wagged a finger in front of him, back and forth like a metronome, "I sought out only the recently retired and the low achievers to confer with. I was not willing to share any of my knowledge with some ambitious Indiana Jones, oh no. I am by nature a generous man, but for this, my blood runs like ice. I am what you would call a selfish bastard." His look was triumphant. Donovan felt perversely like throwing up a high five on that one.

"And guess what? Oh, you will never guess because it is the stuff of the movies! The father of the family with whom I shared a room was the son of one of the palace warehouse administrators. I had made a drawing of the drawing, because the books in that section of the library are in and of themselves treasures, so they cannot be loaned out. Anyway, this man saw my drawing and told me he had seen the cup itself! Yes! With his own eyes.

"He didn't know what the writing on the cup meant, but oh, yes, he had seen it. When he was younger, he helped his father crate up the thousands of treasures Ceausescu had 'safeguarded'..." here Roberto made air quotes with his fingers and leered a comic caricature of evil, "in the bowels of the palace. He even remembered what section the crate was placed in because that same box contained this really sexy, ivory Roman priestess. It, too, was valuable, but hey, I am an academic, not a grave robber." He gave a dramatic shrug.

"So I knew." He tapped his temple. "I knew. But how to get at it? If I submitted a request on academic reasons, they would steal my idea. If I tried to visit it, well, no one gets below the surface of the ground at the palace."

Donovan thought of a ploy. "You could have submitted an academic rationale to study the naked ivory priestess and then asked to see whatever else was in the box." It was amusing, watching first admiration of the idea, followed by the pain of realizing $50,000 was the cost of not thinking of such a simple idea.

"Shit. You're a downer, man. Ha!" Roberto exploded with one enormous peal of laughter directed at himself. "You know, that's spilt milk. No use to cry about it. Instead, why don't you make me feel better by letting me have it, and I will give you tens of thousands of dollars. What do you say? Let's make a trade!" He held out his hand holding the thick envelope.

Donovan reached out to take the envelope, opened it, and counted out five hundred one hundred dollar bills, noting they weren't in sequence. He reached into the opened bag and dropping the ten bundles of bills inside, drew out a pair of plain plaster cups.

Roberto recovered from his initial surprise and accepted them without breaking eye contact.

"Good craftsmanship, no?" Donovan said. "My friend does good work. Well worth the hundred bucks each, I think. Half of your chalice is hidden inside one of these plaster cups, and the other half is inside the second plaster cup."

He got up, went around Roberto's desk, and returned with a wastebasket. Tucking it halfway under the desk, he invited Roberto to hand one cup back to him. He balanced it at the stem and grabbing the heavier end, banged the cup against the side of the desk. Most of the plaster flew off, leaving the dusty base of a gold chalice held between his thumb and forefinger. Taking the second, he smashed it as well; however, this time he held it by the bowl, imposing the violence on the solid plaster base. The other half of the cup appeared, and within moments, Roberto was staring mesmerized at the reassembled bucchero cup.

He shook his head from side to side. "I-I cannot speak for the beauty of it. It's almost as wonderful as the very script that graces its side. Oh, my God." Eyes moist, he turned to Donovan. "I know you are a mercenary, but I want you to know this is a good thing you will have done. You see, the cup had reappeared during the Second World War. Somehow, Ceausescu stole it before anyone could give the Italian people—the world, really—the gift of the literacy and history of the Etruscan language. Who knows what Italy would have been in the absence of its parent culture and language? Nothing! It would be nothing at all! It will take years—a generation—before the Romanian people complete the tagging and archiving of the treasures in this palace warehouse. Shit! No more than thirty people even know it exists! Anyway, I have what I need, and I vow to do good work with it. You say it's a replica? That's okay, as long as it is replicated faithfully."

Donovan drew the cord tight on his canvas bag. "Then I guess it's getting near time to leave." He stood.

"Wait!" Roberto shook his head as if from a reverie. "I promised you a gift."

"Not necessary."

Roberto smiled, some of the emotion subsiding after having seen the cup. "Ah, but this is the gift of business. You still want to conduct more business, right?"

"Actually, I'm choosy about the business I conduct. I say 'no' many more times than I say 'yes,' I promise you, but I can listen politely with the best. So, lay on, MacDuff."

Roberto winked. "Ah, Shakespeare. But your appreciation for a good story will intrigue you, I am confident. Please. Indulge me, if only for the story. And I don't really know anyone like you, Mr., ah, sir. Under other circumstances, I know we could be friends. I can see us sitting across from a plate of *pappardelle* pasta and a glass of good Barbera. But. Okay, so, here is my story." He retreated back around his desk, pulled his chair back to face his guest, and put up his feet.

Chapter Twelve

M ontreal
    A Story For Thursday

Roberto tossed a bottle of water over to Donovan. "Okay, where to begin? Ah. Let us begin in Washington, D.C. and then quickly go to New York City, the Big Apple. And we may even visit the Florida Keys." He winked.

"Okay, let's go back to 1962. The Bay of Pigs debacle was about a year previous, and the beloved president Mr. John Kennedy—JFK—is in a hotel room within sight of the Potomac, and guess who is with him? Marilyn Monroe! Yes! Now, this particular assignation is a bit different. No sex, no 'Happy Birthday' song to the President, it's just a meeting. In fact, there are two others there. Peter Lawford, you know, from the, the...the Rat Pack! He was the one who didn't sing or do stand-up. Do you remember he married a Kennedy? Thus the friendship, I suppose. Anyway, the fourth person was a young Democratic aide named Preston Host." Roberto looked down his slim, denim-clad legs, past his oxblood loafers, and then back up to meet Donovan's eyes and offered an apologetic glance. "I wish I had a drink for you. These occasions are how the seeds of friendships are sown. I am certain we could be friends! Anyway, back to my story—your possible next job.

"Okay, so there they are, having some champagne—I do not know for certain it was champagne, but I bet it was, and they were all talking about Cuba. Peter was talking about how amazing it would have been if he and Frank and the boys could have set up casinos in Havana and Veradero instead of having the communists ruling the country. JFK replied it would indeed have been wonderful. Marilyn could have headlined there, and he could have gone to see her regularly. It was all quite light and maybe a bit juvenile compared with how JFK is perceived. But wait! You'll never guess what happens next."

He stood up and crossed to the door to make sure it was closed and then turned to Donovan, beaming. "JFK up and says, 'This Cuban Crisis will turn out to be just a temporary mess, you know. I'm in talks with Fidel, and we have decided that after two years of posturing, we will have this huge Peace Congress, maybe here, maybe there. Both countries will prosper. Communism will go down the toilet, and we may even end up with a fifty-first state. You never can tell! But the kicker will be our cachet with the people. We could both end up being presidents for life.'

"Ha! 'Ain't That a Kick in the Head,' like the Dean Martin song?" Roberto shifted to face Donovan. "She dies later that year, and he up and gets killed a year later, and that's it. That's all, folks. Game over."

Donovan sat still for a moment and then said, "Sounds like a great anecdote, Roberto. Not sure what I can do with it, but…"

"No! No! I forgot something! The conversation was taped. Ha! What do you think of the story now?"

Donovan sat up. "Taped?"

"You bet. Taped. By that little shit Preston. He was pretty sure he had a future as God's gift to politics. He was buddies with the U.S. president, and at age twenty-one, he had the ear of senators and the wallets of lobbyists. So he wandered around with the tiniest, battery-operated tape recorder of its time, drinking and listening. After a while, the recorder sort of became invisible, so to speak. He had it going that fateful night in the hotel.

"But he was a souse, even at that age. It wasn't long before he pushed his luck and wound up on the outside looking in, especially after Kennedy shuffled off this mortal coil. Couldn't get a job with either party, and later, Host just wound up in Marathon, down in the Florida Keys, a barfly. Pretty wife gone, money gone, everything gone. Everything except his tape. Guess what? He managed to salvage just one other thing, a speck of integrity. He never played that tape for anybody. You see, he did not want the Cuban embargo to stop."

"But he's dead now, right?"

"No, sir." Roberto looked smug. "Here is what happened. Peter Lawford was at a bar in Vegas just before his passing in 1984, and he told the whole story to a hostess friend over a steak dinner. He asked her not to repeat it, and she told me she has kept that promise."

"But?" Donovan knew there was more.

"But there was a Canadian undergrad, a baby-faced history student sitting in the booth behind them. God bless spring break! Fellow named Jarrod Kelly. It turns out he was a big fan of Frank, Dino, and Sammy. So he spotted Peter Lawford and sort of stalked him. A much older Kelly told me the story recently at an alumni meeting. He emphasized how cool it was to have finally met an original Rat Pack member, even if it was over the back of a Vegas lounge booth.

"So, after hearing the story, I undertook to find this fellow, Host. He is still a barfly, but his circumstances have changed somewhat. His brain is mush, and he still cannot, or will not, keep a job. But he is old now, both in years and mileage, and his family tracked him down and brought him back home to New York, to Long Island City, in Queens. He is living with his sister Donna Little, Stan's widow." Roberto's tone changed. "I, erm, had been thinking of writing an essay, maybe an exposé for *The New Yorker*, but my, ah, reputation as a tenured professor is important to me, so I chose not to.

"It seems to me, though, if a person were to acquire that tape, a buyer would not be too hard to find." Roberto's voice went up a tone. "You could either sell it to a private collector, where it would stay buried forever. Or what about creating a bidding war with the networks, make a mint." He paused. "That might ruin your cover, but you'd be rich, so who cares, right? You know, you should come back to visit someday, and let me know how this turns out. Sounds like it would be so fun to see through." His tone was wistful.

"Yeah, about that. No. I won't be pursuing this one, thanks. Seems like a few too many people know a piece of this story, not even counting Fidel and JFK. It's a good one, though."

Donovan stood. "Well, I gotta go, Roberto. Thanks for the fifty K and the bottle of water. *Ciao*, buddy."

Roberto reached over and shook Donovan's hand, who then took this opportunity to leave. The glance he threw over his shoulder as he left found Roberto hunched over his desk, magnifying glass poised over the ancient golden chalice.

Outside the building, Donovan withdrew a notepad from his backpack and wrote down three things: Preston Host. Long Island City. Nadia. *Things don't have to make sense except in my head*, he said to himself, drawing the cord tight on the old green canvas backpack and buckling it. He headed for his car.

Chapter Thirteen

N ew York City
    Monday Morning

He had dinner with Madeleine and David in Montreal on Sunday evening, the night before he left for New York. He made them a three-mushroom risotto laced with saffron and parmigiana reggiana, and finished with a dry Riesling. He paired it with a stuffed-and-seared, oven-finished pork tenderloin filled with cremini mushrooms, wispy-thin slices from a tart green apple, dried cranberries, and a few other ingredients. The accompanying hunter sauce was dark, earthy, and pungent, abetted by a dollop of mango chutney and desiccated mushroom dust.

The couple had brought along a couple of bottles of California zinfandel. A generous splash from the guests' wine infused the sauce with depth. The deglaze drippings from the pork went into the gravy at the end, to bring everything together. Dessert was a simple bread pudding drizzled with a homemade dolce de leche sauce.

He told his sister he was off to New York the next day, on business, and that he hoped to be back within a few days. No, he wasn't certain when that would be. The three chatted about David's thesis, the people in the music industry he had met while researching it, and the good times he had enjoyed during his studies. Neither one mentioned their future as a couple; it seemed it wasn't an issue.

The last thing Madeleine said to him before they left was to share a note of caution. "Life is about balance, Seanny. I know because I have no life, and I have no balance. David is slowly bringing me to a good place." She squeezed his arm as she spoke. "And I believe it's coming around to your time. If you see the opportunity to reacquaint yourself with your London friend, you should. And if there comes a choice between danger and no danger, Sean, you should try no danger. I'm not sure that's what you've chosen to date. I'm just sayin.'"

Donovan smiled to himself on the plane. *I didn't realize she had taken all that in*. But she had. He took the rest of the flight to catch up on his sleep, and in the blink of an eye and the nod of his head, he was flying low over New Jersey, and thence onto the tarmac in Queens, New York City. The City that Never Sleeps.

He dropped his bag off at the Wingate on West Thirty-fifth in Manhattan, not far from Central Park. It wasn't convenient for his new job, but he liked it. The touristy feel, the ability to go unnoticed in a crowd, a reasonable cab ride to Queens, or a walk to Chelsea, the food...yes, mid-town would work out fine.

First off, he visited a security firm in Brooklyn. John David Milne was an acquaintance from his government contract days. The main showroom of the electronics shop consisted of a series of display tables, and the showroom was ringed by a shelf carrying scores of dated electronics equipment, from Geiger counters to radon detectors to cameras and tape recorders. Toward the back, an entrance led to a smaller room with an "Employees Only" sign beside the light switch. Although the plate glass windows could have used a cleaning, every piece of equipment was polished to a high sheen.

He spotted the owner at the back of the room, reading a comic. "J.D.!" he called out. "I thought this was a security store. You know better than to protect your storefront with a WES fifty-four forty. Any self-respecting wharf rat could slide in under an alarm like that."

J.D. didn't even look up. Pointing first with an index finger to the ceiling toward a closed circuit television, he then changed to a middle finger and saluted Donovan with it. "Ya can't sell the good stuff unless you can show the useless shit, Donovan. You know that."

"I guess." Donovan sidled up to the counter, set down a large paper cup, and placed his canvas backpack on the display shelf. He untied the drawstring. "Hey! Remember what you used to say about this business?"

J.D. finally looked up over his bifocals and made a faint stab at a smile. "If I recall, I said we're not in the security business, we're in the *in*-security business." He stood up and offered a hairy paw that must have weighed ten pounds. "How ya doin', Seanny Canuck? Still gettin' rich offa high-tech sales to low-tech countries?"

"Well, I'm less into sales now and more into services, I'd have to say." He leaned over the countertop. "Here. I brought you coffee and a sandwich."

"Uh, oh. What d'ya want this time?" J.D. grabbed the paper cup which disappeared into his hand. He stood up, stretched, came around the counter and without so much as a sidelong glance, shuffled over to the door and flipped the sign to Closed.

"You here on business? Come on in the back room, and we'll sit. Ya gonna take a break with me? What you got there? Ah, a pastrami on rye and a ham and cheese, also on rye? Where'ja get em? Defonte's, down on Third?" He picked each sandwich up and put them down, settling on the pastrami.

Donovan studied the man who had taught him so much, so many years ago. He didn't seem as tall now, perhaps six feet at most. He had gained about thirty pounds, and his back was hunched over, making the broad expanse rounder between his shoulder blades. His hair had thinned and greyed where it curled from the nape, and his nose was flattened. He carried his reading glasses on a black metal chain around his neck and referred to them all the time.

"What can I do you for? Here on business, or you just can't get enough of Brooklyn?"

"Two and a half million people in Brooklyn; I'm obviously here to meet them. Can you introduce me? No, I'm in need of a couple of products. And since it's last-minute, and I only ask for what I really, really need, I hope you have them."

"Well, try me. All I can say is no. Or maybe, go to hell."

"Tell me to go to hell, but get me my things, J.D. First off, I need an electronic door opener..."

"Done. Traceable back to me as the vendor, or is it okay for it to have a shady past? Need it to be wiped?" J.D. finished the pastrami sandwich. "These are some frikkin' good, by the way."

Donovan took the remaining sandwich from the bag. He sank deep into a worn recliner, slinging one leg over the tattered armrest. "Doesn't matter if it can be traced. This time it's for business," he lied. "Okay, now for the hard stuff. I need the chemical that makes steel brittle and ashy so it can snap with a sharp tap. Annnd...I also need a green box." He looked sideways at the shopkeeper.

"The, ah, green box for singing bad Chinese karaoke? Or the one you used to not be able to afford? And do you need to take it back to Canada, or can I get it back after?"

"How do you know all this? Jesus. Anyway, yeah, I need the chemical. And yes, I need the security system green box—the one that tells a security system everything is all right even as I'm wandering around where people don't so much want me. You can have what's left of them both after I'm done. They won't get much of a workout. Do you have this stuff on the premises?"

"Well, yeah. You never know who's gonna come through the doors wanting to break into Fort Knox. I'll wipe them anyway. I'll sleep better. Wanna tell me what it's for, or is it like every other time you needed shit?" The trace of a smile returned.

"It's exactly like every other time. But hey, I'm thinking of retiring, and if I do, you can come visit me in Mexico, and I'll tell you lies for a month. Deal?"

It was J.D.'s turn to cast a sidelong glance. "Really? Lissen, if you are the least bit serious, I'll go. Hell, I'll go be your friggin' cabana boy. I'm all done here! My nephew over in Queens wants to buy me out, and I'm thinkin' I'll let him. He's a good boy, wife and a kid. It could be a win-win, if the bank lets him go into escrow."

Donovan scratched his cheek, staring at his old friend. "I'll keep that in mind, buddy. I don't have enough people in my life who'd watch my back. And who doesn't need a cabana boy?" He took a bite.

"Man, you are the best non-answerer who ever fed me pastrami on rye. Anyhow, if it's warm and doesn't involve lifting, gimme a shout." He stood and rubbed his hands together as if they were cold. "Okay. What were we talking about? Green box, door opener, that chemical that denatures the chromium, nickel, and manganese in high alloy steel. Wait a few. I'll get back to you in a minute. Talk among yourselves, and don't sell anything while I'm gone." He arose, but Donovan stopped him with a raised hand.

"Um, I have another thought. I need a few spools of tape."

"Tape? Duct tape, electrical?"

"No, audio. Preferably from the sixties. Three inch, five inch. One inch, if they exist. Where can I get three different-sized open spools of audio tape, like from a reel-to-reel? Doesn't matter if it's used or virgin. Got any ideas?"

"I believe I do. When you leave here, cross the street and head over to Audio Everywhere. It's up the street a bit." He pointed through the thick pane of his storefront. "Vintage audio stuff. They can fix you up, I bet." He shuffled off to the back room, on the hunt.

Donovan picked up J.D.'s comic book; it was an old *Turok, Son of Stone*, episode thirty-five. The dinosaur killer. He noted the price of twenty cents, and it was worn almost through. Ten more minutes of small talk, and he was in a cab, backpack once again bulging.

Back at the Wingate, he changed into a business casual navy suit, off the rack and inexpensive. He paired it with a boring pair of sensible black shoes and a belt with an oversized buckle. Donovan picked up a slim briefcase that contained a smart phone, some fake business cards, a generic insurance application form, and a sheaf of insurance company letterhead. He also stuffed jeans and a few other items into his backpack.

He was off to Long Island City to visit Donna Little. It was mid-afternoon, and the sun warmed the sidewalks and the pedestrians. Time for a phone call.

"Hello, Mrs. Little? Ah, you're home. Glad I caught you. It's Devin Koulos, from All Medi-Mutual Insurance. Well, actually, I'm calling on behalf of GSMIP, the government insurance program for civil servants. Is Mr. Host home? I understand he lives at this residence. No? I'm sorry to hear that. As I said, I'm calling on behalf of the U.S. government, and we're exploring the possibility that Preston Host might be eligible for a small veteran's pension. Now wait, ma'am! This is very preliminary. Very, ah, preliminary. We're just fact-finding at this point. I'm here in New York from our Washington office, just for the day. Yes, ma'am, driving back first thing in the morning. Anyway, I'd sure love to drop by this afternoon, maybe ask a couple of questions that could get us started down the road to getting your brother a little something for his dedication to the country. I'll be back in two months, or I could swing by shortly. I could? Well, that would be excellent, Mrs. Little. Okay, Donna it is. I'll be ah, an hour or so, sound okay? All right then, see you in an hour."

Donovan took the subway as far as he could, but given his unfamiliarity with Queens, he decided on a taxi. Subway was quicker in Manhattan, but the further from the heart of it one was, the taxi became the go-to mode of transportation. Once he got to Brooklyn, he rolled the rear window down a crack to let in the warm fall air. In a bit, the cab pulled up to an unassuming sixties-era bungalow whose lawn could have used a trim. After a few words to the cabbie, he stepped out, straightened his jacket, and went up the walkway to the house. A woman approaching retirement age stood in the open doorway, watching.

"Hello, Mrs. Little? Devin Koulos. We spoke briefly about an hour ago. Here's my card." He offered a hand and was surprised at the firm grip she returned. Her skin felt dry and rough, yet her face contradicted the rougher life story her hands told. She smiled a welcome.

"I'd sure like to ask the cabbie to wait outside, if you thought the neighbors wouldn't mind. Being unfamiliar with this borough, I wouldn't know how long it would take to get another taxi, and I'm sure we won't be too long at any rate." Donovan was certain the presence of the cab would reassure Donna Little; maybe help her to drop her guard just a bit.

"That will be no trouble, Mr. Koulos. Come on in. Would you like a cola or a glass of water? Some tea?"

"No thank you, ma'am. We might as well get right down to it. Where can we...oh, at the kitchen table? Great." They sat, and he opened the briefcase, just far enough to let her peek in. He noticed she sat facing the entrance. Was she nervous or expecting someone?

As if on cue, she said, "I'm sorry, sir, but I have to keep an eye on the front door. I'm expecting my grandson shortly. I take care of him after school weekdays."

"That's great, and you call me Devin, okay? Keeps the family together, doesn't it, childcare arrangements like that? As I said, I won't keep you long. So...just a few questions, if you don't mind. But first, just to recap, it's our understanding that Mr. Host—may I call him Preston?—worked in the civil service in Washington, D.C. for two years. He also worked an additional year at the beginning as a student intern, is that correct? Yes, ma'am, that was some time ago. And he is how old now? Seventy? Good for him! He's retired now, so he collects social security. Well, that helps with the family income, I'm sure."

Donna leaned in toward him and didn't quite meet his eyes. "Actually, my brother's a bit of a drinker, I suppose you'd say. He's at the bar now, drinking his social security. There's nothing I can do about it, shy of kicking him out, which of course won't stop him. It'll just take it out of my sight, but not out of my mind, right? I expect it'll get the better of his liver one day soon, but until then, any additional dollars would sure come in handy. Do you really think this," she waved toward the briefcase and the promise within it, "could come to something? My Stan passed two years ago, and even with the babysitting money my daughter gives me, some months..." Her voice trailed off.

Donovan felt a pang. *Might as well keep going—if you can't get out of it, get into it.* When he spoke, even he was surprised at the soothing, confident words swirling into the air around the fall kitchen table, warming it. "We are going to try, ma'am, ah, Donna. This potential pension income, by the way, is for accommodations for seniors, so it would, in fact, be going to you. As long as he is staying with you, that is." *A lie, but Host is a senior, so it sounds plausible.* "Okay, just a few more questions. Does he have any government documents or mementos from his Capitol Hill days? It would really be helpful if we had any documentation about his working days. Sometimes our records can be a tad, ah, uneven in their accuracy." His offered one of his hopeful looks.

She appeared doubtful. "He sold or pawned most everything he had before he moved back north, but he did keep a small steel box with his only possessions in it. I'll go get it. You sit." And off she went, eager for a few more dollars a month.

While she was in Preston's room, Donovan called in to her, "Donna, I was wondering if you have a recent photo of your brother. It would be nice to be able to get a sense of the gentleman we're trying to help. I don't actually need it, but it helps to picture the person you're helping. You do? Wonderful."

She was back in a moment, carrying the photo atop a cartridge magazine case. The picture showed a tall, thin old man squinting at the camera. Veins spidered across his cheeks and his nose, blooming into a rosea blush you just knew would never fade. Yet his weathered cheekbones were still as high and proud as a Mongol's and intelligence shone under his bushy eyebrows. At this point, though, the ravages of drink had long since burned his particular bridge at both ends and left him stranded in the middle, uncaring.

The dusty box on which the photo rested was iconic. He'd seen military green cases like that in war photos. If you want to carry a belt of bullets, you get this box. It was about a foot long, eight inches tall, and six inches wide.

Donna saw Donovan's interest in the box. "He was never in the army, but he always kept this once it was given to him. The army probably bought a few million of them over the years, so I don't think it's worth anything, and frankly, I don't expect to see much in the way of treasure inside of it either. It's not locked, so you go ahead and open it, Mr. Koulos." She handed it over. Any doubts he had about her trust in him were quashed, and Donovan felt another pang.

He pulled the metal bar at one end and the lid opened upward lengthwise. He looked at Donna, and then they both peered in, foreheads almost touching from either side of the tiny kitchen table. It's interesting, the things a man treasures and thus uses to measure a thrown-away life. On top was a Purple Heart. "That's odd," Donovan said. "I hadn't realized he had seen action, let alone gotten injured."

She replied, her voice diffident. "No, no, that belonged to his buddy, Tommy Yorkness. Tommy gave that to him when he went off to Washington. Tommy said it was for all the bull-crap injuries he would suffer in Washington. Well, he didn't really say bullcrap, you know."

"I know, Mrs. Little," he replied, charmed. "What else is in there?" He reached in and pulled out a wad of papers curled up in a rubber band and then put it aside so as not to detract the two of them from his real mission—finding the audio tape. His hand dipped in again and right back out, this time with a chunk of brain coral. "Hmm. From the Florida Keys, I guess. What else is in there?"

It was Donna's turn. She withdrew a plain woman's ring, with no stone to distinguish it. The inscription on the inside read: "You, me, and Washington."

"How queer is that, Mr. Koulos? I wonder if it was Chrissie's. She was his wife back in those days and is up in Maine now. Place called Camden. Nice girl, still sends me a card with a note every Christmas."

At the bottom, they found a four-inch square book of scripture (an inch thickness of wisdom), a social security card, a pair of silver dollars, a thousand worthless Confederate dollars, and a postcard from J. F. Kennedy inviting

Host to come visit Cape Cod sometime. Donovan noted the invitation was vague. It sounded like an empty gesture to him, what the French call a "*politesse*." Hemingway's *The Old Man And The Sea* lined the bottom of the box.

And that was it.

Preston Host's life in a can. But no tape. Donovan made a show of riffling through the papers, but it wasn't there.

On the way along the walkway to the taxi, he spied a man, three yards down, taking his dog for a walk. It was a basset hound, low slung and rear legs spread even closer to the ground. The man turned away from Donovan in embarrassment, a recyclable plastic shit-catcher bag in his right hand. Donovan smiled. At least somebody got something out of this afternoon. He swung into the cab, welcoming the warmth within. "Hey, buddy, could you take me to the nearest bar? Should be walking distance from here. And take your time. I need to change my clothes."

SEAN DONOVAN WALKED out of the brilliant fall sunshine—*why is it that the late afternoon, fall sun can create such a distinct light that brings every object within sight into such crisp relief?*—and into the dusty-light entrance of The Laughing Rogue. John Prine and Iris Dement were singing something about the Chevrolet set from the far corner stereo speakers. He couldn't hear much of the words but figured the song had a kernel of wisdom and a catchy melody because all of Prine's music did. He headed toward the back of the bar, passing several empty seats before coming upon a few customers.

The bar itself boasted thirteen stools lined up against a chunk of oak carved into the likeness of a guitar, frets and all. He'd seen a bar top like it in a Hard Rock Cafe in Ottawa, Canada once. Before he picked his spot at the bridge pickup or the machine heads, he spied his target in a booth, alone. He kept walking and sat at a stool right at the end of the guitar, next to the booth. The bartender floated over and without even looking at his customer, took Donovan's order of a Pabst Blue Ribbon, bottle, no glass. He took a long pull at his beer and sat for a minute before pretending to finally notice Preston Host.

"Hi buddy, pretty amazing weather we're having, huh?"

Host looked up and met Donovan's curious, open glance with red-rimmed, wet eyes. He gave a wink and said, "Eat it up, Boss. You know what's coming next." He raised a glass filled with half-melted ice cubes and a little amber staining the bottom. "Here's to the ice age. Maybe it'll get me this year." He drained it, smiled with most of his teeth, and offered up another wink, no charge.

Donovan faced him full-on, without leaving his stool. "I hear you, brother. Hey, that drink looks as lonely as a front row church pew. Lemme freshen her up. Bartender, can I get a drink over here for..." He raised an eyebrow.

Preston identified himself and attempted to get up from the booth, but his motor skills had either left with the previous two drinks, or perhaps a few years back, Donovan wasn't certain. He left the stool and leaned across the table to shake the firm grip of Preston Host, barfly. His hand registered the rough-hewn strength of his new buddy. *Like brother, like sister.*

He slid uninvited into the other side of the booth and put his back up against the wall at the end, just as Preston was doing. He ordered another beer right away, to give the impression of settling in, and then offered up a sidelong glance. "Preston Host, huh? Mr. Host, I am starved. Are the burgers any good here? Let's each have one with these excellent drinks, whaddayasay? Okay, two burger platters and, uh, some deep-fried mushrooms with ranch dressing, sound good? Sounds good."

He began chatting, not even interested at first in Preston's responses. Preston, meanwhile, had just received his newest best friend in the form of a shiny, sweat-rimmed glass filled with ice and bourbon, so his attention was torn.

Donovan continued. "So, you from New York originally? Me neither. I'm still not from here. I'm just in visiting my sister. What a pain in the ass she is. All up in my business, telling me this, and ordering me that. I needed a break, brother. I'm basically in hiding for an hour, so don't rat me out, Big Guy!" He took another appreciative drink from his beer. "Where did you come from before landing here?"

The old man took an appreciative sip and then sank deeper into the banquette seat with a sigh. He rolled up the sleeves of his faded tan shirt.

Donovan noticed a distinct ring circling the man's forearm, just below the elbow. The ring was dug in perhaps a half inch. *A rubber band! What the hell? How can you wrap a rubber band around your arm and forget about it?*

Preston said, "Well, before I came here a year ago I lived in the Florida Keys, in Marathon. I was in Key Largo for a bit. Nice place, maybe a little too prim and proper for me. I set out for, you know, the one at the bottom, Key West. But, you know, I found a nice coconut shack in Marathon with a nearby bar, and I basically set up shop."

He didn't seem to have any accent in particular. It was as if nothing from the four regions of America he had lived in had touched him.

"Oh, yeah. What kind of business were you in?"

Preston's eyes narrowed. "Things, you know, came into the shack, things left the shack, money happened. Had to keep everything on the down-low though, shhh! Because I didn't want to draw attention from the good or the bad, or the really bad, you know what I mean? So I kept it on the down-low, did I already say that? And kept my nose clean. Mostly. But I was having fun there.

"Hey! Ever eat off a hubcap? The best fish I ever ate was cooked on an open beach fire on a hubcap down in the Keys. Might have been ahi-ahi, might have been mahi-mahi, might have been a tired ol' catfish, what the cripes do I know? It was white though. And you know? Spoke hubcaps don't work so good for cooking on." He cackled. "But all good things must come to an end, and I got a stomach ache. Yeah, some bastard gutted me with a fish knife. How`s that for a stomach ache?" Another wet cackle.

"I was healing up pretty good in the hospital when I heard the really bad guys—remember them?—came 'round, cleaned out my coconut shack, and burned it. Right to the ground. Say, why is it if you burn a coconut shack down, or you burn it up, it's all the same frickin' thing? Pisses me off, you know? Cripes.

"Anyway, there I was with a brand new hole in the area where my spleen used to be and no home to go home to. The beach is nice and all, but a fella still wants to be inside walls if a gator comes a-calling. So my sister who, by the way, sounds like your sister—sure she isn't the same one?—came and got me, brought me home. Now I'm a New Yorker." He opened his hands and held them out as if to ask, "Don't that beat all?" and then folded them back in his lap.

Preston continued. "Am I happy? Well, I'm happy-*er*, long as my loyal pal Jim Beam here visits me regularly, you know?" He tapped the glass with an index fingernail that was split almost all the way up the middle to the cuticle, pleased with his perceived cleverness. Attention refocused on his loyal friend, he drew it to his lips and took a long swallow in honest appreciation.

The conversation went that way, with each man trading stories in turnabout fashion. They could have been true; they could have been outrageous lies. Neither cared, they were just killing time. The burgers came and went; several beers and several glasses of Jim Beam made brief visits to the booth. It was time for Donovan to raise Preston's suspicions. If the tape wasn't at his sister's place, it might be at his home away from home. Perhaps he'd reveal whether the tape was somewhere in the bar.

He waited until Preston's drink was gone and then started another story. "Okay, my turn. Ever have this happen to you? I was in London, England, in a bar. I had this thing, a small pistol, I was holding for a pal. The bobbies came into the bar. Yeah, they call the cops bobbies over there. I think they used to call them rozzers a long time ago and then peelers. I don't know if they still do. Anyway, in come the bobbies, and they just stand in the entranceway, staring us down. I kept my cool, I ain't no fool, but I gotta tell ya, that gun was burning a hole in my pocket.

"Anyway, while they're staring everybody down, I up and saunter over to the end of the bar, just beside the little boy's room. The gun was in a baggie, so I lifted the jug of bleach cleaner and dropped the pistol in behind it. I went back to my seat and minded my own business until they left. To this day I don't know why they came in the bar, but I was a very happy gunrunner when I saw their blue serge asses headed out the door."

Throughout his story he kept glancing at Preston, checking for any signs of nervousness. The lip-chewing began when it got to the part of his story where he unloaded the gun. It was time to order another round, but Donovan waited. Would he see a connection between Donovan's story and the story of the hidden tape? He looked for any sign the old man had caught on, and then Preston's eyes widened. Preston got more agitated, glancing toward the bathroom area and then at the floor. Donovan guessed he had his answer.

He stood up and with profuse apologies, confessed the minutes had got away from him, and it was time to return to his dragon lady sister. He ordered another round for Preston, which seemed to absolve everybody of everything. Once it seemed Preston appeared to have forgotten the story, he headed for the sunlight just outside of the door. On his way out, he noted just one closed circuit camera, which was pointed at the rear exit. The lock on the front door was electronic. Perfect. *Gotta like the neighborhood bar where everybody knows your name and nothing ever happens. Guess I'll be back.* He walked out, hailed a cab, and that was the last time he ever saw Preston Host, barfly.

Dusk had fallen so hard you could have heard it. *That's what I get for forgetting it's autumn.* Outside the bar, he grabbed the blue jacket from his backpack and pulled it over his long-sleeved tee. On the way back into the city, he thought about the experience in the bar. He'd just spent two hours with what used to be a very intelligent man. They say most American families are fewer than four paychecks away from losing everything, and Preston must have slid down a steep slope to have landed in his alcohol-fueled heap. One minute you're chatting with the President's mistress, and the next, you can't even get your hands on a president's likeness on a dollar bill.

Thinking about Preston's plight made him ponder his own. He didn't seem as happy these days, so why was that? Was it the work? The fact Nadia was now on the scene? The fact she technically wasn't? And why was he even thinking about these circumstances, anyway? These thoughts hadn't sprung to mind in forever. This wasn't about getting beaten up. Or was it? Or, maybe it was about getting beaten up regularly. In every damned country. That was part of it, but hell, he could take a kick in the ribs; it had happened before. Why did it seem to be different now? Was he any good at this business and did that even matter? Had something happened other than personal fatigue—something that changed everything?

"What's up with that?" he murmured to himself, causing the cabbie to glance back but say nothing. He needed some time on a park bench, or in a bar, mulling this whole thing over. They were on the Queensboro Bridge, crossing over to Manhattan. Not far now. He hummed the "59th Street

Bridge Song," associating the song with the location. Traffic was jammed up about ten blocks from his hotel, so he threw some bills over the seat and hopped out. The walk would do him good.

It took him four blocks to figure out what was wrong. He was a prick. "I'm a prick!" he exclaimed as he strode along, backpack on one shoulder and briefcase in his hand. Nobody even glanced at this revelation, it being rush hour in New York City. He stopped talking, knowing the likelihood of getting arrested or punched was somewhat lessened by keeping these thoughts to himself.

What was wrong? Well, he did bad things for a living. Until now, he didn't seem to care who got hurt or whose lives were damaged or altered by his actions. He didn't even think in terms of good and bad. It was all in terms of success or failure, achievable or impossible, profitable or unprofitable. He made a lot of money—a *lot* of money—by taking advantage of opportunities, of situations. For that read: *taking advantage of others*. But now this whole consequences thing seemed to matter, to the point where he wasn't sure he could carry on this way.

Whoa! I am really good at what I do. Or, am I? Then why do I keep getting beat up? I make a lot of money at what I do—being a prick. Enough with being a prick! Let that...go. Besides, what else can I do? What else is there for me? Go back to the security business? The in-security business. Nope, can't do that, can't go back. Then go...where? Move forward. What the hell does that mean, really? Move forward. What a stupid, New-Age term. His pace accelerated. *Which way is forward? And when you get...forward...where will you be? Surrounded by strangers, and they're not even my strangers. They're other people's strangers. That's how alone I am.* Donovan shook his head. He had no confidence with this dance. He could see his hotel a block away; time to cross the street. He let the biomass move him along with them—the flow of humanity, the rush hour crowd, the Great Unwashed. *I am the Great Unwashed!*

Once across the street, he stopped dead, eliciting a curse from the man behind him. He craned his neck, looking up to the tops of the buildings, feeling the weather turn to a chill October breeze bearing down on him like a bad debt. "Huh. Funny thing, here I am knowing exactly where I am, and yet, I still feel lost." Not knowing what else to say or do, he permitted the flow of humanity to wash him up West Thirty-Fifth.

He strode across the foyer of his hotel and straight to the bar. "Room 419. Three beers, not Coors, not Bud." He took three strides and then turned and said, "Charge my room for the beers, this is for you. Thank you. Sorry. I'm a prick. Sorry." He dropped two twenties on the bar and headed for the concierge and handed him a small envelope together with some more bills. He made a request and then headed for his room.

Once out of the shower, he opened his wallet and pulled out a scrap of hotel stationery from London. He dialed a number and waited. And waited. Six rings and a familiar voice came on the line.

She jumped in first, before he could say a word. "You're calling from a New York phone number. Hi! Before we begin, I just have to say, I would have been surprised if you hadn't called, but I'm kinda surprised you called. Hello, Sean. This week has been a month long. How are you?"

"Well, to be honest, I seem to be wrecked. It appears the weight of twenty years of not being a nice guy has sort of descended upon me, and I'm feeling kind of crushed. So, I'm not calling my gorgeous, wise, maybe girlfriend for a date. I'm actually calling my only friend for a chat."

There was a pause on the line, and Nadia's voice lowered a register. "Are you okay? Want me to come over?"

"No. At least, not now. Tomorrow, I hope. I'm just calling...to hear your voice. But before we go any further, there is something that's come between us. Well, actually, I've placed it between us, and I need to make that go away first."

"Go on." Her voice was neutral.

"I stole your good luck necklace and replaced it with a fake."

"Yes, you did, dear, and a very good fake at that, might I say. Did you do it for the money? Because other than my questionable fame as a fading starlet, the pearls are really not worth more than two hundred fifty, three hundred bucks tops." He could hear the laughter in her voice. "The question, for me anyway, is, am I going to get it back? It has a sentimental value to me, you see."

"Of course." Donovan was confused. "You're not mad? You don't...this doesn't seem to be going the way I anticipated. I was pretty sure you'd say goodbye, or maybe not even want to talk to me."

She interrupted him. "Excuse me, Sean, there's someone at my door, can you stay on the line? Just stay on the line." There was a pause, and then she returned. He could hear the sound of paper ripping. "Oh, you're good. You do have excellent timing," she said, admiration in her voice.

"You got the necklace?"

"Yes. Sean, I missed it so. Don't steal it from me anymore. Seriously, do you need any money? I could make it a loan or a gift, your call."

Donovan smiled, relief washing over him, but he was still careful with the words he chose next. "Oh, Nadia, you are a special person. I have lots of money, even by Hollywood's standards. The, ah, bad news about the necklace is I took it for a not nice reason. I've got to explain the whole thing to you. In detail—all the gory details of which I am not proud. But I have to tell you face-to-face, if that's okay. You can deal with me however you want to once you hear the whole thing, but it's got to be me looking you in the eyes when I talk. Do you think that would be okay?"

"Um, yeah, that's the way I'd want to hear it, so sure." She hesitated. "When? I don't know if you noticed, but it's Monday night, the beginning of a fresh new week, and here we are, the two of us, in New York City. The city that not-so-much sleeps. We could grab a coffee, or I bet we could find a place to eat. Hell, we could just go for a walk down Madison Avenue." She waited. Donovan could hear Eva Cassidy singing "Songbird" in the background through her phone.

"I *want* to." He could hear her sigh, in the pause that ensued. He started again. "I have to work tonight. I'll be all night. I could see you as early as five tomorrow morning, but why don't you let me do this properly? The way things are going, I may actually be fully retired, as in unemployed, by breakfast time, and that's a very good thing. Seriously. So how about you let me finish my work, grab a couple of hours' sleep, and I'll be at your doorstep with a bouquet of flowers and a shiny, fresh-washed face tomorrow at, say, seven? We could go for a walk, I'll tell you a story that, if it's not fun, will at least be interesting and true, and then we could grab a bite to eat, or you can kick me to the curb. Nadia, I am truly, truly hoping for the meal and not the other, I've got to tell you." It was now his turn to wait.

"What hotel are you at?"

"The Windham, West Thirty-fifth."

There was another pause. He heard a strange, faint clicking and guessed her to be playing with her necklace, the pearls brushing against her cell phone. "Just down the street. Okay. Come see me at seven tomorrow. Know where I'm staying? The Algonquin, Forty-fourth West? I guess you do, if you sent me a necklace by courier, and therefore, you also know it's not terribly far from where you are."

"Yeah, by Times Square. I would have thought you'd be a little more distant from your fans." He couldn't help the little teasing.

"You mean, am I cheap, or am I starved for attention? Come stay at the Algonquin and you'll see why I love it so. And if it's good enough for Dorothy Parker, it's good enough for me. So there."

Donovan couldn't help but smile at the warmth he heard in her voice. "Dorothy Parker, eh? She was a firecracker, just like you."

"Oh, Sean, you'll come to know those words are true. Too true. Okay, I'll let you go do what you have to do, and I'll see you tomorrow evening at seven, if not sooner." She rang off and Donovan opened a beer, took a sip and stared out the window as New York passed by.

HE WAITED UNTIL TWO-thirty and then headed back up West Thirty-fifth. After a few blocks, he hailed a cab and threw his backpack into the back seat, following it in. "Long Island City, please."

He asked to be dropped off a few blocks from the bar and walked the balance, feeling the middle-night air. Once he arrived within sight of the bar, he unbuckled his backpack, aware of every alley, every shadow, every streetlight glow.

Fifty yards from the darkened bar, he leaned into the shadows, withdrawing the electronic door opener and a facemask. Without pausing at the entrance to see who might be watching, he placed the deactivator over the lock, turned the doorknob, walked into the bar, and closed the door behind him. The beep! beep! of the alarm filled the dim-lit room. He had the green box ready and placed it over the alarm pad, knowing that after the two seconds it took to get inside, the green box had eight more seconds to disable the electronic warning to the alarm company agents. The meter showed the final two seconds before the insistent beeping stopped. The monitoring staff somewhere in Alarm Central would not be notified this time. The apparatus had told the system everything was cool, so no reason to wake up anyone. Still, Donovan could feel the sweat begin to stain his shirt and pool along the inside of his mask from forehead to chin.

He moved away from the windows, heading to the bar, aware that if anyone else was present, they would already have called the cops. Donovan ignored the main area and walked past the closed circuit television. He smiled. The thing about closed circuit TV is it is automated. Night after night coverage of nothing happening to the very same door really doesn't make for riveting viewing. There needed to be a reason for someone to go out of their way to review the video tapes. Barring any stupid break-ins in the next two weeks, his masked face would be erased, and he would be the tree that fell in the forest—if nobody saw him, it didn't happen. He didn't happen.

He checked the back. Bathroom stall doors open, office door open as well, storerooms clear, janitor closet as tidy as can be. All good. He was alone. It was time to go back to the front. He started with Host's booth, reaching down the cracks between the vinyl banquette seat covers and wooden frames. Donovan cracked another smile. He made almost two dollars in change, which he pocketed. He noted there really wasn't enough space in the cracks to cache even the smaller tape spools. He moved to the bar: lowest shelf, middle shelf, behind each of the cupboard doors. Nothing. He found an almost full tip jar into which he put the two dollars in change.

He almost stood up, but something arrested him. He looked up and saw a faint light playing across the long mirror behind the bar. He eased himself to the floor, holding his breath. Who was holding the light? It seemed less powerful than a floodlight coming through a street-side window. Someone was checking out The Laughing Rogue at three-thirty in the morning. Was it police, a security company, or somebody up to no good? The light traveled from left to right, the length of the mirror, two feet above his head. *What is less than not breathing? Do that.* He tried to will his heart to stop, just for a moment. The sweat from his throat spilled onto his shirt front.

He took inventory of the weapons in his backpack, a task that didn't take long. Nothing. All of the space had been taken up with security equipment, and there was no room for even the smallest trick. *To be honest, I was certain I wouldn't run into anything. Or anyone. Next time, if there's a next time, I'll bring something. Man! Getting caught defenseless on my last job. That sucks.*

The flashlight moved on. In the dead of night, you can hear the furnace, the refrigeration units, the mice, if there are any. Donovan was listening for a very specific sound. Between breaths, he listened with all his might. A key, however, was not inserted into a lock, the doorknob did not turn, and the door did not open. He waited three more beats and then stole a peek. Nothing.

He thought about the office and shook his head. *Nobody is in here with me, so it's got to be the police. Not a good thing, but the least of the three evils.* He crept to the window and peeked over the sill. Three doors away a squad car idled its way down the street, tail pipe huffing in the cool night air, blue-white light flitting from the front window, passenger side, to illuminate every second shop window. Donovan realized he had begun breathing once again.

He headed to check out the restroom. Looking up, he spotted the air vent and decided to save that for the last. He went for the toilet reservoirs first. Damn! Each reservoir lid had a tidy three-eighths inch hole drilled into it and was fastened with a bolt and washer. Knowing how bar toilets are used, and therefore, how prone they are to breaking, he went behind the bar. He looked under the bar top, but it was too dark to see. He reached in, behind the bar towel, past the shot glasses. A pair of pliers lay flush to the back. He grabbed them, hurried back to the restroom, and went to work on the toilet lids.

He found it in the second stall reservoir in a baggy, taped to the inside of the lid. Donovan opened his bag, removed the smallest spool of audiotape, and swapped out the rolls of tape. Three-inch black spool for three-inch black spool. Done and done. On the way past the camera, he opened his coat, so the imaginary viewer would see there were no cash boxes, stereos, or televisions hidden. He left the front door the way he found it, walked at least a dozen blocks before hailing a cab and was back in his room by four-thirty.

Blinds drawn, Donovan was almost asleep when he heard three gentle knocks on his door. A little concerned, since people aren't supposed to be wandering the halls *unless they were on official police business.* He looked through the tiny peephole in the door. She rapped again, once, at the moment he opened the door to her.

"Hi. I miss you. I stayed up all night, so we could sleep together. Just sleep."

Without a word, he opened the door wide and with a kiss, led her to his bed. "Politeness be damned, Nadia, I get the right side." It was her turn to not speak. She had stepped out of her shoes at the door and dropped her topcoat and sweater on the floor on the way to the bed. Tugging off a charcoal pencil skirt, she walked up the length of the bed, kicked the linens down with one toe, just enough to crawl in, and slid down into the middle of the bed. Off came her bra.

Donovan eyed her just before she drew up the covers and then whispered, "Good enough, you can have whatever part of the bed you want. Ah, the middle, eh? Fair is fair, then. I'm getting the middle too. Meet you there." Both were asleep in two minutes.

Chapter Fourteen

New York City
Tuesday Morning

Donovan woke first. He turned over onto his side, the better to watch her sleep. At some point, she had moved to sleep on her back. He took time to study the details of her face. The straight and narrow slope of her nose looked perfect to him, and he cherished those almond-shaped eyes he had come to know for their intelligence and warmth. Her cheeks and forehead were high and pronounced, and her chin meant business, but her full lips softened...everything.

He slid out of bed and padded over to the window where the drapes were opened a crack. Welcome to New York City on a spare, chill Tuesday. The sun was trying but failing to offer any warmth to the thousands of noon-hour pedestrians. They clutched their jackets with one hand at the throat and held the other balled into a fist to their bodies in what appeared to be a vain attempt at keeping warm. It must have been gusty because a few frigid souls walked sidelong into the wind, hunched over to protect themselves. Donovan shuddered.

"Well, anyone would get a chill standing naked beside an October hotel window. Come on back to bed, you." Nadia's voice warmed him, drew him back to bed. They lay still, studying each other's face as if they had never met. Finally, she began to trace the tiny, and the not-so-tiny, scars on his face. He almost couldn't feel her touch. Almost.

"What do you see?"

"I think I see you. Maybe for the first time. Sean, you're a real person."

"I hope to be."

"Seriously. I am a career actress who has spent, um, twenty years in Hollywood. After a while, nothing seems to be real. Not the boobs, not the promises. Not the relationships. Nothing... You seem real. Except for some of your words. You're a bit of a liar, Sean, and liars lie to keep secrets. I don't like secrets. They add unnecessary layers that end up choking you. Maybe I should say some of the time lying comes easy to you. Which puts me in a pickle." She touched the scar on his chin and then placed her hand over his heart.

"I think important things could be shared between us, if we could get past that little issue. Do you think, if my heart was on the line, you could tell me your story, no lies, no bullshit? Because then we could maybe think of today as day one?" Her hand rested over his heart, and he thought that his heart warmed her hand. She left it there, light as air.

"Yes. I could do that. You get three levels of honesty..."

"No, Sean. I want it all. Drugs. Hookers. Of course I don't want that, but you know what I mean. Whatever you need to tell me, so we can start from today. Okay?"

He weighed his options. He could lose her, or maybe he could start fresh. Either way, he had to spill. "All right. I'll start when I was ten. My dad was a crappy musician, living on the road and pretending to be in sales. I never much knew him except when he would just show up. I used to think he came home because he needed to beat on somebody. So now let's fast forward to me at age sixteen. I walked in on him whaling away on my mom, and I took a bat to him. Last time I saw him was the last time I really hurt somebody that bad." Her hand, making a small circular motion over his heart, stopped dead.

"So, that kind of wrecked me for a while. I headed to Montreal, learned a bunch of stuff, got some education, and learned a bunch more stuff. I used this to make money in the IT and security sectors. I got in with government, made even more money, legally this time, supporting international government contracts. I never got into arms, by the way. It seemed to me to be a teeny bit safer making money from security contracts, either in sales, or later on in service. And I suppose I should say this aloud. I've never killed anyone, although I've hurt some bad people. See my problem? Most people don't actually need to do a full murder disclosure with their dates. I definitely need to start a new résumé."

He paused, collecting his thoughts as she waited. "Anyway, at some point I was approached to pick something up and drop it off. I was asked solely because they knew I could go places on business, pull off a job, and then disappear. Let's say, for example, I'd be asked for the floor plans to an art museum. I would get them, drop them off, and pick up my fee, no problem. I never asked why or even cared, unless it reduced the risk. I've been doing that for a while." He looked away, embarrassed.

After a while, she nudged him and said, "Go on. I'm still here."

"Well, really, that's it. Would you like to know about some of them, maybe the last few? Because, ah, one of them was...you."

"It's what I was thinking. Okay, let me have it. This one is about the necklace and...Katie?"

Donovan blushed in mortification. He couldn't recall ever feeling the heat of shame come over him like that before. "Yes. Katie. I think it was because she was jealous of your talent, or perhaps because she didn't enjoy sharing the spotlight. Anyway, she knew your necklace was your talisman, and I suspect she felt if she owned it, she owned a piece of you. I thought I was doing a typical job on some stranger, but instead, I fell for the stranger. Since I'd never fallen for anyone, let alone a target, it took me most of the way through the job to discover I didn't want to do the job."

He angled his head to look her straight in the eye. "Once I got to know you, it was too late. Katie would make a lot of unpleasantness if I didn't deliver, and I didn't want to say goodbye to the victim. To you. So I made two copies of the necklace, gave one to each of you and held onto the original. Yours. The only thing I can say to soften my bastardliness, if that's a word, is that Katie never touched it. The real necklace."

Nadia looked up, a half-smile that didn't reach her eyes. "And what about you, Sean? She touch you?"

He laughed genuinely, for the first time in what seemed days. "No, sweetie. You and I agreed she's a brat, remember?"

"I see. And have you had other jobs recently? Are you, for instance, in New York doing a job?"

"Yes. My last one. I'm sick of it. Sick of getting beat up, sick of being lonely. Sick of how I feel afterward. I'm sick of feeling empty in some hotel room in Prague, or Quito, or even Montreal. It's not that I'm *ready* to stop...I've *already* stopped, no matter what happens here this morning. It's done, and I'm done. Retired, like I said."

"It seems to me, and no offense, darling, if you get beat up as much as your bruises and stories tell me, perhaps you might not be as good a spy as you think you are. Maybe it really is time to get out." Nadia's voice carried a trace of sympathy tinged with humor. "So, what were your last two jobs, other than mine?"

"I stole an ancient chalice—an Etruscan cup—from a Romanian palace warehouse and sold it to an Italian history professor. In Canada. And I'm not a spy. I prefer to think of myself as a broker." It felt important to share even the details he felt were inconsequential. "This week I stole a conversation from a drunk. A recorded conversation. It's supposed to be a chat between JFK and Marilyn Monroe. About Castro. I haven't done anything with that one, yet."

Nadia looked at him, fascinated. "Mr. Donovan, you sir, are amazing. Seriously. Part of me is still processing the whole nice guy doing bad things part, and another part of me is saying shit! That's amazing. And of course I need to know a whole bunch of stuff, like, are you being chased? Am I in danger? Did you really stop as of today?" She peered into his face. "Have I heard my last lie from you, and are you hooked on danger and travel and the thrill of the hunt? That last one was probably unfair, since you won't know for a while yet."

Donovan patted her hand that had remained on his chest. "The thrill left me at least two years ago, and the lying left me yesterday, when we were on the phone. I didn't know what else to do, how to stop. The big thing is, mostly, I didn't know why I should stop. Listen, you ask if we're in danger. I don't believe so. I'm a very careful guy, but what does that really mean, at the end of a long, long day?" The shadow of a thought crossed his mind—of a man at Harrods passing him, twice. He pushed it away for the moment. "Something we might consider is, if we do become a couple, you may want to keep us on the down low for a while. Six months, whatever. Believe me, I could live with a lot of conditions to be with you. Just sayin'."

They continued talking in a desultory manner, sometimes with more animation. Donovan was surprised to discover Nadia had stolen a car when she was much younger and had used her new-found fame to bury the story. She also told him she had no brothers or sisters and no parents, having disowned her father. Nadia, in turn, was surprised to discover he had a sister living in Montreal who was the only human with whom he was close. He also told her he sent money regularly and anonymously to his mother, although he never visited her. She advised him one condition she had thought of, off the cuff, was she had to meet Madeleine.

At some point, hunger pangs slowed their revelations. She asked if he wanted room service, or as a joke, asked if he could recommend a nice sandwich shop. He replied he did know of such a thing—a nice deli on the Lower East Side, and would she like to meet an old teacher of his? He had some things to return to Brooklyn after they picked up the food.

DONOVAN FOLLOWED A stiff October gust in through the door and greeted J.D., who was on the shop floor. He accepted his equipment back, raising an eyebrow when Nadia slipped in the door, offering a sack of fragrant goodies from Katz's Deli. J.D. tossed the equipment into a corner, to be cleaned and restocked later. He and Nadia were introduced, and once again John David placed the closed sign on the door. "Come on to the back. For some reason it's warmer there—stupid tenant services. Gonna warn my nephew about them, that's a fact."

J.D. hauled down a bottle of Chianti and three plastic cups from a shelf inside the back room. This gave Donovan the opportunity to tease. "What's this? You never trotted out wine when I used to come here alone! So a guy has to bring somebody gorgeous to this joint just to get a drink?"

"Friggin' right. So, your, um, that last bit of business was put to bed, and everything happened like it was supposed to?" He looked sideways, squinting.

"Yup. It all went well," said Donovan. "Listen. You've been good to me over the years. I swung by to bring your gear back but mostly to tell you I retired. This morning. Gonna open up a bar in Florida. Or Veradero, depending on how fast Fidel's brother Raoul turns Cuba into Miami South. Or something. Maybe I'm going to travel, see a couple of movie sets."

J.D.'s eyes flitted over to Nadia, who winked at him. He looked away, perhaps star struck by her presence.

"Well, all right then."

Donovan pointed to the shelf that circled the room, about three feet from the ceiling. "I have one last favor to ask. I notice you have a couple of old recorders up on the top shelf—"

J.D. interrupted, opening his empty palms. "But I told ya, Seannie, I still don't have any tapes for you."

"That's okay, I brought my own. Want to hear a blast from the past?"

"Chet Baker? John Coltrane?"

Nadia interjected, "Sean, I like this fella. Let's bring him next time we go listening to music."

The big man smiled.

"Yeah, this particular blast from the past isn't exactly musical. Haul down that old Teac, and let's give this a listen." Donovan tossed a black three-inch reel onto the counter.

The proprietor grabbed a clunky reel-to-reel recorder off the shelf, dusted it off, and spliced the tape through the heads and onto an empty spool, sending a questioning glance to Donovan. He pressed PLAY, and for the next fifteen minutes all three were transfixed.

When the conversation finished, they sat without speaking. Finally, J.D. broke the silence. "Was that who it sounded like? Because I have to say it sounded like JFK and Marilyn Monroe. I don't know the other two. But that sure sounded like Marilyn Monroe, and what they were saying made the guy a very realistic JFK. Shit! Who were the other two guys? One was named Preston?"

Nadia spoke. "Peter Lawford? One of them sounded like Peter Lawford."

"Peter Lawford indeed. And Preston Host. It was recorded in a hotel in Washington."

"Is it real? I mean, Jesus Christ, JFK? In cahoots with Fidel Castro? You gotta be kidding me."

"Maybe. I won't know until I get voiceprints of him and Marilyn, maybe Lawford. I have a suspicion it's the real deal, though."

"So, what're you gonna do with it? It must be worth a couple million at least."

Donovan scratched his cheek. "I don't know. First, I need to know if it's real, and then I'll see. Anyway, what I'd like to do now is get a copy, preferably on a thumb drive. Got something I could use? In the meantime, let's finish eating."

Sometime later, a cabbie picked them up, and then they were dropped across the street from one of the entrances to Coney Island. The rides decorated the skyline to the right and on the left sat the aquarium that had been there for decades. Once on the wooden boardwalk, Donovan looked around. The steps down to the beach were flanked by a double bar railing J.D. had said he had played on as a child—first crawling through the lower bar and then later balancing on the upper bar as a teen. They descended the stairs to the beach. He noticed that, like the song, one really could be under the boardwalk but only if they hunkered down. Great for teens to make out, he supposed.

"Geez, Nadia, nothing's open, why are we freezing our butts off here?"

"Suck it up, Sean. Geez, aren't you a Canadian? I mean, how often do you get to Brooklyn? You have to go to Coney Island, try and find a Nathan's red hot!"

"Well, yeah, but the end of October? Didn't we see Christmas lights in that last shop back there?"

"See? Now you're exaggerating. We won't see Christmas decorations for at least another week." She caught his arm and pulled him toward the steps. "C'mon, it'll be fun. I'll keep you from freezing. Let's go down to the water. Maybe it's warmer there."

"I have to tell you Nadia, your acting skills are way better than your meteorological skills. But okay, let's go down to the sea, and I'll let you dip your pretty toe in the water. I kind of suspect the weather's about the same a hundred feet from here, though." She punched him and tugged him down the steps to the sand. They passed a man searching with a metal detector for lost coins and rings, but other than that, the beach was theirs.

JUST BEFORE DUSK, THEY grabbed a cab and headed back to Manhattan. Neither spoke for most of the ride. They were within sight of her hotel on Forty-fourth when Nadia spoke, low, so her voice wouldn't carry to the front of the taxi. "Did I mention you're a very interesting guy, Sean? Also, you told me you really don't have friends, yet J.D. seems to be a great guy who cares for you. I have to say, we should stick together for a while. You look to have some redeeming features. Hey, I'll be Saturday, and you can be Sunday, and we'll be a great weekend. My friend Victoria says a bad weekend is always better than a good weekday, so we will always be better than that, right?" He just took her hand and nodded.

They went to her hotel apartment, and Nadia rummaged around for a couple of candles. She left a light on by the entrance, and the candles flickered in front of the couple. The dusky illumination soothed him, bringing him to a state of calm, and they pulled the drapes back to welcome the evening New York skyline. A bottle of Syrah, opened but untouched, sat on the coffee table even as the seven o'clock city lights puddled on the carpet under their feet. He noticed her hair, which had been silky smooth and as straight as could be, had morphed into languid waves. It softened her features and made her look younger. He could see her as a rebellious teen, a willful young woman, and he couldn't help but reach over to feel it. It was so feathery soft he wasn't sure if he was really feeling it. He thought it would be what a woman's hair would be like in a dream.

She broke his reverie. "Yeah, my hair goes all wavy when I'm out in the damp. Sorry."

"It's better this way. Really. Women straighten their hair to impress other women. Men don't want straight hair unless it was straight all along. Just saying."

She didn't believe it and told him so, and then she changed the subject. "What do you think of New York City?"

"To live in or to visit?"

"Yes."

"J.D. once told me to never visit him in New York. He says once I do, I'll never want to live anywhere else."

"And what happened, once you did visit it?"

"Now, I love New York. Probably as much as Montreal. Not that I've given it much thought. I guess I just take it for granted, you know? It's here, and I take extra time to stay over whenever I'm doing business in New York," Donovan said.

"Really? Montreal as much as New York? Maybe I better visit Montreal. Know anyone who could show me around?" She cocked her head at him, curious to see if he would take offense.

"Yeah. They both have their charms, New York being bigger and well, more, but after a bit, I always have the urge to leave here to see somewhere else. That doesn't happen with Montreal. I have to say, it also never happens in the Bahamas." A trace of a smile. "You?"

"I must confess I kinda like New York. But I like warm as well. Warm works for me. But you know, we both have money, unlike when we were young, so that means we don't have to choose. We could just become gypsies. Or in our case, we could just stay as gypsies, since we never have actually settled anywhere."

"Peripatetic."

"Peri-what?" She looked at him, confused.

He explained. "People who prefer to wander about, not really sticking to one place. That's us, I guess. Hey, can I add something?"

Nadia faced him.

"If I really liked NYC before I met you, it would definitely be more attractive now. If you were here." Donovan caressed her forearm with the back of his hand.

"I'm not asking that."

"That's okay. Are you asking anything, at the moment?"

"Well, something has crossed my mind. Not sure if it's my place to ask this of you. How about I put it in the form of a suggestion?"

He hesitated. "Sure."

"I was thinking, Sean, that if you undid the last three things you did, it would maybe give you some closure. Make you feel like you really did close a door or something. It would almost be like three wrongs making a right. Does that make sense? We both know two wrongs don't make a right. What about three wrongs?" She smiled at the illogical insight, and her words came out in a rush. "Hey! I'm not telling you what to do. This isn't some stupid fairytale where you get the maiden if you sail off on some quest. I'm just thinking twenty years of doing a certain thing could cause a guy to not believe he could or should stop."

Donovan scratched his chin. "When I set out to do something, I make it a habit to think it through. It reduces errors and slipups. I understand how something like what you're suggesting could close a door, so it does appeal to me. But I have to think about it. I'll need some processing time to work out the hows of it. It's a very attractive thing, at the moment, to just walk away. Do nothing at all." He thought for a moment. "It would be a little ironic to get caught putting something back, as opposed to the original stealing of it."

"Yeah, that would suck." She laughed. "Sorry, it's a nervous thing. I laugh whenever I finally find someone and then suggest things that'll put his butt in jail."

"Okay, here's a question, Nadia. How do you propose I reverse the theft of my friend's talisman necklace? I've already given it back to you."

"Sorry, pal. I'm not the spy, I mean broker. It's up to you to come up with something. How about I just say I'll take it easy on you, and whatever you come up with, I'm sure will meet the rules of the game? Because it's not about details, it's all about closure, as far as I'm concerned. It's about intent, not execution. How you go about it is really only important to you, I think. So, if you accept, what would you undo? The necklace, the conversation, and...?"

"The bucchero chalice. Those are the last three things. And you'd have to stay away from me for a week or three, to keep things clean. Make sense?"

She conceded it did. "You do seem to be fun to have around, though. I'll miss you. I've never met anyone else I'd want to take a freezing walk along the boardwalk in Coney Island with. Too bad Nathan's wasn't open, and they're *never* closed! I wonder if their hot dogs are better than the ones we ended up with. We'll never know unless we go back."

"As long as you pick a warmer day, I'm in." He switched topics. "So what will keep you entertained in the meantime?"

"Oh. Well, I have a press gathering and party to promote the movie that's coming out very shortly, a week from today. And I have an offer in the drawer over there I suppose I should sign. I'm dreading doing it, in fact. The script is dreadful, at least, the role I'd play. Although they'll probably rewrite it a hundred times before it gets made. I just don't want to do it."

She turned to face him, finishing all but a sip from her glass of wine. "You know, I've never turned down my manager's instructions to sign. Not once in twenty years. If I said no to this, it would be the first time. So, between working on another set in London—again with London!—or opening a bar in the Bahamas with my man, I'm leaning toward flipping off the script and heading south." Her eyes widened. "Sean, are we planning? Are we having a discussion about us?"

"I think so. Yes. You all right with that?"

"Yeah. You?"

"Yes. You know, I always wanted to be a somebody, but I ended up being a somebody else. Maybe I can fix that. All right, then. I'll get started tomorrow. Don't sign that script yet. Think about what you want and make a decision in a few days. Remember, I've only been retired for twelve hours. I probably have to prove myself, so don't buy any sunscreen just yet." They both leaned forward at the same time to fill their wineglasses. Planning was over.

THAT NIGHT THEY ATE in to avoid the paparazzi but became a bit more adventurous as the evening wore on. After dinner, Donovan had a suggestion, so at eleven they went to B.B. King's bar. Around midnight, the old bluesman came on and walked over to a stool in the middle of the stage. He sat down, hugged Lucille so as to prevent banging her headstock against the mike boom, leaned in toward the mike and said, "I'm almost eighty now, so I don't have to stand up no more for nobody. And hey, stick around. Introduce yourself to the good folks sitting at the next table. My young friend Susan brought her little green Tele to town. She's gonna help me out a little later." Amid the cheers, he struck the first notes of "Four O'clock Blues." And so went the night.

Chapter Fifteen

N *ew York to Montreal*
Wednesday morning dawned as crisp and fresh as the jump blues of the previous evening. Nadia was the first to leave. She grabbed a cab and was off to the airport to catch an eight o'clock flight to Chicago. Donovan's flight didn't leave until noon, so he took his time over coffee, walked the four blocks back to his hotel, and packed methodically, as was his habit. His was an international flight, so he arrived a little early in order to account for the inevitable delays. After checking in, he pulled out the newspaper he had cadged from the hotel and sat down to wait for his flight.

Something made him look up, turn around, and stare over the heads of the people seated behind the wall dividing the passengers from the rest of the inhabitants of the airport. On the other side of the glass, he had spied...something. A doleful, fifty-something mother tried to tell something critical to a teenage daughter who was trying to ignore her. Beside them a very fat man texted something that appeared to require all of his attention. Between them a man was studying him.

It was just a glimpse, and the man turned away as soon as eye contact was made, and then he was lost in the crowd. But Donovan recognized him. It was the man from the passport photo he had dismissed, back in Bucharest. The mysterious one...Galen? Galen Attanasio. The man people called Gaia. He felt a tickle of disquiet in his gut. "This is not a coincidence," he whispered. A moment later his flight was announced, and he decided, against his better judgement, to board.

MONTREAL GREETED HIM like an old friend. He landed in Dorval and took a cab back to his place. After asking the driver to park down the street from his apartment, he sat there for a full minute, waiting, staring at the cars on the street around the apartment entrance. It took him almost ten minutes to cross the threshold. At that point, he was certain his street harbored no surveillance team, his foyer was empty, and the hallway to his door was bare and as quiet as a Wednesday evening. Moments later, he had also confirmed no one had entered his apartment in his absence, not even his sister.

Once inside, he sat at his desk, reviewing every step he had taken from before his last trip to Romania. Every couple of minutes he eased over to the window, surveying the street from behind his drapes. He took the time to look into all of the ones nearby, recognizing most as cars from the neighborhood.

He made a mental note of every individual whose acquaintance he had met, from Katya in the Romanian Ministry of Labor, to the waitress who had sidestepped his question about Turks versus Italians, all the way to the staff at the Brooklyn deli. Thankful for his eidetic memory, he reviewed every conversation he'd had, including the one in the bar with Preston. Nothing. How did Gaia find him? For he had. And if he did (*and he had*), why did Gaia want him? Was it all about the passport, or did it have anything to do with the Romanian gig? Was this about the bucchero chalice? He didn't think so, but then again, he hadn't thought he was being followed either. He had a feeling, though, that he'd better get this one figured out. Someone like Gaia had serious resources.

Since this line of thinking could lead to nothing useful, Donovan thought about the job at hand. Of the three things that had to be undone, which should he start with? The necklace was the quick fix. He had an idea, and all it would cost him was a phone call. Easy. Next? It had to be the cup. Odds were it was the source of his current worries, perhaps it should be his next priority; better to make it go away fast. He headed for the bedroom and used one of his cell phones to book a flight. He spent the rest of the evening plotting, working out logistics, and scheming back door exits and Plans B, C, and D. This was a time for deliberation and care.

THE NIGHT HAD DELIVERED a brief snow squall. By noon, it had warmed up to melting. The sun offered a sullen light that turned the pristine snow to grey slush, but didn't quite break through the clouds. A brisk breeze drove the cold air up from the St. Lawrence Seaway and dampness chilled to the bone. He checked the snow dusting on his second-storey balcony for footprints, but there were none, nor on the lawn beneath it. Donovan had got up early and chatted with the night staff before they booked off for the day. Luc at the desk confirmed it had been an extra quiet evening. The tenant in 712 came in unusually drunk at two-thirty, managed not to puke in the foyer, an event that would have offended Luc to no end. Other than that, no one came or went until the residents started going to work. A boring night, really.

His car was in the underground garage, and there were wet spots and a bit of slush by the driver's side door. There was no other evidence of his being followed or watched. Some of the other spaces where vehicles had been parked earlier also revealed traces of melted snow, so he couldn't be sure if his car had been visited. He threw an overnight bag in and headed downtown, stopping at one of the large office supply stores to pick up a laptop.

HE CHOSE TO TRAVEL business class this time, flying straight through to Bucharest and not bothering to mitigate his jetlag by staying the extra day in London or Hamburg. It was noon when he arrived, and with no complications at customs, he hopped into a suicide cab that ignored all traffic lights as it took him straight to The Intercontinental. He grabbed a nap and forced himself awake at three o'clock. After a quick shower and a change of clothes, he headed off to the Ministry of Labor to see Katya.

Protocol dictated he contact Petruscu first, so he phoned him from the cab. The man picked up on the first ring, and Donovan's explanation for the unexpected visit was fluid and brief. He had forgotten one tiny security detail, and since he was in Hungary on business—practically next door—he felt obliged to swing by and tidy things up. Razvan was grateful, both for the visit and the lack of responsibility for yet another *delegati*. He was a busy man, and after all, Donovan had offered to take care of himself.

Donovan smiled as he rang off. It would have been a natural thing for Petruscu to confide in a security expert: his computer had been hacked, and he had lost a lot of money. But how to explain how the money had gotten there in the first place? "Between a rock and a hard place," Donovan murmured as he got out of the cab.

It should have taken a bit longer to enter the ministry without official papers, but the guard at the foot of the winding staircase recognized him and made that wonderful, sweeping gesture of the hand that could mean "Go away," or "Let him pass." In this case he assumed by the result it was the latter. He went up the stairs to the offices.

Nothing informal happens within the Ministry of Labor, or in fact, within any department or level of the government of Romania. So Donovan accepted that to get to see Katya, under normal circumstances, it would be necessary to chat with Razvan, the director. But in his absence, he would meet with the manager, Maria Cuza.

He knew her well from his first trip to Romania a year earlier. However, she had been out of the country two weeks earlier, in that instance in Australia on business. But she had now returned and greeted him at the office door as if they had met many times more than his brief visit a year ago.

"Mr. Donovan! Sean! Welcome back. What an unexpected surprise and a great pleasure, too, of course." She proffered each cheek to kiss and gave him a quick hug. She made him think that if he lived here, he would be on her list of preferred dinner guests, no matter the occasion.

Maria was about five feet, two inches, proportioned, handsome with chiselled features, a perfect complexion and a smile that seldom left her face. It was difficult to listen to her melodic voice and picture her managing an international operation, but he had been able to watch her with her staff a year earlier. He had been impressed by her insight. Every decision she took on his behalf was logical and above reproach. She turned to fetch a cup of coffee for her guest, and he took a moment to admire her two-piece suit, beneath which she wore a simple white blouse.

She brought over a coffee, softened with a hint of milk. He noticed her nails were trimmed back. "So. Razvan says this is a quick trip?" Her English was perfect. As they chatted, he noticed Maria kept one eye on operations through the director's glass wall.

Donovan replied. "Yes, but first, I have two gifts for you. Actually just one, but maybe the second item can be perceived as a gift. You be the judge." She smiled as he withdrew a plastic container from a gift bag.

"All the way from Montreal, Canada, I bring you one small cheesecake, still cold from the travel gel packs, and just big enough for you and your two daughters. But if you decide to eat it all before you get home this evening, I would understand."

Maria clapped her hands in glee. "You remembered I said Canadian cheesecake is the best kind! How thoughtful. Thank you, and yes, it may be difficult to save some for my daughters. But they are still my little girls even though they are all grown up, you know?"

Donovan reached into his oversized briefcase and pulled out a smaller one. "Well, the second gift isn't much of a gift. I brought along a laptop..." he cast a quick glance to see if her open smile had changed in any way, "which is actually for my work. I've programmed it to test your security systems once each week. I'll show Teresa how to synch it up to your servers, and it'll do the rest. But for the other ninety percent of the time, you could use it for your own work. I am leaving it behind after the project closes, so please consider it yours. You work every evening. Maybe this will be helpful. It has all of the office software you might need, plus an adaptor to convert electrical power to your system. What do you think? Might you have a use for this? Otherwise, it will just sit around the office waiting for Monday morning to chat with your servers for less than a minute." While she thought, he waited. *Their computers are four generations behind Canada's. Such an inexpensive gift would be so helpful to them, but they are proud. I hope she buys my excuse.*

"Thank you so much, Sean. You have been more than kind. I'm not sure if such a gift could be best used by me, or if perhaps it should be used by Petr. You have seen the equipment he is working with. I think maybe it will be Petr's, with me taking, of course, all the glory for his rise in productivity." She laughed so that several of her staff looked through the glass wall to see the reason for her levity.

The discussion with Teresa took only a few minutes, and Donovan had timed the length of his visit to correspond with the team's exit for the day. As they all headed down the staircase to the exit, Donovan swung in beside Katya, who gave him a megawatt smile.

"I didn't think you would be back so soon." She linked her hand into the crook of his elbow.

"I had a little bit of business to conduct. It's nice to be back. Left or right?" he asked as they exited the building and entered the last minutes of sunshine. They headed right, toward the bustle of the city center. As they approached a restaurant, he asked if she had time for dinner.

"Not tonight. My mother is expecting me in an hour or so." Her voice was tinged with regret. "Tomorrow?"

Donovan countered, "I'd like to speak with you about something. Do you have twenty minutes for me?" She nodded, and they went in.

They found a quiet spot near the back, and he ordered a couple of glasses of the house wine. He noticed Katya had a broad grin, and her eyes danced. "What?" he asked.

"You. That is what." Her smile broadened, and he took a second to admire this stunning young woman.

She continued, "You and I, we began to maybe take a special notice of each other the last time you were here. It's the same this time, but here it goes again." Her hands flew up in mock frustration. "Always I can't be available, or you have to fly away quickly. Do you know what I think?" She didn't pause for an answer. "I think you have a girlfriend at home, and you are too much the gentleman to fool around. Am I right?" She tossed a significant glance at him, nodding once to reinforce her guess."I say this in part because you seem...somehow different this visit. Warmer? Is that the word? I think warmer this time." She nodded again, confident.

He agreed with her. "Well, you're gorgeous. Who could blame me for falling in love with you? But it wouldn't be right, to see you if I have a girlfriend. However, I do think of you as a friend. That's okay, right?"

"Of course."

"Well, I need some help. I have a little project I need to accomplish while I'm here in Bucharest."

"Of course. If I can do anything..." She waited.

"The last time I was here, I met this Roma beggar. He always carried a little girl—a blonde toddler—on his hip wherever he went. Have you ever seen them?"

"Of course. They were always around *Le quartier Française*, not far from here. His family is named Purrum...it means onion...why, I do not know. But the boy was killed recently. Why are you asking about the Purrum boy? Do you know him? His family?"

"No, not really. I met him the day before his death, just briefly, but I feel, um, badly for the family. He—I heard he was always accompanied by the very young blonde girl, his sister, was it?" he questioned.

"Yes. Ana. Very dirty, but underneath all of the dirt, she is a very pretty girl. I bet she could be a child model, if she wasn't Roma."

"That would make a difference, being a Roma?"

"Yes. Of course. The Roma don't get hired to do real work. Almost never." She looked up from the table where she was wiping an imaginary spot from the table.

"I don't hate the Roma, believe me. I just have a difficult time when people beg, and they don't work even when most of them can work. Romania is a very poor country, and to fix this, everybody has to work. This is just my opinion, but it is how I feel. If you want to know more about the Purram, you should talk to Maria Cuzo. She knows a lot about the Roma families."

"Okay, tell me this. Do you think maybe, if the boy's family had some money, I mean a small pot of money set aside, do you think that would help them to get out of the begging business?" Donovan watched her smile, but it seemed this time to be tinged with an edge, since it didn't make it to her eyes.

"Sean, I am so sorry for what I am about to say because it may sound not nice, and for that matter, we don't usually talk about such things, but do you recall I said the boy's name was Purrum?" She leaned over the table and made her voice confidential. "In truth, there are many of them, and all of their names are Purrum, except for the girls who marry outside and leave. That is a big family. An extended family. And when the days get cold, maybe in a few weeks, the Purrum Roma will go to the Black Sea, or maybe the Mediterranean. They will stay in lovely homes, and they will bathe the child Ana, and she will be beautiful and warm—did you notice she is a healthy baby and not skinny? Next spring, Purrum will be back in the *Quartier Française* again, with black hands and faces, begging once again."

Katya's eyes were sad. "So, ten minutes ago you walked into this bar with a pretty girl, and I had romance in my brain. Instead you forced me to reveal to you that I am ugly and horrible inside. You will go home with that picture of me. You see? They were right. Do not tell outsiders about your culture. We have a saying: 'Families eat together because they know each other's food.' You don't know the Roma. It's not your fault. You are just a nice man from far away, trying to fix something that cannot be fixed. Because, you see, it is not broken."

Donovan noticed her eyes were glistening. She smiled and then asked him how his work had gone. His moment had passed. A few minutes later, she contrived an excuse to go, leaving him alone with his glass. As the restaurant door opened to let her out, he noticed a familiar figure leaning against a furniture repair shop, across the street. His eyes narrowed as he stood and then headed for the window beside the door. He could readily see the smaller brother, Janos. The man stared at Katya but didn't attempt to follow her and then, leaning on the building behind him, returned his attention to the restaurant. Dobra wanted someone else.

Donovan waited a moment or two and then left the restaurant, crossing the street. Katya was no longer in sight, but Janos was leaning against the building, smirking. His mouth was turned down into something cold, dangerous. He waited until Donovan drew up and then stood away from the building, attempting to be as tall as his small frame would allow.

"Mr. Donovan."

"Little boy murderer."

Janos shrugged. "He lived on the streets. He knew not to interfere with other people's business."

"You're still scum."

Again, Janos shrugged. "It is of no consequence to you." He smiled in satisfaction. "Do you know this is my city and not yours? You have just made a very bad error, Mr. Donovan, but we are fair, my brother and I."

Donovan's face lost its color. Remembering what he had done to the nose of Tomas, and knowing what the brothers were capable of, he grabbed the man by the lapels of his greasy jacket. "What have you done?"

"Oh, I haven't *done* anything." Janos bared his teeth. "But you know, my arm is still tender from having been cut. And my brother's face is quite uncomfortable, not to mention unattractive." He looked hard at the Canadian. "You, on the other hand, are reasonably healthy." He paused and smirked. "I wonder how your woman friend is, right this minute?

Donovan reached to grab him again, but the man stepped aside, putting up one hand.

"I wouldn't push things too far. Wait one moment, and you will see the woman. Ah! Here she comes now." Janos pointed to a wheezy grey Dacia that huffed up the street and came to a stop in front of them, his brother driving. "Get in, dog."

Donovan squeezed into the back seat, beside Katya.

"Are you all right?"

Katya nodded, her eyes wide. A bruise swelled across her cheekbone. She breathed in shallow gulps. Inside he raged, but the gun pointed an inch from his face prevented any action as the car sped away from the city core.

"Mr. Donovan, I know you have no gun on you, so sit back and make no moves. We have to go somewhere private, as we have something to discuss."

"Okay. Why don't you let this woman go, and we can discuss whatever you want."

"Come on. You think I'm stupid?" He looked over at his brother, who was concentrating on driving. "We will let her go...later. Now, shut up and don't act out."

Donovan knew they were going to be killed. He suppressed panic, willed his heart rate to drop, and thought of the only weapon at his disposal. In the toes of each of his shoes rested a pulse-powered, non-incendiary explosive device the size and shape of two pairs of peas. Three of the peas had a red dot on each, and together, they comprised the explosive part of the bomb. The fourth pea had a green dot on it. It was the detonator. He was confident he could slip off his shoes and retrieve the peas, but to set them off in the car would be suicide.

Not knowing what was to come, he had to decide where the explosion would be most effective, and yet not kill Katya and him. He decided he'd drop two of the red dot peas on the floor of the car and keep one pea, plus the detonator, in his back pocket. Over the next ten blocks he negotiated the movement of the peas out of his shoes and into his hand. He took pains to ensure which pea was the detonator, so he could drop the two bombs without looking at them. He motioned to Katya to talk to Janos, which she did in Romanian. Donovan assumed she was pleading for her life until the meaty, heavily-bandaged hand of Tomas swung backward, glancing off the side of her head. He straightened in his seat and continued on. Whimpering, Katya stopped talking while Janos laughed at her. At that moment, Donovan dropped two of the three explosive peas onto the floor and pocketed the remaining one, plus the detonator.

Donovan noticed the apartment buildings began to thin out, and they drove into an industrial area. A minute later, they passed through a fence whose chain link gate had rusted and fallen off. They drove to a side entrance and turned off the motor. It was silent for a moment, and then the brothers exited the car and hauled the two captives out as well. Donovan saw Janos grope Katya as he pulled her out of the vehicle and once again was overwhelmed by a sense of rage and utter helplessness.

As Tomas watched, Janos patted Donovan down and found nothing. When Janos once again began to feel Katya's breasts, Tomas cuffed him on the side of his head and cursed in a low voice. Unchastened, Janos hustled the captives into the factory.

Once inside, they crossed a dusty factory floor. The random slices of marble lying along the walls and in heaps of rubble suggested this was a marble processing plant. Everything, however, had fallen into disrepair, and the layers of dust revealed no one had worked here in a long time. Donovan noticed one spot in the middle of the factory where the dust was scuffed up. At the edge of the scuffmarks, he saw a dried rusty stain at the foot of the foreman's tower. *Dried blood? Have these two bastards been here before? More than likely.* The footprints of the group made fresh marks into the dust. They entered an office on the far side of the factory floor, and Donovan dropped his last remaining pea just outside the entrance to the room.

Tomas closed the door and pointing to a corner, growled in Romanian to Katya. She cowered and then hunkered down, back to where the two walls met. Making herself as small as her long legs would permit she waited, eyes averted. Tomas then approached Donovan, who stepped forward and got the first lick in, driving his fist as low into the abdomen as he could. It took the giant by surprise, and he grunted, doubling over. Donovan swung his left foot in a brutal Muay Boran strike that caught Tomas on his ear, dropping him to the ground. Before Donovan could do any additional damage, Janos smashed Donovan on the head with the barrel of his pistol, tearing a two-inch rip across the back of his skull.

He went down.

A minute later, his head stopped swirling, and he found himself curled up on the floor, a piece of Katya's sweater stanching the blood from the back of his head. A seated Tomas glared at him.

Janos began. "It's time to talk. You have something of ours, and we want it back. You have no idea of the harm we will do if you choose to be uncooperative. Do you understand?"

Donovan nodded, wincing at the pain in his head.

"Good, then. Okay. You have a passport belonging to Galen Attanasio, and we want it back. Do you have it on you?"

Donovan weighed his options. He had only one, and it was a desperate move that relied on both timing and luck. He looked over at Tomas, who now stood, and he knew the punishment would begin soon. "All right. Yes. I have it. It's at the hotel. One of you can go get it while the other watches over us. The key to my room is in my pocket, and you will find the passport inside one of my shoes in the closet."

He watched the brothers confer. A trickle of sweat slid down his back. *Why the hell did I mention shoes? It may give them ideas to search me again. Thankfully, I dropped all of the peas except for the detonator.*

Tomas finished speaking and approached Donovan. "Give him the key," Janos said, and Donovan handed it over. Janos continued in English, so Donovan could understand, but this time his words were for Tomas. "Phone me from the hotel if it isn't there, so I can kill the woman immediately."

Tomas headed out while Janos took a position near the door, his eyes trained on his captives. Donovan whispered to Katya to stand and then sit. Janos screamed at them to shut up and be still. The vein beneath his ear pulsed, and they knew they had pushed him as far as they could, but by then, Donovan had the detonator in his hand.

Donovan's plan depended on the reach of the detonator. The pea outside the door would go off, for better or worse. If the distance to the car was too great, the detonator wouldn't reach the impulse bombs he had placed on the floor of the car. He had been counting the time he guessed it would take for

Tomas to reach the car, and a few seconds before that imagined moment, he pointed to the door. "What was that?"

"What was what?" A nervous Janos broke out into a sweat. He backed up until he hit the wall and then slid over to the door while staring at Donovan. "Shut up!" It was whispered, and both his voice and the gun barrel trembled. Still facing his captives, Janos reached behind him, found the doorknob, and went to pull it open, but...at the last second, he froze.

Donovan, out of time, twisted the detonator and then covered Katya's head with his arm. The force of the single pea blew the door inward. Shards of glass and wood transformed into weapons that shot toward Janos. They ripped the clothes off his back and sent scores of glass fragments deep into his back, neck, and the back of his head. His body, now a projectile itself, flew across the room toward his captives, landing on Katya's legs. Deafened and shrieking, Katya pushed him off her, and she and Donovan staggered to their feet. Donovan picked up the pistol and hauled her through the dust and over to the foreman's tower.

And then they waited. Either the bomb in the car had worked, and their troubles were over, or Tomas had gone on his way to pick up an imaginary passport that was actually in Canada.

Or...

Or, he had heard the bomb go off in the factory and had returned to see what had happened. They waited some more. Nothing. Katya started to say something but quieted when Donovan put his hand over her mouth. After a moment, she nodded, and he dropped his hand. Another few seconds passed, and Donovan watched the door they had entered ten minutes earlier. *We will be sitting ducks if we stay here any longer.*

Tomas chose that moment to burst through the factory door, pistol waving and running at top speed toward the still-settling dust and the hole where the door had been. He screamed, "Janos, Janos!"

Donovan thought once again about his options and knew he had only one. He shot the giant through the heart as he approached the foreman's tower, and Tomas dropped right there, knees first, and then face, beside the dried, rusty stain.

THE POLICE WERE SYMPATHETIC at first and then very curious at the explanation of the explosive. Donovan wasn't very helpful. "Seriously, Inspector, I have no idea what kinds of explosives they were playing with. It was a complete surprise to me when the bomb went off. It must have been a booby-trap they set to clean up things after they got what they wanted. What did they want? It was obvious. Ransom. They wanted to kidnap a Canadian tourist, didn't they?"

Katya kept mum. She told Donovan she couldn't remember the name of the person whose passport was asked for. She told the police she, too, thought the kidnapping had something to do with a ransom. She had never met the two assailants. She just wanted to go home. When she left the station to be checked out at the hospital, she came over to hug Donovan.

"Thank you for saving my life, Sean. Thank you for getting into the car at the restaurant. Do I have anything else to worry about here?"

"No, both brothers are where they belong. They were just very bad people. It's all over now, Sweetie."

NEXT MORNING DONOVAN headed back to the Ministry of Labor. He entered the office and went straight to Maria's office. She greeted him at the door, and he brought up the incident. "About Katya, I am so sorry for what happened."

"Yes. She was checked over at the hospital, but I have, of course, given her the rest of the week off. She will be okay." Maria's forehead furrowed in worry. "They don't have any idea why it happened. Not a clue." She returned to her desk and sat, fiddling with a pen. "Are you all right, Sean?"

"Yeah, I'm fine. A little shaky and my head aches, but I am well enough to work."

After a few moments of small talk, he worked his way around to the point he needed to make. "Tell me about the Buchuresti Roma."

She smiled, still preoccupied by her employee's recent experience. "Such a long story to tell in ten minutes! What do you wish to know, Sean? I would like to think I know a fair bit about the Roma people, having studied them in school. Let's be honest. They are our neighbors, as different as they are from us. Do you know, for instance, where they came from originally? India. Yes! It's a long tale beginning from a great distance away. I am sorry. You wanted to ask me something about them?"

Donovan began again. "Well, do you know if some of them are wealthy? Do they stop begging when winter comes?"

"That's true. They do stop," she conceded. "I must say most of them are not around in the winter. But there are different possibilities and scenarios as to where they go. It is popularly thought they head for the Mediterranean to spend the large amounts of money they acquire from begging. Popularly thought," she repeated, her voice dry. "I suspect there is more truth to the second possibility—that they go somewhere warmer and beg there." She shrugged. "It seems probable to me. But either way, they are warmer and safer in the south than if they stayed begging in the Romanian winter. We have already lost our best weather, only bad things like snow and ice to come." She shivered and then smiled a cheerful smile. "What else do you wish to know?"

"Do you know the Purrams?"

Maria's face saddened. "Yes, the Purram family. They lost a little chap a few weeks ago. We called him Telal, or Old Clothes Man. He was very bold, this Old Man of the Forest. I knew him from a baby and his sister Ana as well. Such a shame."

"Did the newspapers say why he died?"

"Yes, it was horrible. They said he fell from a bedroom window and landed on a wrought-iron fence. It seemed odd to me. His family—he has no parents—stated he would have had no business in the house he supposedly fell from." She opened her hands and shrugged in resignation. "What can you do? There isn't even an investigation for the Roma. But why do you ask about this family?"

"Well, you know I was here at that time, and I have been treated very well by the Romanian people. I was just wondering if there was anything I could do for the little boy's family. What if I offered to sponsor the little girl, Ana?

Would they be offended? I could set up a college fund…support her at school here or in Canada, their choice."

Maria stood up and paced, her forehead creased. "My first thought is this is not necessary. However, it is not my decision to make. The Purram should of course be the ones to decide. I assume you wouldn't offer if you couldn't afford this? That's correct? Wonderful. So. Would you like me to speak with them? I could see what they think."

He nodded. "Do I have to worry about where the money will go, once they receive it? I could set up a trust fund, so it doesn't disappear over the years." He waited for her answer as she pondered the best response.

"A trust fund is always helpful to keep things absolutely clear. You should know they love their children, so they would in all likelihood do what is best for her. But they are relatively uneducated, so it's better to have a legal document stating this is to be used for Ana's education. That is simple, and simple is good.

"There is but one complication, Sean. The Roma do not have a culture of work or study, at least not in the way we think of those terms. I must caution you when the time comes for Ana to begin school, the family could be torn. How hard do they push her toward studies? Do they send her off to school? Will she be persecuted at that school if they find out about her heritage? They will think these things through, of course, but little Ana is a gypsy, a Roma. She has many proud generations of wanderlust in her blood, so which will win? On the one hand, she is tough, so she will be able to take any abuse her schoolmates can offer. But the wanderlust? I cannot say, Sean, but we can try.

"Will you be staying in Romania long? It may take one day, or it may take five before I get back to you." Maria paused. "You know, even if they agree, this could take time. Why don't you go about your business, go to Hungary, or wherever your work takes you, and I will let you know what they say." She offered a kind look, resting both hands on his forearm and giving a gentle squeeze. "This is beyond generous, to support someone whom you've only met once. May you be repaid twice what you offer, Sean."

HE ORDERED FROM ROOM service that evening and then went to the Romanian Athenaeum to take in a concert. It was billed as an evening of Strauss waltzes, and his intention was to disappear into the crowd and just...be. Once inside, however, he was overwhelmed by the sensuous frescoes covering the domed ceiling. Art blanketed the walls between the rounded beams arcing from the floor to the rounded theatre dome. Even the floor presented mosaics of musical iconography. Every seat was filled, and everyone wore their best clothes, each face graced with a smile. The seats surrounded the stage, embedding the George Enescu Philharmonic into the middle of the audience. The music began, and it was the orchestra that captured his senses. The look of the hall itself and the sound of the philharmonic were very complementary. *The word for it was "opulent" or perhaps voluptuous.* He'd bring Nadia here one day. He sat, drunk on the music until the final notes wove through the circular staircases leading out to the foyer. He was the last one out of his seat.

Chapter Sixteen

B *ack In Montreal*

Next morning he caught a flight back to Montreal and again went through an elaborate series of surveillance steps to ensure his apartment was clean. Satisfied, he caught up on his sleep and awakened mid-morning. He drove downtown, following the signs marked "Centre Ville" until he hit Outremont. Changing direction, he headed out to Boulevard St. Laurent—Saint Lawrence Boulevard. It wasn't difficult to park, find a quiet cafe, and choose a table by the street-side front window.

Donovan waited until the second cup of Greenwell Farms Kona coffee was served before he punched a familiar number into his cell phone. "Nadia? Hi, Sweetie. Yeah, I know. Wasn't supposed to call. I could tell you it's because I missed you too much," he grinned at her snort, "but no, I have a favor to ask. Do you have any talk show interviews coming up, you know, to sell your movie? Yes?" He shifted in his chair as someone squeezed past him. "Well, here's what I want you to do."

All that was left now was to wait for the show to air and see if his suggestion had the desired effect. He and Nadia took a minute to catch up, and then he turned his attention to a pair of omelette crepes. They were smothered with tomatilla salsa. Montagnolo triple crème cheese oozed from one end, and chives and red pepper jelly garnished the top.

Off went his phone, so he could enjoy his meal. Earlier, on the ride downtown, he had gotten a call on his Devin phone from someone who knew of his work. They mentioned something about the floor plans to a small art gallery in Boston. He interrupted the caller, saying it must be a wrong number. He had turned the phone off, and his Donovan phone was also retired for the day. He was alone, save for the weak sunlight that brought no warmth, and the indifferent passersby who had much to share with their companions as they strode by. But nothing, of course, for the man watching them from the cafe window.

What did Gaia, the Greek, want with him? Was it just the theft of a passport? *I must study it with more care once I get back to the apartment.* No, it had to have something to do with one of his last three jobs. And who was the man at Harrod's? Where was the connection?

He pulled out a notepad and began making lists, this time of the events surrounding the gigs. Once he'd finished his meal and started a third cup of Kona, he paid up, left the warmth of the cafe, and took a stroll along St. Lawrence Boulevard. As he walked, he tore little strips off his list, rolled them up, throwing them some down gutter grates.

The temperature had dropped, so he bought a sweater and wore it out of the shop, not having dressed well enough for the weather. Then he frittered away the afternoon, walking, thinking, walking some more. At five, he hit the gym at his apartment building and headed up for a shower. He hadn't contacted his sister Madeleine because there had been too much to think about. He called her now. Yes, she was fine. Would she like do go to dinner? Of course. Would David like to come with them? No? They were "on a break?" Okay, he would pick her up at seven for an early dinner. They'd go to Garde Manger, Chef Chuck Hughes's boisterous restaurant that was as famous for the dancing on the tables later in the evening as the amazing cuisine that could be found on them earlier. At seven o'clock, it would be much less exciting, which suited them both.

He met her at the corner of Rue Saint Francois Xavier, and they walked the half block of stone buildings to the restaurant. As usual, her greeting was unrestrained. He made a mental note to tell her he really didn't care for public displays of affection, but then reminded himself, as they walked arm-in-arm, he thought of that every time they met and then forgot all about it every single time. It was a weeknight, so getting a last-minute table this time had been possible. They slid into a corner.

Donovan noticed she was quite sombre and brought it to her attention. "Oh, stuff happening. Changes on all levels. I don't like changes, Sean, except in energy levels. I'm a big fan of excitement but not negative excitement, y'know?"

"Sounds quite vague, Madeleine. Got an example for me?"

"Well, isn't that just like life? Crazily, I have examples from all of my unique areas, believe me." She held out the slender fingers of her left hand

and began counting from the baby finger inward. "First, my love life. I no longer have one, since we've gone from 'on a break' to 'completely broken off.' I sort of mentioned to David it would be nice to see some sort of, I don't know, direction to his life. Not necessarily a job but maybe a direction toward a job. He said that maybe we weren't on the same page anymore, and I guess I agreed. Next thing you know, off he went, and I heard from Anne-Sophie he'd moved to Toronto. He's joining a band. For research, apparently. Bullshit. But hey, I was probably too old for him." She cast a weary, knowing glance toward her brother and held up another counting finger.

"Next up, my famous work life. Guess what? You'll never guess. I've taken up modeling. Yeah! Who knew? It's just catalog work, some of the other larger department stores. It's part-time, and I've kept my day job, but I must say it will be nice to have the extra money. Sean, where the hell does money go? You finish your week with a reasonably fat paycheck, and thirteen days later, you're eating cereal for supper. How does that happen? Man. Anyway, my new part-time job almost doubles my income if I don't get fired. And plus, the agency says they have lots of business for me. Apparently, I have a unique look, whatever that is. Frigging Quasimodo had a unique look, too. Whatever, I'll take it. So that change balances out the No-David-Anymore change.

"Third," she folded another finger, "I had a visitor at my work. Some foreign guy. I forgot about it until just now. He came into the office the day after I saw you last. He had an Italian accent, I think. He smiled a lot, and he was quite hot, I must say. He asked about you. That was kind of strange. Nobody asks about you, Seannie." Madeleine stopped chatting as the server deposited drinks and a shared appetizer.

Everything had gone very quiet within Donovan. He was overcome by that out-of-body sensation he had read about, of being in an operating room looking down on himself, watching as his life hung in the hands of strangers, his spirit drifting away from his dying body. He clutched the edge of the table, focusing on what he had just heard, with a horrible fascination. Madeleine reached over to sample the fish and chips-style fried calamari.

"This man," Donovan thought his voice didn't sound like his at all, "what did he look like? How old? His hair, did he speak quickly?"

"Yes, exactly! He did speak quickly. And his hair! Brother, that man had gorgeous hair. He'd be somewhere in age between you and me, tall and slender, had a melting smile which he used a lot, and he wore a corduroy jacket. Who wears corduroy anymore? These calamari rings, Sean, they're across the river and into the trees good." She dangled one that dripped chipotle tartar sauce in front of him. A single drop hit the bare table, ruining everything.

"Did he say anything specific?"

"Nothing much. He said he was a friend of yours and asked if you were out of town. I told him I have never kept track of you and had no clue if you were even coming back. He said 'coming back from where?' so I said New York. He thanked me—he was very polite—and he left. So is that strange? Probably not, right? Not as strange as me getting a modeling job, right?" She tugged the appetizer plate closer and began to show her appreciation for the seafood.

FIRST THING THE NEXT morning, Donovan made his way to Concordia. No, Professor Umbra wasn't in. He had a family emergency and had returned to his home in Bucharest. Not Italy? No, he and his wife Stefania were gone to Romania for the rest of the semester. He would be returning after Christmas break.

Donovan walked away puzzled. Weren't all of Roberto's ties to Italy? What was the tie to Romania? There was none. But if there was, did it take him to the Etruscan cup? Or to Gaia? It seemed like it had to be one or the other. It also seemed like things were closing in on him.

WHAT TO DO? DONOVAN had felt panicky only a few times in his life. He knew how vulnerable he had made Katya, and now Madeleine and Nadia were in danger. Two of the most important people in his life—the only important people in his life—and he didn't have a clue as to how to keep them safe. He had one option. If the mountain wouldn't come to him, he'd have to go to the mountain.

Chapter Seventeen

A *Cell Phone Call From Montreal to New York*
"Hello. Mr. Attanasio? Yes, it's Evander. Everything went well in London. I made sure he saw me at least twice in different settings and then followed him to Canada. No sir, he didn't see me here but left clues around to make him know he's being watched, as instructed. I placed some slush on the ground beside his car, but unfortunately I couldn't leave a puddle outside his window on the balcony. Yes, sir, I'll tell you why in a moment. As for him, I couldn't get close enough to place a GPS on him. Nico will have to track him the old-fashioned way in New York. Oh, he'll go to New York, for sure. He's getting upset, I can tell. I know, the tracker would have been helpful, I suppose, but what can I do?

"Well, everything else is going well, except I cannot seem to get into his apartment to grab the item you sent me for. If it's even there. Since we don't know for sure, Nico will need to keep track of him in New York. I don't know! It seems he has this male friend, or associate, or house sitter. I don't know that either. The man won't leave the apartment."

Evander listened for instructions. "All right. I enter the apartment and kill whoever is there and find the item. If it is there, and if it is secured, I leave it alone until Donovan returns with you to get it. Okay.

"So you'll meet me here in twelve to eighteen hours. Okay. I'm powering off this phone now. No phone contact until you walk through Donovan's door with him. You will leave the place with the item. I'll take Donovan from there. *Ta leme*. Later."

Chapter Eighteen

M *ontreal to New York to Montreal*
Sean Donovan was beginning to put the pieces together—Gaia in the airport in New York and Umbra visiting his sister. Someone hanging around his apartment. It occurred to him these were indicators of a lack of caution on his part. Did he sign up for one job too many? Taking the passports wasn't wise, in hindsight. Something else occurred to him. If someone like Gaia wanted him dead, he would already be dead. Something else was going down, and the most probable scenario was Gaia wanted something he had; maybe the passport, maybe the cup. But if not, then what? Umbra's presence pointed to the chalice. Damn! Was it his toss-off comment about the bucchero cup being a mere copy? Umbra didn't seem concerned about Donovan keeping the original. Then what? If he could maybe get himself into the neighborhood of whoever was after him, perhaps he could find out, maybe even manipulate the situation to his advantage.

He was concerned, though. If they knew about Madeleine, he was certain they knew about Nadia. How could he keep them safe? Their value as trade bait seemed obvious to him. If he was being targeted by Gaia, his situation looked a little bleak. Gaia had all the resources a hundred million dollars could offer. That was a lot of resources. And, if Gaia wanted to send a legion of hit men out to get him while he hid somewhere near the ends of the earth, well, he could do that. It seemed his only real choice was to return to New York, kick up some dust, make a little noise. See what, or who, came out of the woodwork.

He decided to again stay at the Wingate, not far from Penn Station. His half-assed plan was to surface, make some kind of fuss, and see who turned up. It made sense to appear in places he had been to before—the Wingate, mid-town Manhattan, the Garment District. He had stayed here before, so maybe he could let it be obvious he was making himself available. It was less of a trap and more of a coin toss, but to be honest with himself, he wasn't so sure how to proceed otherwise. It seemed, he thought, that his *modus operandi* all along had been to enter unannounced, do his dirty deed, and then disappear, wiping off fingerprints and erasing footprints behind him. This time the cat had been let out of the bag. Donovan's business card had been found, so to speak, and he was up to his hairline in unfamiliar territory.

He had chosen to stick within the Garment District. After dinner, he found a place not too far from his hotel to grab a drink. It was one of those bars that suffered from a personality disorder. It was evident it wanted to be a sophisticated, urbane purveyor of cocktails and martinis, but the businessmen in the area who frequented the bar insisted it was really a beer lounge. So by way of a concession, management had displayed, among the swish chrome-and-glass design hardware, little signs on each table that offered three beers for the price of two. Under ordinary circumstances, this dichotomy offended Donovan's principles of order, but this evening he didn't care. He just wanted a drink, so Shaken, Not Stirred was as good a bar as any in which to think. He did, however, take a quick look around, and slide the little cardboard beer sign onto the floor under his table.

And there he sat, thinking, alone among seven million people, staring into the deep red within a glass of Cote du Rhone. He knew no one in the bar, and no one knew him, as far as he could tell. But in light of recent events, he imagined a shoulder holster inside the jacket of every man in the bar. At one point, an over-dressed woman stopped by his table and asked him if he'd like some company. She was his age, didn't wear much makeup, and didn't need it. Everything about her spoke of money, and he was curious as to why she would hit on a stranger in a New York bar. A chance comment left him with the impression she was not a hooker but had, in fact, been stood up by her date. Either way, he wasn't in the mood for sex, or sad he-done-me-wrong conversations, so he shrugged off her overture. Sometime after eleven, he left the bar and headed back toward West Thirty-fifth. The chill autumn weather had moderated, so he walked the few blocks back to the hotel.

Donovan was within sight of his hotel when an ash-grey limousine pulled up right beside him. The passenger side rear window rolled down, and a voice invited him to step in. The very large man who appeared at his left elbow encouraged him into the vehicle with a firm hand on his shoulder and a slight push that seemed difficult to resist. Next thing, he was in the car, sitting beside Galen Attanasio, famous Greek multimillionaire playboy. The limo pulled away from the curb and accelerated in the direction away from the Wingate.

"Mr. Koulos. You are a hard man to get hold of." It didn't sound like a question, so Donovan didn't reply. Gaia continued, "Koulos. Sounds Greek to me." He stared at the back of the driver's seat. "You don't look Greek. Perhaps you were adopted?" His English was effortless, with a trace of an accent.

Gaia leaned over toward him, close enough to enfold him in cloying, vanilla cologne. Gaia was a large man, six feet tall, and well over two hundred and forty pounds. It seemed obvious he had been very handsome years earlier, but his eyes were now sunk in fleshy softness. They carried a perpetual weariness. Everything else from cheek to gut had also softened—everything but his intentions. Gaia spoke again, his voice audible, but just so. "So are you, Mr. Koulos? Are you a hard man to get hold of?"

"Really? I wouldn't have thought that of me. It was easy enough for you to find me in a crowded airport and later on a busy New York sidewalk." Donovan faced Gaia. "I would have thought folks like you had armies of staff to do that kind of surveillance." He noted the direction in which they were travelling and realized he wasn't being blindfolded. That could be a good thing or a very bad thing.

Gaia smiled without warmth. "Right, right. You're the kind of man who nobody sees, even though you are out in the open. The Invisible Man. You pick up things lying around, and nobody sees you because you have arranged for them not to be looking for you. It's your, your 'shtick.'" He mouthed the word as if he had never used it before. It sounded distasteful, coming from him. The lines on his forehead deepened. "As for the airport, well, I like to take care of all of the business personally affecting me. If I have an unpleasant task to perform in, say, Montreal or Budapest, I'll go there myself. If my hands get dirty, I can always wash them."

The big man settled deep into the leather seat. "Do you have your passport? No? Then we will have to go back to the hotel to fetch it. Donald, please return to the Wingate. We have to fetch Mr. Koulos's passport. How inconsiderate of him, Donald, not to have anticipated our desire to leave the country." The driver made a series of left turns, and once again, Donovan was headed in the direction of the Wingate.

On the way to the hotel, he ventured a question or two about their destination and what it was Gaia sought, but the Greek ignored him, instead using his smartphone to text. Donovan sat back on the soft black leather, studying everything around him.

The bodyguard who had encouraged him into the limo accompanied Donovan up to his room. Just before they left the limo, the bodyguard made a point of opening his jacket to reveal a lethal-looking semi-automatic Turkish Akdal Ghost. Donovan's inquiry as to whether he should check out of his room received no response, so he didn't bother to pack. He grabbed his Devin Koulos passport—his real one was already in his jacket—and picked up his cell phone. The bodyguard shook his head no and then took the cell phone from him, powered it down, and laid it on the windowsill of the hotel room, just behind the drapes. He then gave Donovan a cursory pat down, and a few moments later, they were back in the limo and off to JFK.

But they weren't.

Instead, the limo headed north and drove for an hour without Gaia uttering a word. He spoke once to Donald the driver, requesting classical music. Once the suburbs began to open up a bit, the limo eased onto a secondary highway, and soon after they approached the general aviation area of an upstate airport. An executive jet waited on the tarmac. Once they were in the air, Gaia became chatty once again. They were powering along in a Dassault Easy Falcon, a comfortable executive ten-seater. "It's usually for business, but you can imagine I quite enjoy traveling this way." He swept his arm, as if to present the plane's interior. "It beats going by train, that's for sure, and the air conditioning is always just right for me." He laughed as if that was the richest joke in the world.

"So, where are you taking me, Mr. Attanasio?"

Gaia paused. "Montreal, Mr. Koulos. We are going to visit your apartment. You have something I want." The look on his face revealed his curiosity. "You know, you haven't resisted in any manner. So you are not, at this stage being kidnapped, hey? You are my guest! I wanted to point that out." He gestured for a drink. "Some wine, Mr. Koulos?" He raised his voice. "Nico. A glass of pinot noir for my guest. He prefers Australian."

He took a sideways glance at Donovan. Two drinks arrived, and Gaia took the one that had been poured into a Glencairn whiskey glass with a couple of whiskey stones resting on the bottom. Out of deference to the act of flying, Donovan supposed, his Reidel crystal wine glass had no stem. It nestled in his hand as if custom designed for it.

As he studied the bottom of his glass, Donovan wasn't feeling very optimistic about this turn of events. He knew very well there would be few opportunities to influence the outcome of the next two hours. Right now, the only possible way to gain the advantage would be to overpower Gaia, Donald the chauffeur and the bodyguard, Nico. His only weapon was a stem-less wineglass. He settled deeper into the creamy leather seat, thinking about his attempt to draw Gaia's attention. *Be careful what you ask for.*

Having nothing by way of a weapon, he thought perhaps a better understanding of the situation would be helpful. He looked over to his host. "So, Mr. Attanasio. What do you want, really? It can't be money. You have so much already."

The big man looked annoyed. "Are you a child? Mr. Koulos, you can never have too much money. That's a naïve thought, and I don't for a minute believe you to be naïve, but that is incidental to your question. No, there is something else I want. I want the golden bucchero chalice. My grandfather received it for his efforts in Italy in 1943. Afterward, it was stolen from him by some escaping Romanian prisoners of war, and it seemed at the time to have left the face of the earth.

"Next thing you know, my people in Bucharest heard of the cup resurfacing in Montreal. Some petty thief—you, as it turns out—found a way to steal it back from the Romanians. How did you do that, by the way?

"And as you can imagine, I desired to get it back. It is a matter of pride. It's nothing against you. You're just a pawn as even you must appreciate. I should thank you, but I won't, since in reality you weren't acting on my behalf. But I am grateful for the circumstances that have placed the cup within reach. I must say, it's exciting to think I am an hour or two away from retrieving it. Of course, I also want my passport back. It is less important, but still..." he shrugged.

"Mr. Koulos, I'm telling you this to explain why under these circumstances you should be in less danger than one might think. This is another reason why you should just go along with me, compliantly, and let me have my way. Hell, I almost feel like paying you a commission. Of course, I won't, but it did cross my mind." He bellowed a roar of pleasure.

Donovan paused to consider what he'd just heard, setting aside for the moment the fact that Gaia appeared to think the chalice wasn't a replica.

"Okay, that makes sense. But why all the mayhem in Bucharest? This could've been such a simple transaction. I go to the palace, grab the goods, and I go home where you could've bought it from me. There was no need to murder a little boy, let alone a British government official. Was that just to make things interesting?" He hoped if he could rile the Greek, something useful might slip out.

The corner of Gaia's mouth turned down, but his voice remained unperturbed. "Ah. The street urchin. Who on earth would care two cents' worth of salt for a nameless beggar boy and a gypsy at that? But I'll answer you anyway. He was in the wrong place at the wrong time. The first thing is he met you. That alone makes things messy. Nobody likes witnesses walking around, willing and able to sell their thoughts to anyone who wants them. You have heard the expression 'knowledge is power'? He knew things. And that was not acceptable." Gaia sat back in his seat, took a sip and continued.

"But far worse, he ran afoul of one of the men I own, as well as our Mr. Edward Yorke. Yorke was busy scooping up lots of money for me when the beggar boy was interviewed by a Romanian program officer. He told the official that his family, who were supposed to receive scholarships from the grant money Yorke administered, never received a *sou* from the agency set up by Yorke. As you can imagine, this was about to spark an investigation. The agency would not stand up to scrutiny. So I was very reluctantly obliged to send in more of my staff to tidy things up."

"The brothers with the shared apartment."

"That's right. Tomas and Janos Dobra, who, by the way, would have been under the employ of our Mr. Petruscu, who I understand has also made your acquaintance. Employed by Petruscu, that is, if they hadn't met an untimely death recently." Gaia glanced sideways at Donovan. It was a serpent's flicker.

"Now, before we go any further, please be aware there are no ties that connect me to them or vice-versa. At least, there will be none once I get my passport back. No souvenir for you, Mr. Koulos, I need my passport. No evil plans to implicate me, if you find yourself wandering around free after this, as you well might."

Donovan didn't believe this for an instant. To do so would be folly. Gaia knew of the fate of Tomas and Janos. Would there be repercussions? Of that, Donovan was certain. Events were drawing in around him. Despite having been reminded the possession of knowledge was dangerous, as far as Gaia was concerned, Donovan had to press further. "And Edward Yorke? Why did you kill him?"

Gaia's shoulders relaxed, and he shrugged, averting his gaze. "I do not really know much about that one. Perhaps it was the Romanian police who killed him. They are all bastards, you know. Anyway, I'm bored by this. That is enough. I have things to do." He pulled out his smartphone and began texting again.

THEY MADE A QUICK WORK of Customs, and in no time, Donovan found himself in front of another limo. "Does your ass ever touch anything but leather?" he asked Gaia with some asperity as Nico the bodyguard, Donald, Gaia, and he climbed in. The big man just smiled without looking up and continued texting as Donald pulled away from the Montreal airport.

Finally, the man put down his phone and stared at Donovan. "Don't you find this a very unique situation? I still do, after a lifetime of interesting adventures. When I was young, I could not conceive of encouraging a stranger like you to fly to Montreal to give me something that, I'm sure, you do not want me to have." He waved a hand as if to dismiss the gravity of the situation. "Do you know this quote? 'Behind every great family is a great crime.'"

"Fortune," Donovan muttered.

"I beg your pardon?" Gaia leaned towards his captive.

"It goes, 'Behind every great fortune.' Balzac used the word 'fortune.'"

Gaia frowned and then laughed. It came out as a great roar. "You know, I have always heard it my way, but the way you say it makes more sense. Now, with my family, it makes sense either way, so why would I question it? You see, our family fortune has its roots in the Second World War. My grandfather was helpful to the Nazis. He would identify the whereabouts of several of a country's great art pieces, Italy for example, and his reward would be to retain some of the smaller ones. His career is not so different from yours, Mr. Koulos. He was born poor, educated himself, and vowed to extricate himself from the morass of poverty by whatever means necessary. The Nazis would ship him to various occupied countries to perform similar business. Turkey, Romania, Allies, foes, it didn't matter. He was in Italy, for example, until 1943."

Gaia's voice became animated. "Then one day at the beginning of 1944, he disappeared and turned up in France, fighting for the French Resistance. You see, he could smell the winds of change." He touched the side of his nose. "It was time to choose another side.

"He went to school in Paris after the war, learning more about art. He opened up a small gallery, 'discovered' the odd Greek painting, the occasional Romanian artifact, the very rare Turkish gold piece. He became very rich and then doubled these riches. He seemed to those who followed his activities to be very fortunate, very lucky in turning up these small, exquisite pieces, always from Greece, Turkey, Romania, and Italy. And always, I heard the story of the cup." Gaia winked, counting the countries off on his fingers.

"In the eighties, when I was younger, there was a fuss from one of the countries, but by then all trails leading from these artifacts and sundry pieces to my grandfather had gone cold. Besides, when on those rare occasions the trail of a piece seemed to lead to my father, my grandfather having passed on, the family's considerable fortune paid for a tender war story of this French Resistance fighter and impoverished artist who had built a new life in France. And since my family owns many newspapers across Western Europe, it wasn't difficult to have the story we wished to see splashed across the headlines of an accusing country. Now, let me ask you, who can resist such a romantic ending?"

"Why are you telling me this?"

Gaia eyes locked with Donovan's, and his lips thinned until they all but disappeared. "Because that is why my ass always touches leather." He offered a small, sly glance toward his guest. "Because it's what I want. My grandfather took advantage of a situation, showed tremendous courage, and I am the grateful recipient of his efforts. I suppose I must take care to avoid traveling to those four countries, but isn't that a small price to pay to be me? You of all people surely understand."

Donovan said nothing. He knew no good would come from rousing the ire of someone who held your fate in his hands. The limo slowed and then pulled into the parking lot beside Donovan's apartment building. It glided past a moving company cube van parked at the corner of the building and pulled up to a spot at the very back of the exterior parking lot. Donald turned off the motor, and all was quiet.

Gaia turned to his guest, studying him for thirty seconds. "We are going into your apartment. You, me, and Nico. If you act up, Nico will break your neck, and we will take what we want anyway. If you don't, you may actually live. I don't necessarily want a messy international ending to this. I just want what I want. It's like the leather seats. I always, always get what I want. At this moment, I don't want you to die, but I may change my mind. Do you understand? I hope you do. Just understand this." A strong hand struck him on the side of his head. "One errant move, one twitch, and you will fly out the window of your own apartment. Now, get out."

The three men entered the building, passing a less-familiar face at reception. "Where's Luc?" Donovan asked the young woman. She shrugged. Nico's hand gripped his elbow, and he felt a sharp twinge in reward for his inquisitiveness. As they passed the young woman, Gaia murmured Luc had received an unexpected cash bonus and had chosen to visit his girlfriend in Sherbrooke today. It was at that point Donovan understood he might be out of his league. This was a level of thoroughness he could never match. They marched down the corridor to his apartment door.

The next moments became a blur. Nico, who entered first, took three muffled shots to the heart and was on his knees in the doorway, already dead, one hand affixed to the door jamb. The compact stain on the front of his white shirt spread outward from the one tiny hole in his chest. The man's back, however, revealed a crimson stain the size of a softball. Gaia made a frantic grasp for his pistol but was slammed so hard from behind he tumbled over the bodyguard and lay sprawled on the floor with two Romanian agents standing over him, silencers just inches from his shocked face.

Donovan heard a familiar voice murmur in his ear, "Let's step inside, shall we?" The small group entered the apartment, each stepping around the bodyguard and out of reach of Gaia. Not knowing what else to do, Donovan sat in a nearby chair, watching and waiting as Roberto Umbro closed the door behind him.

"Good work, gentlemen. Let's have Mr. Attanasio sit on this kitchen chair, and yes, pat him down well. Let's be thorough, no mistakes, no second pistol. Tie him for the moment. Is the limo secured as well? Yes? Good." He sat on a nearby chair and nodded toward Donovan. "So, you're probably wondering what the hell is going on." He looked over to Gaia. "And you, you are wondering about your poor late friend Evander. I can tell you both some things in just a minute."

He spoke a few quick words in Romanian to the two agents, who then left the room and returned with a hand cart carrying a large wooden box into which they placed the unfortunate Nico. Roberto produced a pistol with a silencer, which he pointed at Donovan. "I apologize for the gun. This scenario looks so desperate I feel obliged to deter you from taking any extraordinary steps which I assure you are unnecessary. If I point this gun at you, you will not try to jump me and get yourself killed."

"You're very considerate of me," Donovan muttered, which elicited a hearty chuckle from Roberto.

"Well, I like you very much. You really would be welcome at my table under other circumstances. Anyway, this ended well," Roberto continued, his tone cheerful for the gravity of the scene before him. "The problem is contained, the two most dangerous individuals have been dispatched, the prey has been captured, and you, my friend Sean, are unharmed. This is great. All that's left is cleanup, which will hopefully also go well. Um, there's one other thing, though." His voice carried an apologetic tone. "I have to ask you for something. May I have the passports and the tape, please? No, don't get up for the moment. Just indicate where I can retrieve them."

Umbra followed his captive's gaze toward a tall black lacquered chest with a hammered bronze Asian latch mechanism. Roberto waited until one of the Romanian agents finished with Gaia and could cover Donovan with his pistol. Then Roberto stepped over to the cabinet. Just before opening it, he turned back to Donovan. "Will I be harmed by opening this, Sean? No?

You know this gentleman will kill you if I am harmed? And really, you haven't had the taped conversation long, it's just a trinket at this point, hardly worth your life to protect, am I right? Great, here I go, then."

Roberto opened the chest and swung the door wide, wincing when it bumped against the wall. With the care of a surgeon, he pushed aside the first item, a derringer. Resting against the back of the cabinet was a pebbled glass box filled with artifacts. Umbra peered through the pebbled glass at the arcana resting within the box. "Okay, what's that?" He stepped aside, so Donovan could see the object he was pointing at.

Donovan glanced into the cabinet and noted the object he was pointing to. "It's a monkey's paw. You shouldn't play with it or even handle it. It's not nice."

One of the Romanian agents said something to him in a low voice, and Roberto nodded. "That's the beast that got Tomas. It's nasty. You have a nasty side to you, Sean. Okay, so where is the conversation? Ah, here it is." He turned from the bowels of the cabinet to face Donovan, holding up a small reel of tape. "It's this one, right?"

"That's the one. What do you need that for?"

Without saying anything, Roberto took out a disposable lighter and burned the celluloid ribbon in a ceramic bowl. He then slipped Attanasio's passport into his jacket pocket and turned to Donovan. "I'm sorry, old man, but it had to be done." He returned to the center of the room and sat down, ignoring the man tied to the kitchen chair. Donovan noted the pistol with the silencer was still pointed in the general direction of his gut.

"Are you ready for another story, my friend? First of all, might I say your sister is very lovely, very nice, and she cares about you. You may rest assured she's as safe as anyone can be—at least safe from us. Okay. The passports. The unlucky Edward Yorke stole some passports while trying to be clever. Thieves, yes? They always want a little more than they can safely steal, no offense to you.

"At any rate, he had the brothers Janos and Tomas steal a number of passports, including Gaia's, which is how Yorke got himself murdered. It was ironic because Gaia had made a rare visit to Hungary, and we almost got him there. Edward Yorke had gone to meet with Gaia and had somehow managed to nab the man's passport, but that was as close as we came to grabbing the big fish. Doesn't that take a lot of nerve, to steal a passport from your boss?

"Anyway, it gets more complicated. Somehow, the little Roma boy ended up with the passports, and Gaia hired Tomas and Janos to get them back. It got messy, and for whatever reason, they ended up killing both Yorke and later the boy, that night in the rain. They got back the passports, the same passports you later grabbed. We couldn't implicate Gaia in the murder because we needed to keep things quiet if we were to have another go at him.

"Now, do you recall me telling you about our friend Preston Host? And do you recall his propensity to tape everything, useful or not? It transpires that in his role as a government official, he taped more than just Marilyn Monroe, the president, and Fidel Castro, which is valuable to some but of no consequence to us. This Mr. Host also sat in on a meeting between our then head of state for Romania and one of our spies who at the time was working in the United States. In that conversation, our head of state revealed his intention to have Romania work in concert with other communist countries to seek to undermine the United States, including the assassination of the president. Imagine the impact of such a statement, foolish though it was, given it was recorded a few months before JFK was, in fact, assassinated."

Roberto pulled up a stool from the bar and lit a cigarette. "While this is merely some historical fact for you North Americans, it is a painful embarrassment to my people, so when we discovered the tape's existence, we had to retrieve it and make it go away forever. But..." Roberto wagged a finger, "we couldn't really go to the United States to rob an old man. Better to, erm, encourage someone to get it for us. So sorry, my friend."

"Okay, I get that, but why destroy the whole thing? You could've just separated the tape into two conversations and given me my part back."

Roberto eyed him with genuine humor. "Are you serious? I save your life, I have the opportunity to erase all of the evidence of my visit..." he opened the palms of his hands to sweep the room with a grand gesture, "including you, might I add, and you complain about a few dollars? Sean," his tone was that of a mentor chastising his apprentice, "we can't have any stories floating around, can we? What's more, you don't see me asking for the money back from the blackmailing of my agents for Mr. Yorke's passport, do you? You should cut your losses, my friend."

Donovan looked over to where Galen Attanasio sat. "What about him? How did I get involved in this? I didn't know him until I got hold of his passport, and passports get lost all the time. Why would a lost passport be important?" The agents had boxed up the bodyguard and were donning moving company coveralls.

Umbra smiled and chided, wagging a finger. "How did you get involved in this? Please don't sell yourself as an innocent, my friend. You walk into a government scam run by a powerful multimillionaire, steal a hundred thousand dollars from one of his agents—not to mention his passport—kill two of his employees, and create a shambles of his Romanian operation. No, not so innocent.

"To answer your question, however, the passport had a smudge of blood—an obscured thumbprint on it. Janos had marked the passport with Edward Yorke's blood in a blackmail attempt. It was too clumsy to work, but it did tie Gaia to crimes in Romania. This wasn't acceptable to Gaia." Roberto glanced at his bound captive then back at Donovan. "You would be wise to forget you've ever seen him. Don't ask. Above all, don't tell." Roberto's face took on a severe look. "He murdered Edward York as soon as their relationship soured, or his people did. That caused us a lot of trouble. Further, he has stolen so many of our Romanian artifacts we cannot possibly recover them through diplomacy. It's time to take graver steps. Again, forget all of this, my friend."

Donovan thought of another point that had puzzled him all along. "You're Italian, right? So, what's the connection between you and Romania?"

Roberto's good humor returned. "Ah, yes, how am I Romanian?"

Donovan had a thought and interrupted, "Stefania is that Transylvanian chick. The one in your story whose father worked in the palace warehouse!"

Roberto smiled. "Yes, she is my Transylvanian *chick*. I left her in August, but I returned to her in October that year. I'd fallen in love with her and her country. We moved to Bucharest shortly afterward, and I soon went to work for the Romanian government as a spy, even as I continued my education. I work for the university in Bucharest to this day, although I kept dual citizenship with my mother country, Italy. And as you've discovered, I'm a visiting professor at Concordia for the school year." The conversation was interrupted by the return of the two Romanian agents, who had brought a second wooden crate, which they placed in front of Gaia.

Roberto Umbro stood and stubbed out his cigarette, closing the conversation. The two agents first taped the Greek's mouth and his feet at the ankles. They then helped him into the crate and nailed it shut as Roberto oversaw. Gaia had not uttered a word between the time his bodyguard was shot and his mouth was taped. Roberto put away the pistol and gave a brief salute as the men left, closing the door behind them.

Sean Donovan stood alone in his living room, staring at the small pool of blood that had gathered beside the hall stand. He watched the blood track outward to follow the grout lines across the tumbled marble tiles of the foyer.

Chapter Nineteen

New York City
All Souls Day

"Seriously? You cooked this for me?" Nadia brought Donovan a glass of Kim Crawford Pinot Noir. She leaned over to smell the wok filled with pad Thai. They had borrowed an actor friend's apartment in Chelsea, and it was the first time they'd met since Donovan's trip to Montreal.

"We're alone here, and I can't eat it all by myself." He kissed her neck and then, placing his hands on her hips, eased her aside, so he could spoon a dollop of sweet Thai chili sauce into the wok. He filled a pair of ramekins with crushed peanuts and rested chopsticks atop each.

"Okay, time to take stuff over to the table. I'll hand you the food. We'll start with a watermelon tomato salad with feta and basil, drizzled in aged balsamic vinegar and olive oil. After that we'll move on to the pad Thai, and for dessert, we'll have something really sweet and delicious, like you, to take the chill off. It's called Poor Man's Pudding; kind of a pineapple upside down cake, hold the pineapple, but made with maple syrup. If I can get it to you while it's still warm, it would be reason enough for you to stick with me forever. Basic ingredients, but decadent."

"That sounds amazing. So when are we going to get caught up on all of your recent adventures? Can you tell me anything about your trips to Romania, Montreal, and who you met? And frankly, I need your final assurance you're retired. Come. Let's sit down and chat."

"Can't sit down for another ten seconds, love, pad Thai waits for no man. We can chat in a moment." Finishing up the last of the cooking, he moved over to join Nadia at the table, sitting beside her. Their view was through a fifth storey bay window overlooking Central Park. Donovan toasted her, and then he told her everything.

He finished, and Nadia was quiet, taking it all in. "So the guy who was after you is gone? Where?"

"Just gone." He didn't elaborate. "We may read about him in the news, or we may never hear about him, other than he's disappeared. We'll see."

"And the tape is gone?"

"Actually, that was my only worry. These are really professional people. They stood a good chance of knowing we had made that copy in Brooklyn. But here's the thing. They seem to have anticipated everything, and as I thought of it, they had already dealt with it. After they left, I went to a payphone and called J.D. to see if he was okay and if the tape was still there. He was, and it was. So the Romanian agents may have slipped up because I had J.D. edit out the additional piece they were worried about and told him what to do with the JFK part of the tape. It's gone now." He took another sip.

"Gone?"

"Well, you know of Nadia's Challenge? You know." Sean smiled. "Nadia's Challenge to make me a good guy, or at least a better guy."

"Ah. *That* challenge. I'm so sorry. I regret laying that on you, Sean. I almost got you killed."

"Not at all. People make their beds, and then they lie in them. I made that call when I was sixteen, and then years later, I met you at the same time as I was sick of old me. So it's not on you, it's on me a hundred percent. Anyway, back to Nadia's Challenge. Your challenge. Do you remember precisely what it was?"

"Sure—three wrongs make a right. I wasn't serious about that part—don't tell me you managed to achieve it?"

"You be the judge. First, the chalice. It was a copy, planted for me, so the Romanians could get me to steal it and tease out the attention of Gaia, knowing he's a hands-on guy when it comes to family business. But the payday was real. Anyway, I put the money for that job into a scholarship for the Roma boy Telel's sister, Ana. You remember, the little boy who was murdered? His little sister. I got a business acquaintance who is a friend of that family to administer it.

"Here's the only difficult part of the whole Romanian incident." He told her of the events leading up to the explosion in the marble factory, taking pains to reveal his fears for Katya if he had let the two brothers live to continue to wreak havoc in Bucharest.

Nadia was quiet for a moment, pondering this revelation. "I see. It seems to me your hands were tied, and after you killed two murderers, people are safer over there." She set the confession aside. "Okay, let's hear how you solved the next one—the case of the stolen necklace of the beautiful and talented actress!"

Donovan looked at her. "I'm going to have to give you that one, Sweetie, since you're actually beautiful and talented. Okay, so you're already aware of how the necklace job went. A couple of weeks ago, you recall me asking you to make a statement on one of your interviews? Well, as soon as you did that interview where you'd announced your necklace stolen from the set of your London movie, you took half of Katie's pleasure away, since it's clear you're aware it's gone. Her only pleasure is the knowledge she has the original necklace which, as you know, she doesn't, since I gave it to you. She's got the fake." He picked up his wineglass, and they touched the bowls in salute. "And you always have the option of rattling your jewelry, as John Lennon once said, next time you meet her in public. I bet it'd make her wonder."

Nadia got up and dragged her chair a bit closer beside him. She picked a chunk of salty Balkan feta from the dish. "This watermelon salad is amazing, Sean, but I must say, you do tell a good story. I'll just pick from your dish as you tell me the last part. I cannot imagine how you undid the conversation. But you're gonna tell me, right?"

"Of course. The truth will set me free. Well, there I was in Brooklyn, having just made that duplicate tape, and I thought about the political implications of letting such a controversial issue go public. Would it harm the Democrats? Would it end up delaying the inevitable thawing of relations with Cuba? I must say, Nadia, I just don't get why the States would continue to punish such an impoverished little island as Cuba fifty years later. It beats me.

"I contacted a friend of a friend, an ex-baseball star named Tito Soca. He just retired from the Twins. He hopes one day to return to Cuba to visit his mother and sister. Anyway, while he was playing for Minnesota, he continued to study modern history, majoring in Cuban-American relations, pre-embargo. He expressed a strong interest in the conversation and offered a neat twist. If I wouldn't open the bidding to other parties, he'd make me a one-time, take-it-or-leave-it offer."

"And did you take it, love?" She had tucked her hand into the crook of his arm.

"Yup, I did. He sounded sincere when he told me he just wanted to keep it as a collector. It would give him hope in the cold days of waiting for relations to thaw. I mean, how long can Castro live, right? So, I set up a modest pension in Preston's sister's name, and his so-called pension becomes his rent money to her from now on. It's not a ton, but it will help immediately, and won't get drunk up. Oh, and I gave J.D. a handsome commission, so he can retire. He's already training his nephew to take over after Christmas."

"That's great. Three wrongs do make a right. And...?"

"And I'm retired. Sweetie, I've had a hard life so far, and I'm looking forward to some peace and quiet. Not six month's worth—a lifetime's worth. I want to reinvent myself. Start over. And I want to start over with you. You can act or whatever. I just want to be part of whatever you offer. I can't guarantee this, but I'll try not to complicate your life."

"Sounds good to me. What're we going to do, and when can we start?"

"My thinking is we need to go away, and we could just be that Saturday and Sunday couple you mentioned, for a few months. And," he continued, "I have an idea, if you're game. Afraid of hard work?"

"Never!" she chuckled. "Bring it on!"

"Like wine and the idea of being around wine all the time?"

"Oh yes!"

"Okay. Then we're going to a vineyard in Niagara-On-The-Lake, in Canada. We're going to learn to make wine. Is that okay with you?"

"That would be amazing. Well, for my part, I'll offer to quit acting since I already did. I told my agent a few days ago I needed a rest from the business." Her voice turned playful. "So, I'll pay our room and board while we're learning the ropes. What will you give me?"

"All I can give is all that I have, Sweetie. That's probably worth a new life. I hope so."

About the Author

C huck Bowie graduated from the University of New Brunswick in Canada, with a Bachelor Degree in Science. He still lives in on the East Coast of Canada, an hour East of Maine. His writing is influenced by the study of human nature and how people behave, habits he picked up as his family moved nineteen times in his first twenty-one years. Chuck loves food, wine, music, and travel, and all play a role in his work.

His writing will often draw upon elements of these experiences to round out his characters and plotlines. Chuck is involved in the world of music, supporting local musicians, occasionally playing with them, and always celebrating their successes. Chuck will at times share his thoughts with a brief essay, some of which can be found on his website. http://chuckbowie.ca

He is working through the second novel in the suspense-thriller series: Donovan: Thief For Hire. It is titled *AMACAT*, an acronym for the three elements of the plot.

Chuck is married, with two adult musician sons. He and his wife Lois live in Fredericton, New Brunswick.

Did you enjoy Three Wrongs? If so, please help us spread the word about Chuck Bowie and MuseItUp Publishing. It's as easy as:
- *Recommend the book to your family and friends*
- *Post a review*
- *Tweet and Facebook about it*

Thank you
MuseItUp Publishing

MuseItUp Publishing
Where Muse authors entertain readers!
https://museituppublishing.com
Visit our website for more books for your reading pleasure.
Meet our authors and staff, have a chance to win a FREE ebook,
and get special discounts on upcoming releases by joining our Readers
Club:
http://ca.groups.yahoo.com/group/MusePub_Readers/
You can also find us on Facebook:
http://www.facebook.com/MuseItUp
and on Twitter:
http://twitter.com/MusePublishing